PRAISE FOR

ADULT CONVERSATION

"Ferner's book is at times laugh-out-loud/so-funny-you-have-to-repeat-aloud-to-the-person-nearest-you, and at times viscerally poignant in how accurately she portrays motherhood, as well as how tenuous working outside of the home can feel! Most of all, she reminds us that no matter how many children we have, where we live, or how we live, we as mothers are more alike than we are different, and that we are at our strongest when we band together."

—DR. DARRIA LONG, best-selling author of *Mom Hacks*

"Reading *Adult Conversation* is like having a friend who is both funny and 100 percent real walking beside you on the heart-bending and life-upending path of parenthood. You will see yourself within these characters and find humor and solace on every page. Brandy has somehow captured the sometimes soul-crushing reality of parenthood in a way that makes you laugh and feel deeply seen, while providing a bit of therapy all at the same time!"

—BRITTA BUSHNELL, PhD,
author of *Transformed by Birth*

"This gripping story is so relatable you'll wonder if Ferner pulled pages from your journal. *Adult Conversation* is a much-needed antidote to today's perfect Instagram mom."

—LAURA MULLANE, author of *Swimming for Shore: Memoirs of a Reluctant Mother*

ADULT CONVERSATION

ADULT CONVERSATION

A Novel

by

BRANDY FERNER

SHE WRITES PRESS

Published 2020
Printed in the United States of America
ISBN: 978-1-63152-842-2
ISBN: 978-1-63152-843-9
Library of Congress Control Number: 2019913852

For information, address:
She Writes Press
1569 Solano Ave #546
Berkeley, CA 94707

Book design by Stacey Aaronson

She Writes Press is a division of SparkPoint Studio, LLC.

For A and J.
When I met you, I met myself.
And there we were together, finally.

CHAPTER ONE

It Was Small,
But It Was Something

The banging was relentless. And then came the screams. I curled my body inward, as if shielding myself from a bomb about to detonate on the other side of the door. I sat there rocking sideways, wringing my hands and cursing in a low whisper with eyes closed, wishing the attacks would cease and that this relationship wasn't so abusive.

The screams turned to low, loud wails and the banging intensified. I felt my feet vibrating against the cold tile floor. The bangs became a full-body assault against the door. It would not be standing much longer. I knew what I must do. The last thing on this precious Earth that I wanted to do.

I clenched my anus and accepted the demoralizing fate of a half-taken shit and opened the quaking door to an incensed, tear-covered toddler with doll-like eyelashes and gorgeous wispy curls.

I gritted my teeth and began with step one from the "Peaceful Parenting" article that Facebook had forced upon me that morning: validate your child's feelings (even if you'd rather tell them to suck it).

"What I'm hearing from you, Violet, is that you want Mama to be done in the bathroom."

Violet nodded a firm yes.

"I understand that, but there are things that mamas have to do and those things include going to the bathroom. And sometimes we want a little privacy." I smoothed my dark, shoulder-length hair behind my ears. One side of my hair hung a little longer than the other, and at a sharp angle, for when I needed to feel edgy at Bed, Bath and Beyond.

"No!" Violet dropped her arms to her sides as if they had fallen out of their sockets, and stomped her bare feet.

I took a breath and steadied myself with a hand on the wall. This was resistance number forty-four of the day.

"Your words tell me that you disagree with Mama, but remember when you go poop, you also like to have some priv . . ." But before I could finish Mom-splaining in third-person—always an act of desperation—Violet threw herself to the ground, hitting her head on the way down, now crying even harder than before. I instinctively moved toward my girl to console her.

"No!" she raged, amid tears and kicking, pushing me away.

At that, I hit my threshold for bullshit. I stepped over the crying mess and tiptoed to the nearby fridge for salvation. The upside of having a small home is less square footage to clean. The downside is the kitchen's too-close proximity to the crapper.

The afternoon sun beamed through the kitchen windows like a laser. I opened the fridge door with the quietest tug. I stealthily pulled my chocolate bar from the covered butter inlet, knowing that toddler ears would perk up at the detection of any wrapper rustling. I whisked around to the little corner where the fridge bulged out further than the kitchen counter, making a perfect hideaway cove for freebasing sugar while my children were in the vicinity. I closed my eyes, savoring a medicinal bite of dark chocolate. It was small, but it was something.

Suddenly, my eight-year-old son threw open the door from the garage. I choked the rest of the chocolate square down to hide the evidence. Before both of his feet were even fully inside the house, his pants were off, laying in a human-shaped heap on the ground, as if he had spontaneously combusted inside of them. This was my Elliot, lanky and with sparkling blue eyes that could see right through you. He liked comfort above all else, a trait we shared. In high school, I lasted two days as a smoker before I realized you have to do it outside in the cold and rain.

I licked my chocolate-covered lips and turned around. "Hey, Honey!" I forced myself to sound upbeat, despite having been debased on the toilet moments earlier by Violet.

Elliot came in for a hug, and I rested my chin on the top of his head while we squeezed. Our puzzle pieces fit just so, but his next growth spurt would change that. He looked up at me with a chiseling grin. "Can I play on the iPad?"

I paused, paralyzed by this trap. Saying yes would make my life easier *now*, but I would pay for it later because surely there was homework to be done. Elliot had a master's degree in sensing a possible opening.

"Please, please? I finished my homework at school." He jumped frantically in front of my face and I barely dodged a skull to my chin. Violet, who had suddenly aborted her hostage situation outside the bathroom, came running over holding my chiming phone.

"Mama, phone." She carefully placed it in my hands like it was the Heart of Te Fiti.

There was a text from my husband, Aaron. I read it, leaning into the counter for support as my eyes filled with tears, which I stifled. I was always stifling something. His was a message I'd received countless times before, yet it still brought me to my knees:

> I'm gonna be late tonight, April.
> Label mishap. God forbid people
> have to wait until mid-
> September for their paleo
> pumpkin pancakes. PEOPLE
> LOVE FALL. FML.

Aaron was a packaging designer for "Market Street," a specialty grocery store chain on the West Coast that valued form more than flavor and preyed on the insecurities of the urban hipster with its open-air European vibe. The original store had laid out actual cobblestone only to realize that grocery cart wheels and bumpy stones don't work together. But Market Street was wildly successful and it was Aaron's job as head designer to create quirky sketches, ironic themes, and appetizing fonts to sell mediocre, overpriced ego food.

Because it was spring, he was preparing for the onslaught of fall—the season of everything pumpkin-flavored. Their star employee, Aaron was outgoing, rarely said no to higher-ups, and had an insanely powerful knack for pairing fonts and food. His bosses exploited him on the regular, which I could see, but Aaron, somehow, could not. As a design school graduate with more eagerness than edge, Aaron loved his job and the art he got paid to create, especially when he threw in a microscopic obscenity or two—a secret that only we shared.

But hijinks aside, if there was one thing I wished I had been told before becoming a mother, it was that even with all the immediate, whine-soaked, child-induced atrocities violating my personal space and sanity as a stay-at-home mom for eight straight years, the one person who would consistently dole out the final push over the edge would be my husband. All the parenting books had left that minor detail out.

CHAPTER TWO

Royalty

*N*ine hours earlier, I had woken up consensually—a rare parental victory.

I reached my arm below our Nate Berkus line-art sheets and rested it on Aaron's broad chest, purposefully avoiding the lower zip code of obligation. He opened one eye, sleepily smiling with male optimism. The pink morning sky blushed behind the shutters as if it were eavesdropping.

Aaron and I lay on our sides, face to beard, the ends of our pillows kissing, our legs pressing against each other's. His soft, green eyes widened as he looked around. He must've been confused since we were both awake and touching without the air-raid siren of children. On the nightstand, his phone lit up with a simultaneous alarm blare and reminder ding. We had enjoyed ten whole seconds of uninterrupted marital connection.

He made his way to the bathroom, phone in hand, as I peeled myself out of the warm bed, walked into the closet, and slipped on my light blue fuzzy robe—the one I'd worn during labor with Elliot. The one Violet referred to as "Mama wobe."

I opened Elliot's door, drinking in the image of my

sleeping boy, who woke up at 5:30 a.m. on weekends, but slept in on school days. The wall above his bed was adorned with a row of green "Kindness Kounts" awards he'd received for being an upstanding citizen at school. I moved his robot covers aside and sat in bed next to him, rubbing his back. "Time to get ready for school," I whispered, kissing him on the cheek.

Then came the melodic, "Mama. Ma-ma," through the wall from Violet's room. Past data showed that her murmurs would quickly escalate into Guns N' Roses–esque shrieking if I didn't attend to it within ten seconds, so I went.

Upon seeing my face, Violet's lit up and her tiny, two-year-old legs rocketed her to standing. Her slept-on hair flipped to the sides like Lisa Rinna's and her diaper rustled inside her footed, pink owl jammies. I plopped us both into the fuzzy, worn glider—a distant cousin of Mama wobe's. She laid her head on my chest and the two of us snuggled as we greeted the day together. I breathed in the peaceful moment and Violet's sleepy, sweet head. No one needed asinine things from me yet.

"Mama, I have jelly beans?" Violet said, lifting up her head. And just like that, the first "no" of the day was administered. *Did I even get three minutes?*

The kitchen greeted us with its standard décor of kids' art, yesterday's dirty dishes, and a rustic sign that read "This Home is Filled with Love and Laughter"—more of a threat than a boast. As I passed the thermostat, I forcefully tapped the "cold" button to the "off" position. Aaron wished we lived in a casino, blasting air conditioning at all times, while I was considering buying a nice property on the sun.

I set Violet down on the tile floor. I would need both

of my hands to make breakfast—a reasonable request—but it was a fact that she couldn't accept, so she leveled herself against the ground, sobbing at the injustice. It was far too early to deal with this shit, so I picked her up, knowing it would immediately flip her toddler volume switch to "off."

And it did.

I grabbed a bowl of strawberries from the fridge, trying not to think about the fact that I'd cheaped out and gone non-organic this time. Seared into my memory was the day the too-cute-to-be-a-produce-manager had so graciously bestowed his berry prophecy on me as I reached for a tub of pesticide-riddled red beauties. "Strawberries are like little sponges. Always go organic on those." Since then, any time I so much as saw a conventional strawberry, his words, "Little sponges . . . little sponges . . ." echoed in my head, evoking deep shame.

"Juic-ee," Violet mumbled with a messy mouth that dripped strawberry juice down her chin and onto the front of her full-price Hanna Andersson pajamas. She'd snagged one while I was meditating on toxins.

I groaned, reaching down into the sink cabinet for my forever friend, OxiClean. Violet jerked forward and knocked the canister and its lid to the ground. The tiny white and blue grains of poisonous sand spread all over the floor.

"Dammit, Violet!" is what I wanted to say. But I didn't utter any words. It felt wrong to be at the end of one's rope so close to where it started. So instead, I swallowed my irritation and pulled the vacuum out from beneath a scattering of board games and Shopkins in the closet. The weight of it was almost enough to make my uterus drop directly out of my body.

There was an insistent yell coming from somewhere, competing with the deafening whir of the vacuum. I looked up and saw Elliot mouthing something with urgency.

"MOM!" he was still half-shouting when the vacuum subsided. "Can I have a waffle?"

Shit. Breakfast.

I popped a waffle in the toaster and scooped Aaron's favorite beans into the coffee maker.

A layperson may think that Aaron took twenty-minute showers because that was how long the water ran. But the actual time Aaron spent in the shower was about four minutes. California state officials had talked a lot about ways residents were wasting water, but one avenue they had not publicly explored was the amount of time husbands spent masturbating with the shower running. But this was something I knew better than to complain about, or else the job would fall on my shoulders. Or knees, rather. Sex was scarce these days, but exhaustion and two-year-old tantrums were not.

A horn honked outside.

"There's Liam," Elliot called, stuffing the last of his waffle in his mouth and bolting from his chair.

"Did you say goodbye to your dad?" I asked as Aaron came galloping down the stairs, freshly showered, like fucking royalty.

"Bye, El," Aaron said, hugging Elliot.

"You brushed your teeth, right?" I asked. Elliot flashed a guilty, stinky grin as he grabbed his backpack and fled. I sighed the sigh of a thousand mothers wishing their kids cared about stank mouth, and then ran over to my purse and grabbed a mint.

"Take this," I said, chasing him outside.

"Can I have two?" he asked with a sly smile. My eyes went cold. He'd pressed his luck and he knew it. "One's good." He quickly kissed me goodbye. He was not yet too cool to show me public affection, but I knew the expiration date on that was just around the corner.

I walked back inside to see Violet cramming two discs into the DVD player. *Could you not try to break everything we own?*

"I watch?" she asked.

"No, Sweetheart." I scurried over to her and gently took the discs even though I wanted to run out the door, away from the day full of toddler resistance and mother rage that I knew awaited me. Like always.

She moved on to a more favorable option, Aaron. "Dada, I watch?"

"Sure, Baby, which one?" He held out the two discs for her Highness to choose from. Both of them were royalty and I was the fucking servant.

"Seriously?" I said, trying not to go full wife on him before 9 a.m. "She can't watch a movie now if I have any hope of showering later. A movie is the only thing that grants me clean pits."

His head turned toward Violet, lulled by her small voice singing along to *Alice in Wonderland.* "You need to relax about this stuff," he said, pointing to a euphoric Violet as if she were evidence. I felt words escaping my mouth faster than I could swallow them back down.

"I need to *relax*? You swoop in here, give a hug, put on a little movie and you don't have to deal with any of what happens before or afterwards."

"Fine. I won't put movies on for her when she asks anymore, jeez." He reached to press the stop button.

"No! You can't turn it off now," I said, grabbing the remote out of his hand. "You've already said yes. This now has to play out. You get to drive away from it. I don't."

He couldn't argue with that. After all, I was wearing Mama wobe and he was wearing real human clothes. He pulled me toward him, for a hug. My arms hung limply at my sides. Anti-hug.

"Sorry, A.B.," he said.

That name transported me back to college, when our new love was so electric that we couldn't keep our hands off each other. Spending summers apart were torturous, as if we were living in a Shakespearean tragedy. In addition to daily two-hour phone calls, we stayed connected by sending each other quirky care packages. Aaron would send me detailed drawings signed by him, "A.S.," along with mixtapes, and pictures of him as a round, shiny-faced Stewart kid at Medieval Times. I would reciprocate by sending him homemade Chex Mix, pictures of me in fourth grade with mushroom hair like Carol Brady's, and my attempts at art, which I would sign with my initials, "A.B." Although marriage had made me an "A.S." like him, he sometimes still called me "A.B.," which was a sweet reminder of how we began, and who I used to be. But it didn't work like a Magic Eraser or anything.

"It's fine, whatever," I said.

His phone buzzed. He looked down at it while still embracing me. He grimaced.

"What?" I asked.

"Today I get to design a label for pumpkin-scented tampons," he said, with a terrified stare.

"I didn't realize I could experience fall vaginally."

He ran over to Violet and playfully showered her head

with kisses as she giggled. I wished I could be the dad. I poured him a to-go mug of fresh coffee and shoved a kid's energy bar in his hand. I never intended to be a doting housewife, but it seemed to be an unadvertised side effect of being a stay-at-home mom.

As I stood in the doorway watching him sit in the car and scroll for the perfect drive-to-work music, I couldn't help but wonder what it must feel like to have all that autonomy. If the giant smile on his face every day as he backed out of the garage was any indicator, it was fucking paradise.

He rolled down his window, Snoop Dogg's nasally voice wafting from the car. He cranked it for effect. The high-pitched synthesizer and heavy beat took me back again to when we were young together, when our only real responsibility was acquiring a giant burrito at some point in the day or night.

"This is for you. Hang in there, A.B.," he yelled out the window of his Prius. He cranked the music even louder, bobbing his head like a white man in a Prius.

"Only twelve more hours to go," I said, giving him a slow and sarcastic thumbs up, and then I pressed the garage door button to guillotine his flaunting of freedoms.

CHAPTER THREE

All Roads Suck Balls

Something I couldn't shake, but never knew how to accurately verbalize to Aaron, was my quiet resentment about his daily life having changed very little since we had the kids, whereas mine was now unrecognizable. Parenthood had exacted something from me that it hadn't exacted from him—not even close. His morning routine, his leaving the house, his job, his luxury of coming home late if needed, his weekend surfing, all looked nearly the same as it did before the kids. I, on the other hand, was filling my days with wiping ass, bleaching vomit, feeling shame about conventional fruit, and generally serving as everyone else's snack bitch and more—a far cry from my past duties as owner of a handmade clothing line.

Our inequality and my jealousy of Aaron's balanced life made me feel like a dick because I chose to be a stay-at-home mom. No one forced me. We both agreed that we wanted to raise our own kids. Sure, that choice was made blindly, and "we" really meant me, but I had made my bed and now had to lie in it. Ironically, I never got to literally lie in my bed anymore. And I also hated Aaron's face some days because he reaped all the perks of parenthood without having to do the heavy lifting of it. Also, his nipples didn't resemble chewed gum.

The next task of the day that wasted my college degree was grocery shopping—that is, after clothing a small, angry person. There is no on-the-job training that prepares one for the task of wrestling a shirt and pants onto a person who is running. Working with the severely mentally ill was the closest thing, but caretakers were legally allowed to use tranquilizers. The only tranquilizer I had was an essential oil called "Serenity," and Violet's room reeked of it.

My dad, Wayne, who always had a story on the tip of his tongue about his three favorite things—snakes, Harleys, and the Florida panhandle—had once told me a tale wherein a swampy, backwoods town had a local anaconda they were trying to capture because it kept eating people. The town's solution? Sew incredibly thick jean material together and create a giant tube that they would try to catch the snake in. That was the whole plan. But they saw it out and the snake did, in fact, find its way into the denim tube—and this is the part that I especially remember—the snake thrashed inside that jean tube in such a violent way that the town's people weren't sure if this anaconda was about to burst the seams open and eat all of them. That visual is what I thought of every time I tried to put pants on a bucking Violet.

But today, I won the war on pants. She stood up from the fracas wearing her hot pink leggings with puffy diaper butt and soft grey smock dress covered with smiling rainbows. I was sweating.

The necessary supplies for leaving the house with Violet included a smattering of snacks in containers that couldn't be dumped out, sippy cups that couldn't spill (which were none), copious amounts of hand sanitizer, animal figures that would be immediately dropped on the backseat floor, and of course, cloth grocery bags, which were going to save the Earth at the expense of the sanity of mothers everywhere.

I hauled Violet and her provisions into the garage, making sure to leave the big garage door down until she was strapped down in her car seat. A strategy existed for every task with her. I knew that an open garage door plus an unrestrained toddler meant the high likelihood of a Benny Hill–style wild goose chase down the street. These were the things Aaron did not know, because he didn't have to.

With Violet shackled into her seat, the tranquil island that was the driver's seat of the minivan welcomed me. I closed my eyes and let my head fall back against the squishy headrest, taking my first break of the day.

"I needs 'Baby Shark' song!"

There was never silence. Or stillness. Why hadn't minivan manufacturers added glass partitions yet, like in limos? They'd rolled out the in-car vacuum, so why not double down on what us parents really want—silent children at the push of a button?

The peppy beats of a shark family rave flooded in. It was either that or the sound of screeches and sobs, and my entire parenting philosophy basically hinged on limiting both of those things so that I didn't actually lose it. What was I like unstifled? I was scared to open the floodgates because I wasn't sure I could close them.

The manicured flowers and shrubs of the Southern California suburbs ushered the local minivans of moms and their youngest spawn to and from morning errands. This time of day was called "before nap." I was not a So-

Cal native, but Aaron was. After college in the landlocked Midwest, where we met, he couldn't fight the siren song beckoning him back to the ocean. So I obliged, knowing that there were worse places to live, but I didn't quite fit in with the women around me who seemed so fixated on fancy handbags and eyelash extensions. I wore very little make-up, mostly because a small person was usually screaming at me while I got ready each morning. But when I was bestowed a moment at the mirror, one coat of mascara was my upgrade of choice. Eyeliner occurred maybe twice a year.

We parked at the grocery store and the shark jam ceased, finally.

"Noooooo!"

My neck stiffened at the sound of resistance. And then my phone dinged. A text message from my own mother.

> How are my perfect
> grandchildren? Perhaps we can
> FaceTime later?

My mom's given name was Donna, but she always felt it too ordinary, a mismatch with her self-proclaimed "crackerjack" personality. She turned the whole *picking what you want to be called as a grandmother* thing into an entire name reset and insisted that all of us, including myself, Aaron, and the kids, call her Marnie. My whole life she wrote with a straight-edged ruler to make sure her letters looked impeccable. Her eccentricity was not new. So I called my mom Marnie. And Aaron and I laughed our asses off about it when we weren't rolling our eyes.

> Here's your perfect
> granddaughter.

I pressed the video record button, capturing Violet's raging perfection for her—seat kicking and all.

> Oh that's not my granddaughter.
> Must be someone else! 🫠 🖤

In addition to being quirky as hell and using ill-fitting emojis, Marnie was in Grandma denial. She had never uttered an unkind word about either of her grandkids, and pretended that any challenges the children presented for me were either not happening or misunderstandings on *my* part. And despite seeing live footage of my struggle, she always brushed it off—a form of gaslighting I had experienced forever.

In sixth-grade music class, after we'd blown the shit out of "Hot Cross Buns" on the recorders and my teacher was going around collecting them, he would frequently drop one in front of me, bend down to get it, and linger. This only happened on the days I wore a skirt. His moist stare made me feel sick and ashamed, and when I told Marnie, she barely looked up from her newspaper.

"But Mom, it never happens when I wear pants."

"That's a big allegation, young lady. Mr. Dane's never been anything but nice to you," she said, retreating back behind the six-foot paper.

The rest of that year, I wore only pants. It never happened again.

My independent streak as a "young lady," coupled with Marnie's unwillingness either to believe me or to be bothered by my emotional needs, didn't make for an intimate mother-daughter relationship. But despite that crater in our bond, she had always shown up for me in the most practical sense. After babies, when she came from Florida to visit us, she would clean my entire house, order in dinner every night, and pay for summer camp, swimming lessons, or whatever else the kids were into. It was hard to argue with that, so I learned to be grateful, while also trying to ignore the other more primal ways I longed to be loved by own mother.

I lacked the will necessary to formulate a text response that could cut to the heart of thirty-plus years of mother-daughter baggage, so Marnie got what she wanted.

> Yep, everything's just
> great. At the store now.

Wonderful! Keep checking those
to-do's off your list! 😜

Positive attitude + productivity = Marnie nirvana.

I skeptically eyed the lines of carts at the entrance of the grocery store, as did the other approaching mom. *Which cart handle didn't have the latest stomach flu virus?* One couldn't know, so we kept our heads down and played grocery-store Russian roulette.

I had a clear plan of what I needed to get and where, without having to backtrack at all. Marnie's efficient DNA was coursing through my veins, after all.

"Mama, I have dat?" Violet pointed toward an array of bright bell peppers.

"No, Violet. You don't like those."

"I waaaaant one," she whined. And then the crying started up again. I paused. My child *was* begging for a vegetable, and experts did say it can take a few consistent tries to get them to like new things. Never mind that this happened every single time we went to the store.

"Which color do you want?"

"Lell-low!"

Violet put her lips up to the yellow bell pepper, exploring the waxy smoothness, and then sunk her tiny shark teeth into it. "Is ickee," she said, frowning and dropping the pepper straight to the damn floor. I picked up the yellow carcass and put it in the cart, just like I did every week.

Once we'd hit nap time (the marker of midday), and Violet was behind a closed door and caged in her crib, my nervous system finally dared to let its guard down and unwind. If days ended right here, I could totally be an award-winning, sane mother. The second half of the day always tried its best to eviscerate me.

My stomach growled. Apparently eating my resentment and a half-banana three hours ago hadn't been sufficient. *Weird.*

My lips had barely touched a spoonful of fried-rice leftovers when Violet's voice wailed over the baby monitor. I wanted to sink all of our money into a study about how children intuitively knew the exact moment in which their mother was about to sustain herself with food. This had to be the seventh sense. I pounded as much rice as I could before she went apeshit up there. Even though I was a second-time mother and had been through the naptime wringer once before, Elliot and Violet's six-year age gap had caused some sort of a reset and everything felt just as intense and unruly the second time around. I thought I would know how to tweak things to get it right this time, but I still felt powerless.

The booms started. It was Violet throttling the wall from inside her crib. "MA-MA, I NEEEEEEEDS YOU!"

There I was in that familiar corner of motherhood where all the choices that lay before you suck balls, and your job is to weigh which one sucks the least, and then do that thing. *What to Expect When You're Expecting* needs an appendix called "Making Sacrifices: Say Goodbye to Meals."

Violet jumped at the sound of her door opening. And then came the wafting smell of shit.

"Apparently, you had to poop," I pointed out, pushing the blackout curtains aside and sliding the window open for fresh air. The brightness caused her to squint and flop down into a civilization of stuffed animals that had overtaken her crib. It was like a deranged Noah's Ark in there. Kitties with giant eyeballs, a freaky half-giraffe/half-zebra fellow, and a stuffed dog named "Big Fuffy," who was the size of a large piece of luggage. And a purple blanket aptly named "Purple Blanket."

Suddenly, the distinct smell of poop in the raw—not inside a diaper—hit me like a wall. Any non-parent would back up and walk away, but like a bloodhound, I instinctually started sniffing the entire area to find out where the awfulness had escaped the diaper and how far it had spread. The first logical place to search was Violet's fingers, which smelled so strongly that I dry heaved loudly.

"I go poop, Mama," she softly said, matter-of-factly.

"Violet, please don't put your hands in your diaper again."

But it was all pointless. I wouldn't be walking away from this situation with a firm, shit-filled handshake and promise that she wouldn't do it again. In fact, she probably would do it again, immediately. I set her in the running bathtub and added infinite squirts of all-natural bubble bath that didn't quite feel strong enough. *Did OxyClean make a bubble bath?*

"Will you sing the shark song for me?" I asked Violet, who happily nodded yes. This was a trick I'd learned when Elliot was small that let me walk away from the tub for a quick moment. If your toddler is singing in the bathtub, they aren't drowning.

She began.

I bolted back into her room for five seconds and stripped the sheets off the crib at lightning speed. I wrapped everything in the assaulted sheet and set it by the stairs to take down with me after her bath. It sat there like a festering wound, but like always, I turned my attention to Violet, who was singing and delighting in her bubble bath instead of her nap. All I wanted to do was eat, but I sat down on the bathroom stool in front of the tub. *Even prisoners get three meals a day, for Christ's sake.* My weary eyes connected with Violet's brilliant ones. They were the exact same color as mine—deep brown in the center, surrounded by hazel and a ring of blue on the outer edge. They looked like planets.

"Mama, you da best."

I wanted to say, "You are the literal worst right now. Why can't you just go to sleep and not touch your own feces?" But instead, I said, "Aw girl, *you're* da best."

I dumped two gallons of soap on a washcloth and scrubbed her fingers vigorously. She kept resisting, trying to move to the other side of the tub. She broke free and lowered down into a squat. I knew exactly what was happening.

"Violet, wait!"

I lunged to pick her up, but it was already too late. I cupped my hands in the water and caught the brown log because of parental auto-pilot, but then immediately wondered why I'd caught it. How did that actually help things? There were still poop flakes in the water and now my hands were septic. Violet splashed around. Her mouth dropped below the water, and opened.

"Imma whale!" she gurgled as poop water lapped in.

I felt my neck tighten as if it were made of guitar strings, and the back of my eyes throb. Why was caretaking so urgent and never-ending like this? And why did it make me nearly snap? What was wrong with me? Motherhood and mental illness looked far too similar. Also, why didn't I work in a nice office doing straightforward tasks for someone who was potty-trained?

My bed, my most favorite place in the world, teased me from across the hall. I longed to get in it and throw the covers over my head. Aaron and I referred to it as my "nest." On exceptionally taxing days, I would text Aaron with just the word, "nest." He would then know that I had been pummeled by the day and was in my safe place. He also knew that no boners were allowed in the nest.

But instead of holing up, I used my last shred of energy to lift a questionably clean Violet out of the infested waters and dove headfirst into the "after nap" part of the day —on a technicality, and running on fumes.

Every day went something like this—a few truly lovely parenting moments overshadowed by difficulty. I wished I could get used to it like other moms seemed to, but I never could. Instead, I silently interrogated myself. *What am I doing wrong that makes it feel so hard? I love my kids, so why isn't that love enough to soften the sharp edges of motherhood? Do I need professional help?*

The glowing babysitter (aka TV) showed up for me, like always, and played *Storybots* for a finally calm Violet. I stood at the kitchen sink before a mountain of brightly colored IKEA kid cups and bowls. Instead of overlooking a big wooden swing set, vegetable garden, or a treehouse, my kitchen-sink window looked directly at the side of my neighbor's close house, specifically where they kept their trash cans. My childhood home had a huge grassy yard, perfect for doing cartwheels across, and I hated that our tiny concrete patio couldn't even hold a modest birthday party. Size-wise, this house was just adequate for the four of us—minimalistic, as I liked to skew it—and it had a warmth that made it cozy rather than noticeably small. Or so I hoped. The kitchen, dining area, and family room all flowed into each other. Being alone downstairs was nearly impossible, except if you escaped into the warm garage.

"Mama, I needs snacky," Violet called from the couch.

"You could have blueberries, or crackers, or an orange, or applesauce . . ." I hated myself for listing snack options like a waitress listing specials, but yet I continued.

"I needs bluebees."

I fetched and then handed Violet a bright plastic bowl full of blueberries. They were organic, so there was no shame.

She rejected it. "I needs yogurt," she whined, flopping sideways on the couch.

"But you asked me for blueberries." I was firm.

Offended, Violet raised her bitch-slapping hand and sent the bowl flying in the air before my frayed reflexes could stop it. The blue balls hit the floor and radiated toward all edges of the room, a larger version of the Oxi-Clean grains from the morning.

"Dammit, Violet!"

It shot out of my mouth. I hadn't caught myself this time. She went silent until a huge wail came from the depths of her being. My stomach flopped. I felt equal parts rotten and justified mother. I sat down and wrapped my arms around her as she snuggled tightly in my lap like a kitten, crying harder. I felt seasick from the choppiness of emotions—my own and Violet's—vacillating from low to high, all within the same moment, multiple times a day, every day. Mothering was the journey of a hundred daily dinghy rides, back and forth to opposing ports. Why didn't anyone talk about this part?

I wiped the wet wisps of hair out of her eyes. I knew I was the adult here, but I couldn't bring myself to apologize, yet. I felt victimized too and hadn't forgotten the act that caused me to vocalize the profanity in the first place. But I gave Violet the best I could muster in that moment, a consolation prize.

"Let's clean this mess up together," I said through a tightened throat. She contracted into a tighter ball.

I stopped the show. She unfurled herself and sat up. "No, Mama!"

I looked at her and held a finger up, serious. "*Storybots* comes back after you help me clean up the mess. That's the deal."

No deal. She threw herself off of my lap and into the

corner of the couch, bawling and kicking. Her foot struck me square in the breast, leaving a heavy sting in the very thing that had given her sustenance as a baby. The injustice nearly undid me as I mumbled, "Fuck," underneath my breath, clutching my boob and moving away from the hysterics. I seethed as I speed-walked to the only place that held temporary peace as I tried to put myself back together: the bathroom. I locked the door, lifted the lid, and sat down on the cold seat. I couldn't even remember the last time I had gone. Was it this morning? Had I even drank any water today? I pulled my phone out of my cardigan pocket and clicked it on. Only two more hours until Aaron would be home to bear some of the onslaught with me. I felt a hopeful twinge. I told myself that I could make it two more hours.

The wails coming from the couch subsided, but only because they had moved right outside my shithouse of solitude. Then the banging started. And the screams. The half-taken shit. Elliot's out-of-the-pants magic upon entering the house. The iPad finagling. Aaron's "I'm going to be late tonight" text message shove over the edge. The counter holding me up.

I didn't know how to answer Aaron without utter contempt, so I gave no reply. There needed to be an emoji for a wife who was choking down resentment yet again at having to face the pitfalls of the evening alone with children. The face with the X's for eyes seemed like the closest thing.

I had no choice but to reassess the homemade dinner I had planned on extruding through the pasta roller with the kids, like on the cooking shows we watched together. Getting through the evening in one piece was my new mission, and my first order of business was finding the packaged spaghetti. Second was handing Elliot the iPad and third was turning *Storybots* back on for Violet and telling her to pick blueberries off the ground if she was hungry. Fourth was driving away and never coming back.

I needed fortitude of some kind, so I click-click-clicked the gas on for the stove and set a tea kettle on it. Coffee drinking might've been the key to my entire parenting experience, but I would never know because after having kids, my bowels had gone on strike and rioted at any caffeine or alcohol. I opened a bag of loose tea leaves and sniffed hard, expecting (hoping) to smell pot, but I didn't. It smelled like chamomile instead.

An incoming email dinged on my phone. It was from Elliot's teacher, reminding me—not him, but me, because this is how modern parenting works—that book reports were due tomorrow and needed to be accompanied by a list of questions that the kids would hypothetically ask the author.

"Elliot, you did your book report, right?"

"Just a sec, Mom," he said robotically, eyes glued to the iPad.

"iPad down, now." I was beginning to steam like the tea kettle.

"I did it at school."

"The questions for the author too?"

"Ummm."

I looked at him long and hard until he dragged his corpse over to the art supply cabinet, slowly slid a sheet of paper out, and plunked down into a chair at the kitchen table.

"First, we should put the word 'Questions' at the top, don't you think?" I suggested, in that way mothers tell you what to do, but in the form of a question.

He nodded and began. And then stopped. "Mom, I don't know how to make a capital Q."

I looked out the window at the clear blue sky and Violet's half-dead fairy garden below it, as if they could offer me anything. My phone rang. It was Marnie trying to FaceTime with us. I clicked the decline button on my own mother so I could get back to being one myself.

"You really don't know how to make a capital Q?"

"I've never had to write one before," he said, his voice quivering. He looked down at the paper, made an O and put the tail of the Q on the wrong side. I was speechless. How was this possible? How had he gotten through to the third grade—and with decent marks—if he couldn't write a fucking capital Q? Nothing made sense. We had about two more painstaking hours ahead of us and writing a capital Q was probably the easiest part.

"Mama, I needs something eat!" Violet yelled, running toward me.

I contemplated snorting a line of tea leaves, but instead I pointed at Elliot and said, "You, figure out how to write a capital Q." Then I picked up Violet, the packaged spaghetti, and a handful of Goldfish crackers as bait, and said, "You, help me with dinner."

I could do it. The finish line was so close. Also, I had no choice.

CHAPTER FOUR

Parenting for Fifteen Hours
Isn't an Aphrodisiac

*F*or dessert, I rattled two Advil out of a bottle. The mediocre spaghetti dinner had sufficed, and the child abuse in the form of teaching someone to write a capital Q at age eight was now behind us. I had triumphantly made it to bedtime. Not my own, of course, but kid bedtime—the time of night when I had the least will to live and my kids had the most.

Tonight included the usual shenanigans of heavy negotiation, stalling, a bumped ankle, tears, the application of a *My Little Pony* Band-Aid, the removal of a *My Little Pony* Band-Aid, the right pajama drama, slow-ass water slurping, chasing, hiding, hog-tying, and then threats. I turned out the soft light in Violet's room. The lack of nap knocked her out cold.

One down.

Even though Elliot was old enough to have a job in some cultures, his bedtime routine length doubled that of Violet's because he simply would not fall asleep without another human body lying next to his. The whole thing was sweetly maddening. We laid there, in the dark, looking up at the glowing stars I had helped him stick to his ceiling.

"Mom, this shirt's tag is itchy."

I rolled my eyes so hard I went dizzy. Then I motioned for him to get a new shirt because I knew I couldn't hide my exasperation if I spoke. Constantly trying to temper outward signs of my motherly frustration was wearing, but if I didn't, my kids would grow up feeling like they were a burden on me, which they sometimes were by nature, but they didn't need to know that. And fuck, it was hard to pretend to enjoy the unenjoyable parts of motherhood.

Back under the covers again, Elliot pressed his shoulder against mine and said, "I forgot to feed my fish."

I moaned as if I were in labor. "You have ten seconds to feed Slippery."

He beat the clock and returned to bed.

"Good night, El. Love you," I said through gritted teeth. I searched for his cheek to kiss in the dark, finally landing it.

"Love you too, Mom."

I shut my eyes and felt the glory of my body sinking into the bed.

"Mom, I forgot to look for that Pokémon card. Can I just find it really quick?" He was sitting up.

"Lay down, Elliot. It's time for bed. Love. You." It was taking all my self-restraint and goodwill to end this day on a positive note. I knew if he voiced his need to do one more thing I would spew fire this time. *Please don't say another word. Please don't say another word.*

He laid back down and softly rolled over, his legs touching mine. I pulled my silenced phone out from my pocket and ducked underneath the covers to dampen the light from the screen. Elliot made a relaxed, baby-like sigh which reminded me of when he was a toddler, before smartphones existed, when it felt something like suffocation to be incarcerated for thirty minutes or more with a child who may or may not be sleeping, with no line of connection to other humans—kind of like a POW. Now I could meal-plan, buy paper towels, or mindlessly scroll Facebook while lying next to him.

The sound of the garage door buzzed below. Aaron was finally home. I could hear one of his wonk political podcasts booming from his car below in the garage. His every move was amplified in the silence of sleeping children— the car keys clanging in the bowl, the beer bottle top popping, the air conditioning turning on. *Dammit.* I imagined him hungry and tired.

My phone lit up with a text from him.

> Hey. Did you fall asleep with the kids? Or are you in the nest?

Lying in the dark had dampened enough of my resentment so I could at least text him back this time.

> I'm about to attempt my escape from child #2.

When Elliot's breathing turned deep and loud, I rolled over with my arms pinned to my side, moving in slow-motion, maneuvering to avoid the edges—the squeak zone—at all costs. Victorious, I emerged from his room like a bedraggled marathon runner finally crossing the finish line. I came downstairs to find Aaron happily eating the meh spaghetti. His eyes lit up when he saw me, just like my kids' did.

"Hey," he said with a full mouth. He was scarfing down his dinner as if he didn't get a state-mandated lunch break.

Out of the corner of my eye, I saw something move and then vanish. It slowly peeked its head out again. It was Elliot—who had been asleep nanoseconds ago—looking around the corner, like goddamn Houdini.

"Why are you out of bed?" I asked.

"I get scared sometimes." Tears were brimming in his eyes. I looked at Aaron, who was about to take his first bite of garlic bread. Someone had to act quickly before there was actual crying from Elliot that would protract things even longer. Aaron chomped loudly.

"Come on, let's go," I said, pointing upstairs.

"Sorry we didn't get to read comics tonight, El. Tomorrow for sure."

Elliot smiled and shuffled over to Aaron for a hug, just like he had this morning. Bookend parenting. I couldn't bear to look at Aaron and his beard full of crumbs.

Elliot and I laid in bed, take two. The glowing stars were more muted than before, which juxtaposed my irritation level which was at a solid twelve.

"Mom, who was your best friend in third grade?"

"Dude. Sleep."

"I just keep thinking about Freddy." He was referring to an animatronic bear in a game that was a mix between Chucky from your nightmares and Chuck E. Cheese from your birthdays.

"What are some other things you can think about?"

"Nothing, I'm too scared." His tears were returning.

I knew there was one thing that would work, but it would require me to push through the pain. *If I can just do this one last thing, I'm off for the night.* I swallowed hard enough to perform an attitude adjustment and began to sing a song that Elliot had heard through the walls of my womb, and then every night after as a toddler. It was *My Cherie Amour* by Stevie Wonder. He moved his head against mine and snuggled in closely as I sang.

After I finished my last "La la," only the hum of Slippery's tank filter could be heard. But I knew it was too soon to leave, and couldn't bear risking it all again. I retreated to my under-the-covers phone cave. There was a text waiting from Aaron.

> **Don't forget we have Bachelor tonight!**

What a paradox he was. Intelligent but clueless. Political but privileged. Progressive but a reality TV junkie. When Aaron and I first got married, my girlfriends swooned over his ability to do chores without being asked. We'd host dinners and afterwards, Aaron would scrub plates while verbally dissecting punk-rock albums with his buddies in the kitchen, like it was the most normal thing for a guy to do. Raised by his mom and grandmother, he never saw a first-hand distinction between men's and women's roles in his own home. As someone who could change her own flat tire, I was pulled in by Aaron's modern masculinity—strong but soft. My friends assumed that I trained him to vacuum and do laundry, but he came to me that way. Aside from the obvious practical benefits of having a roommate who can clean up after themselves, I saw his thoughtfulness as a reflection of our equality and his respect for me. But after having kids, the immense workload of parenthood and our gender roles within it had muddied things. Even though Aaron was modern, he was still a man. Behind my back, fatherhood had quietly bestowed him the luxury of letting the household and kid tasks fall on me, while motherhood had gifted me with quick reflexes to catch it all.

It was 9:38 p.m. when I surfaced for the second time. I had parented for fifteen hours straight. Aaron sat on the couch munching from a bowl of pretzels, much like his children did. He reached his arms out for me to cuddle with him, much like his children did. I obliged even though all I wanted was for my body to finally be touching no one. He raised his eyebrows as he motioned to the TV with *Bachelor* all queued up.

"Ready?" he asked.

I nodded and grabbed a blanket. What an oxymoron he truly was: equally interested in Noam Chomsky and Chris Harrison. Aaron snuggled up closer to me so we could share my blanket. I wanted to want that too, but the truth was I just wanted some goddamn personal space and for no one to need anything from me.

He lovingly rubbed my leg as we watched train-wreck girls vie for a milk-toast douche. If Aaron had it his way, he would be touching me—even innocently—every second of the day and night. His love language was physical contact, just like Elliot. But my love language was being left completely alone.

I became hyper aware of Aaron's touch and the possible unspoken obligation behind it. My hard-earned *Bachelor* bliss was being taken from me as his hand softly slid onto my lower leg, finding its way underneath my flowy pajama pants. I told myself it would stop, but it slowly moved to my upper leg and then towards the side of my ass. Too much. I leapt up off the couch like someone had dropped a rubber snake in my lap.

"Oh my God, what?" he asked, backing away from me.

"I'm sorry," I stuttered. "It's . . . I just can't be touched in that way after the kind of day I had." And really, it was all the days I've had in the past eight years. A gaggle of women played flirty football against the Bachelor on the TV in the background.

"I was just rubbing your leg, I didn't mean to put you in an uncomfortable situation. I haven't seen you all day," he said, his bafflement turning to annoyance.

"It's not personal. I just don't want to be touched."

"How am I not supposed to take it personally?"

"Because it *isn't* personal. It's not like I want to be touched by some other guy. I just want to be touched by no one."

Aaron sat on the couch, his head hanging down, looking wounded and rejected—the exact opposite of the Bachelor touching the asses of all the ladies. I turned the TV off.

Aaron picked his head up. "April, I know you are overwhelmed. I try my best to understand that you're not up for sex like I am. But it's driving me crazy not being able to even touch you—to connect with you."

I sat silently. He wasn't wrong. Letting him rub my ass on the couch was the last thing on my 10 p.m. wish list, which was the time of day when we were finally alone together. But after being pecked to death by children all day long, I just couldn't take on another pecker.

We sat on opposite ends of the couch in silence, the blanket tossed in the middle. As I stared at the floor, Aaron's bare foot caught my eye, the one with the pink-painted big toenail, the sloppy work of Violet last weekend.

"I wish I wasn't so touched out at the end of the day. I

can't imagine it will stay this way forever." There I was giving comfort after having been pushed too far, yet again.

Aaron sighed and rolled his eyes.

"Why did you just roll your eyes?"

"I didn't."

"Yes, you did. You just rolled your eyes while I was trying to be honest with you."

"Okay, sorry if I rolled my eyes."

"*If* you rolled your eyes? You *did* roll your eyes."

We were at the crossroads that every married argument takes: semantics vs. the actual issue at hand. The only way out was for one person to let the thing go. It was usually the more exhausted person who conceded.

"Never mind, Aaron. It doesn't matter. I love you. And I don't know what to do. But please know this is nothing personal." I moved over and put my hand on his leg. He nodded slowly, as if he didn't believe me. "Like even if Justin Timberlake were here right now with his dick in a box for me, I would not want anything to do with it," I said, testing the tension to see if it could withstand any humor.

He didn't smile.

In the days before kids, a marital argument would've gone on for hours, into the night, with much rehashing and re-explaining. And perhaps it would've ended with some hot 3 a.m. make-up sex. But the smartest thing for me to do right now was to get to bed and save myself. Staying up into the night—especially for a fight—would make the next day even more unbearable than it was going to be.

Separately, we cut our losses and walked upstairs, still remembering to tread softly past the kid's bedroom doors. We brushed our teeth side by side, with sleepy eyes, in silence and disconnect. Aaron stared at his phone while his electronic toothbrush buzzed. We got into bed and turned our lamps off one after the other. I closed my eyes and wondered if there was anything else that I could say to him to make him get it, especially now that the room was dark, and I didn't have to look at him.

I rolled toward him. The cold white light of his phone shone against his face like a flood light. *Guess what, asshole? Our kids aren't the only cock blockers in the house.* I wished I could rise above my frustration and say anything helpful so we didn't go to bed angry. It felt dangerous to ignore the number one piece of marriage advice. What if this was the moment that undid us? But my tank was empty. No reserves. Not everyone's night could end with love.

So I curled up, and turned away from Aaron, listening to the hum of Violet's white noise machine through the baby monitor. I wished I were back where things were more simple—with Elliot, underneath the innocent glimmer of his ceiling stars.

CHAPTER FIVE

Swallowed Up

*M*A-MAAAAAAAA! MA-MAAAAAAA!"

As if last night's argument had brought a curse upon the house, I woke up to Violet screaming my name over the monitor. No slow build. Full throttle.

My body jolted and I looked over at Aaron, who lay in bed still asleep and in the fetal position, completely unaware of Violet's commotion.

How is this my life? I can't keep living like this.

At minute six, when I couldn't bear to hear her yell my name any more, I moved the monitor toward Aaron's stupid head. I snapped it back and pretended to be asleep when he started to wake.

"I'll go grab her," he said.

A nicety. Or was it? Is going to get your daughter a nicety or just part of being a father? I rubbed my temples with a forceful thumb. It was too early to be writing an internal thesis on the existence of double standards in the parenting dyad.

I perked up at the sudden realization that today Violet and I were having a playdate—a forgotten lifeline with the promise of adult conversation. For this, I jumped out of bed.

My friendship with Danielle was fairly new. We met at

a Gymboree class when her bruiser son, Owen, crawled over Violet, giving her a bloody lip. Danielle was mortified, apologizing profusely and offering to buy me lunch after class. It was like the old days of being picked up at a bar, except there was blood, clowns, and tiny bubbles.

Danielle was a lawyer, on hiatus to be at home with Owen, but preparing to go back full-time next month. She was unlike the stuffy lawyer stereotype I had expected. She was open, funny, and sometimes referred to Owen as "This Motherfucker Right Here." One of the things I most appreciated about her was her desire talk about things other than gymnastics classes, Instant Pot recipes, and PTA fundraisers. When the kids weren't constantly interrupting us, we talked about when we lost our virginity, which foreign countries we longed to visit, which drugs we'd tried, and the onslaught of political and racist blights occurring daily. No topic was off limits. We were smart, thinking women first, and moms second. But if Danielle wasn't such a catch, I might've dumped her on account of Owen's constant bullshit.

I pulled into the sprawling mini-mall parking lot in front of the local Barnes and Noble. A Home Goods, Jamba Juice, Michaels, and Old Navy made it a Mom Mecca. Or almost, for there was no Target.

I parked my miniature van next to a pristine, white, convertible BMW. In contrast to our quaint, tightly-packed neighborhood were the million-dollar, gated communities surrounding it. We technically lived in Laguna Beach, but we were at the very eastern tip of it, which meant we were closer to the Hobby Lobby than any fancy Laguna art gallery. But no matter which side of the gates we were on, SoCal's weather didn't discriminate. When the state wasn't on fire, the sky was perfect and the air was perfect, just like today.

I scanned the Barnes and Noble entrance looking for Danielle and Owen. I never realized the number of play-dates that went down in places of business until I had children. Barnes and Noble was like an upgraded library, with its in-house cafe and shelves of shiny new things to distract toddlers with while moms talk. And unlike parks, it had doors to corral escape artists.

Beep. Danielle drove by in her Lexus SUV, smiling. She refused to sell her soul to the minivan—and other parts of motherhood. She parked and hopped out. Everything felt better in the presence of another adult.

"How's my little Violet?" she asked sweetly, scrunching up her face. Violet blushed.

Danielle had rows of box braids and was wearing actual pants. Chinos, to be exact, with a light blue button-up shirt, like adults wear. I was wearing black leggings and a fitted cotton dress with pockets—a slightly more mature version of what Violet was wearing. My post-kids fashion sense had taken a nose dive toward comfort and ease of washing.

"This playdate may have been the only reason I got out of bed this morning," I said, peeking past Danielle, into the car to say hi to Owen. He stared back at me, expression-less. Maybe I hadn't sufficiently hidden the obligation in my salutation to him. Or maybe he was just a dick. Maybe we were both dicks.

I gave Danielle the G-rated/in-front-of-kids rundown of my previous night. She attentively listened to all of the painstaking details while trying to hoist Owen from the car.

"Damn," she said, struggling to shut the door while

holding Owen and her overstuffed bag of toddler para-phernalia.

"Here, let me take that." I swept in and grabbed her bag. "It sure looks like you could use a minivan," I said, trolling her by emphatically pressing the door close button on my key remote. The four of us stood there, watching the magical door slide closed.

"Nah, I'm good," she said, laughing with what sounded like a hint of pity for me.

We walked toward the gilded front doors of the not-yet-open Barnes and Noble. A crew of customers had already formed outside. There was something oddly embarrassing about showing up at a store before it opened, something I'd never done until I had kids who often woke up before the sun. As we found our place within the opening crew, Danielle elbowed me and cautiously nodded toward a woman in purple and electric yellow leggings with llamas on them. The woman smiled desperately through tired eyes, her drooling infant strapped to her chest like a bomb. She was clearly jonesing for adult human contact. And sleep. And a wardrobe not designed by Mormon women entrepreneurs. I smiled at her until Danielle gave me eyes that said "Let's not become part of her day." Danielle was right. Our time together was holy, and we had a lot to cover. I was hoping to get back to our discussion about "womanism," if the kids were chill enough to let us go deeper. No time for scooping up lost souls today.

Once the store was open, Owen stamped his way through the doorway and then bolted for the children's section in the back, but not before straight-arm shoving Violet. Danielle sprinted after him, embarrassed and mouthing, "I'm sorry" to us, as usual.

Violet's tiny hand took mine. I crouched down to her level. "I'm sorry Owen pushed you. I'll keep an eye on him, okay?" Bottom lip jutting out, she nodded. I kissed her forehead and stood back up. I took a big inhale, filling my body with one of my favorite smells: new books. With words. Adult words, with no pictures of bus-driving pigeons or cats who think they're Chihuahuas. I hadn't read a non-parenting book for myself in nearly eight years. Violet yanked on my hand.

The kid's section was a cornucopia of color and whimsy that could sweeten even the most sour adult. And there was exquisite order that could only be experienced first thing in the morning before the toddler ransacking had commenced. It was visual Xanax.

We quickly heard and then saw Owen, who had zeroed in on a bin of stuffed Cliffords and was dumping that shit right out, methodically making his way to the next bin of plushies. Danielle threw her hands up and then bent down onto the hard carpet to put the fuzzy red dogs back. Violet found a baby animal lift-the-flap book on a low shelf and sat down with it on the log bench, away from Owen.

"So why is Aaron always working late now?" Danielle asked.

"Death by pumpkins."

"Right. I don't get all the pumpkin hype. If it were that good, wouldn't people be eating it all year?"

A lawyer had finally exposed the lie of the pumpkin lover. I crouched down next to Danielle, helping her pick up the newly tossed Curious Georges. If the price for in-person chat time was picking up stuffed animals all day, we would gladly pay it. We moved over to the mound of freshly unloaded Very Hungry Caterpillars.

"I know his work needs him. But playing the good wife is taking its toll for sure. I get no relief."

"Have you called Tanya yet?" Danielle was referring to a babysitter she'd kept pressuring me to hire, as if it were that easy. *It was probably that easy.*

"Not yet," I confessed.

"Ap. Ril." She clapped her hands as she said each syllable of my name. "A babysitter is a necessity. What is your hang up?"

One of my other favorite things about Danielle—her way of calling bullshit—was now being used on me. I appreciated it more when it was directed at say, the President or pumpkins. I felt more defensive than I wanted to.

"Well, money. Hard to justify spending it on 'me time.' Then there's the whole letting-a-potential-psycho-take-care-of-my-kids thing. Did you see that video on Facebook?" I dug for my phone to show her horrifying footage of a babysitter sitting on a toddler and whacking its face. Somebody had posted it on one of my sometimes helpful, always catty mom groups.

"Unless it's *my* babysitter giving Owen a beat down, I don't need to see it," she said, holding up her hand to stop me. "I've already vetted Tanya for you. Owen loves her, she's a college student who lives with her parents, and she's still obsessed with Cinderella. How much more wholesome can you get? She's $10 an hour. What other excuses you got?"

Danielle and her husband, Daveed, were financially comfortable, and $10 an hour sounded like chump change to them, where it sounded like "vital groceries" to me. They had a membership to the local swanky gym instead of the rundown YMCA, and vacationed in hotels rather than in friends' guestrooms. In contrast, nearly a decade of me staying at home with the kids had choked our finances, and calculations showed that even if I went back to work, we'd still be strapped because of the high price of reliable childcare and the fact that I couldn't earn a six-figure salary. I shouldn't have felt responsible for our income, but my inner feminist did.

"Aaron thinks a babysitter's going to steal our identity."

"If Aaron were the stay-at-home parent, how long do you think it would take him to hire a damn babysitter?"

"Two hours," I laughed.

"Exactly. And where are you at?"

"Uh, eight years." Saying it out loud made me feel a twinge of shame. "But I can't get over paying somebody money to do a job that I signed up to do."

"At what cost?" Danielle was becoming exasperated with me. "What you're paying for is your mental health. It's either a babysitter or Prozac." She held her hands out like scales tipping back and forth.

Suddenly there was a loud, continuous thud. We looked up to see Owen arm-swiping an entire shelf of books onto the floor. Violet sat contently next to a stack of books by the Dr. Seuss display. Was she really this well-mannered? It felt like I was looking at her through some sort of enchanted glasses.

"Owen, you pick those up *right* now," Danielle ordered, standing up.

He positioned himself for another swipe of the higher shelf.

"You. Pick. Those. Up," she demanded, in a tone that made me realize I was witnessing Courtroom Danielle. She stamped over to Owen, who lowered his arm in fear. She didn't waste any energy agonizing over how she spoke to him or how mindful of a parent she was being. Sometimes I was jealous of Danielle's ability to not give a shit, and other times my mind flashed forward to Owen in therapy as an adult. Her no-nonsense parenting surely affected his temperament, even if it spared her sanity.

"Should we head to PetSmart?" I asked, knowing that Owen was going to keep upping his dumping ante and there was a whole table of *Harry Potter* box sets nearby. Danielle nodded with desperate eyes. I turned to Violet. "Do you want to go see fuffies and kitties?"

"Ya ya ya!" she cheered.

"How about if Owen and I grab us drinks, and we'll meet you over there?" Danielle asked, pointing at the in-house Starbucks.

"Sure. But let me take Owen so you don't have to wrangle him in line." I reached out for his dimpled hand and hoped I could handle it.

"I owe you. Extra pumpkin spice in your tea, right?" She smirked.

"Never!" I yelled like a warrior refusing to go down in battle. She darted toward the smell of coffee and momentary freedom.

The two kids and I marched out the golden doors and through the automatic sliding doors of PetSmart, next door. Suburban playdate gold. The smell of wood chips, dog piss, and birds hit hard.

"Mama, I wanna see fishys," Violet said, pointing to the big wall of stacked fish tanks. I maneuvered them through the aisles to avoid passing the snakes. She and Owen stood in front of the aquariums, pointing. His pointing quickly turned into glass tapping.

"We don't want to tap the glass, Owen. It scares the fishys," I said, bending down between he and Violet. He looked at me blankly and turned back to the tank. His finger morphed into a fist and he punched the glass. The fish scattered.

"Owie, no!" Violet said.

He did it again. POUND! The fish clustered in the back corner. Right as I wondered if I would have to put my hands on Owen's to make him stop, Danielle came up behind us with warm drinks and two pink cake pops.

Again, POUND!

"Owen!" Danielle shrieked, pushing the goods into my hands so she could manhandle him. "Do not even think of touching that tank again." She yanked his fist away from the glass. Violet quickly noticed the presence of pink and cake. So did Owen.

"Mama, I needs pink!" Violet said. Owen snatched one out of my hand.

"This Motherfucker right here . . ." Danielle mumbled, throwing her arms up and shaking her head. She bent down and gave a cake pop to Violet. "This one's for you, Sweetie."

"Thank you, Danielle," I said, urging Violet to say the same.

"Tank oo."

Danielle patted Violet's head. "You must know some parenting secret I don't. She's so well-behaved. Can we trade for a day?"

I looked at Violet proudly and ran my fingers through the sun-kissed ringlets at the bottom of her light brown hair. My fingers stopped, trapped in the knots. "Sorry to ruin the fantasy, but she isn't like this all the time. Or even most of the time," I whispered, not touching the "can we trade for a day" comment at all. Because HELL NO.

"At least she holds it together sometimes, unlike this bulldozer." Danielle jiggled Owen until he giggled. It was nice to see him not in trouble for once.

We sipped our drinks and the kids munched on cake balls as we meandered past the guinea pigs and rats, finally arriving at the great glass wall of doggies in daycare. It was an interesting melding of delicious tastes and atrocious smells. Violet stood there slowly licking her pop, mesmerized by frolicking fuffies amid the fur wonderland. Probably not the most hygienic playdate.

Owen raised his fist to the glass and looked at Danielle.

"Owen Allen!" she scolded. His name sounded like a knock-off furniture store. He lowered his fist.

"What do you guys have going on the rest of the day?" I asked, feeling like we'd spent too much time trying to fix my life. Danielle needed a turn.

"Tanya's coming over. I have a late lunch with the firm."

"Wow, a lunch date. With only adults. Imagine that."

"I have to stay in the loop with work or I'll forget everything I worked for before Owen. I swear, motherhood could swallow me up whole, if I let it." She took a sip of her coffee.

Ouch. I took a long pull off of my tea to soothe the sting of Danielle's words, unsure if her dig was intentional or not.

"I didn't mean that as some passive aggressive comment about you, April. I was fully referring to myself."

I shook my head and looked downward. "Oh, oh no. It's fine."

She reached for my arm, came in close and looked at

me seriously, like a doctor about to give a life-changing diagnosis. "You give so much of yourself to your children. I could never do what you do. You are the most amazing mom I know."

"Thanks." Her compliment didn't feel as good as it sounded. I traced the hot tea cup lid with my finger. "But I feel like I'm on the verge of a nervous breakdown. Everything seems so fragile. I want to do this right for them, but it's so much work. I love them, and I'm trying to like motherhood, but I just can't. The whole thing is awful."

Danielle's eyes widened. I regretted saying that last part. Violet tugged on my leg, but my attention didn't veer from Danielle and the words I'd just blurted out.

"But you've got this motherhood thing on lock," she said. I looked at her, incredulous, but she continued. "You make dinners. From scratch. You put two kids to bed, and you lay with at least one of them until he falls asleep. You change diapers while practicing spelling words with Elliot— I've seen it. You can diagnose strep throat by smelling your kids' breath. You knew that stuff in plastic, um, that stuff that heats up or whatever . . ."

"BPA."

"Yeah, BPA—you knew that was toxic before anyone else did. April, you know your mom shit."

"It's survival. I'd rather not know the smell of strep. I'd rather be reading a novel in silence on the sunny spot of the couch than Googling toxins. I do those things because I have to, not because I want to." *Was I yelling?* It felt like I was yelling. But it was Violet.

"MAMA, OWIE STICK POP!"

Danielle and I turned from my wreckage to see what she was shouting about. The great glass wall of doggies had been blurred by the smears of pink frosting and crumbly cake. Owen stood there gripping the stick and dragging the pop's remains across the glass.

"Give me that right now!" Danielle shouted, prying the stick from his senseless hands. He screeched in anger. "You are going to help clean all of this off the window." She reached in her purse, pulled out a wipe, and shoved it into his hands. He rubbed it on the glass, spreading the frosting around even more. I didn't say anything.

"I should probably remove Owen from public," she said as she stepped forward to hug me, as if I was in a receiving line at my own funeral. "You're an incredible mom. And you need to call Tanya," she whispered in my ear as we one-arm hugged.

"Maybe I will." I tried to sound optimistic even though I felt like I couldn't breathe.

"Well, look at *you*," she said, applauding. Owen joined in on the clapping. And then Violet. Everyone was clapping at me. The doggies on the other side of the great glass wall all barked and jumped up behind me. I stood there like a fool as Danielle and Owen left, when one of the jumping dogs crouched down and took a huge dump on the floor. A PetSmart employee with blue hair and orange Crocs, who was incarcerated in the glass room, walked over with paper towels and picked up the steaming brown pile. The worker's eyes met mine through the glass. We shared an ephemeral glance of solidarity, from shit handler to shit handler.

"Slippery needs food, and you can hold it," I said to Violet. In Danielle's listing of my mom superpowers, she left out that I knew the nearness to empty level of all foods in our house—pet or otherwise.

We walked to the checkout, Violet carefully clutching the small container of fish food, clearly believing herself to be "so big." The cashier, a grandmotherly-type woman with blonde cotton-candy hair, lit up when she saw Violet. When we got closer, I noticed the woman's gold necklace with a heart charm that held three diamonds within it, and her nametag, which read "Lucile."

"Well, let me see what you have there, Sugar Lump," Lucile said, coming from around her post to get closer to the fish food's barcode—and to Violet. Lucile stood smiling euphorically, caught in some sort of fugue.

"Hold out the fish food so she can scan it," I nudged for everyone involved.

"Aren't they just the sweetest things at this age? I had three myself. Did you ever think being a mommy could be this wonderful?"

I halted. This old woman was enraptured by Violet's charming youthfulness, but she was also light years away from the reality or responsibility of having young kids. Did she remember any of the challenges, or had time turned them into only blessings? I felt uneasy and like I might explode all over a well-meaning senior citizen, so I hurried our transaction before detonation could occur.

After Violet's tear-filled campaign to hold fish food that she would've surely dumped all over the inside of the van had I not taken it away from her, I sank down in the driver's seat and peered out the windshield, feeling gutted. Danielle's comment, my own dark admission, and the glimpse into my future (thanks to a random PetSmart cashier/oracle) made me feel like I truly needed professional help. But what condition was I suffering from? In my mind, I was appropriately responding to the feeling of being overlooked and overworked. Anyone in my shoes would feel this frustration. Except for the moms that didn't. *Fuck. Also, they're lying.*

My phone rang. It was Marnie. I picked up, out of guilt since I declined her last three calls.

"How's my favorite little girl?"

"I'm okay, it's just been a rough . . ."

"No, my *other* favorite little girl."

On any other day, I could brush off my mom's noninterest in me. But today, it hurt like asphalt in a freshly scraped knee and all I wanted to do was scream into the phone at her, like the lead singer of a metal band. Instead I offered to call her back.

"Of course, honey. Make it a great day!"

Make it a great day? The fuck? How about you help me make it a great day by tapping into the godamn maternal spring inside your cold dead heart, Donna?

Once home, I put Violet down for a nap and prayed to the Sleep Gods that they would shine down upon me this afternoon.

There were endless things begging for attention in the kitchen—the trash to be taken out, the stack of junk mail on the counter, the kid's artwork to be dated and saved, the PTA donation form to scoff at, and everyone's breakfast dishes still on the kitchen table. I reached for Aaron's abandoned cup of cold coffee and walked it to the sink like a zombie. My mind kept replaying what Danielle had said to me, like a looped audio clip. *I could never do what you do. I could never do what you do.*

Even though it seemed she had sincerely meant it as a compliment, what I heard was, "I *would* never do what you do." My mind swam in a sea of judgment as I robotically tidied the kitchen. Was I doing this mom thing all wrong? Had I let motherhood swallow me up whole?

I was no stranger to self-analysis. It snuck up on me while shaving my legs in the shower or waiting in the car-pool line. I thought they were fleeting thoughts, mental chatter, but today I started believing something was really wrong with me. Modern motherhood looked so much like anxiety, which was which? Maybe Violet *was* an easy-go-ing toddler and I had been too frazzled to see it until to-day, next to Owen. Maybe *I* was the unpredictable one— maybe *I* was the problem. Did I have some late-to-the-game post-partum depression? Was that even possible? And thanks to Lucile, I now worried that by the time I fig-ured out how to really savor these days with my young kids, they would already be over.

Opposite to many of my friends, I adored the newborn and infant stage with Elliot and Violet. I felt like a goddess mother, nursing my babies to sleep, and huffing their pun-gent little heads like a Sharpie marker. I took baths with them and floated them around on their backs, their eyes twinkling as they looked into mine. In the early days, life flowed like a gentle river. It wasn't awful at all.

And now, a part of me felt like I was drowning.

I needed to be saved.

CHAPTER SIX

Mother Mary

*G*oogle stared at me, waiting. I didn't know what to search for, exactly, because I didn't know what I was feeling, exactly. Was it post-partum depression? Was it anxiety? Was it motherhood in general? Or was it me?

I began typing "Orange County" and Google so graciously auto-filled "Breast Augmentation" in for me. *Thanks Google, you dick.* I erased it, typed "Post-partum depression" and hit enter.

The first result read: Mother Roots Counseling and Wellness Center. I liked the sound of "wellness center." Like a spa where moms blow off some steam and do yoga together instead of have mental illness. I clicked the link. A breathtaking image of a large painted tree with a maternal-looking face carved into the knotty trunk welcomed me to Mother Roots' webpage. Multi-colored leaves on widespread branches made up her wild hair. The graphic started to animate and the leaves changed colors, slowly fell to the ground, blew away, and then started to grow back bright green. Something triggered me hard. *Shit April, pull it together, weirdo.* I was half-laughing as I wiped tears away with my sleeve. Crying at a website graphic was a pretty clear sign that one needed professional help. But I knew from my friends that I wasn't the only one brought to tears by basic shit since becoming a mother. So what was just motherhood and what was brainsickness? I watched the tree go through its computer-animated seasons for a good while before I clicked on the "Our Intention" tab.

"We see motherhood as a changing of seasons. As moms, we must rely on our roots to gather the nourishment we need to sustain ourselves, and our little ones. Let Mother Roots be part of your rich soil."

My jaw dropped. *I'll take six of whatever they're selling.* I quickly clicked on the "Our Team" tab. Five marriage and family therapists were listed. I'd never been to therapy before, but the idea of dropping off my emotional laundry with someone else who could aid in sorting, washing, and folding it for me sounded fucking delightful. And the uninterrupted conversation. My desperation level saved me from stewing about any stigma.

I perused the accompanying therapist headshots and bios. A blonde woman caught my eye. She looked to be about my age, with blown-out hair that lay immaculately against her bright yellow party dress and turquoise necklace. The woman's eyes sparkled and her cheeks shimmered from what had to be perfectly-applied cosmetics. The only thing missing from her headshot was a curly handwritten font on a chalkboard, next to a succulent wall. What could she possibly know about the struggles of motherhood? There was a quote under her picture that read: "I am passionate about helping mothers tend to their needs, which often go overlooked in their role as 'Mommy.' I am a Southern California native who loves beach days and sushi dates with my boys."

The sign of a good mother was at least a little bit of

dishevelment, and this woman had exactly none. Her kids ate sushi. She would not do.

I combed the page for someone less perky and polished, not sure that was possible in Orange County. I needed someone who had battle wounds, like my left eye that was scarred with a permanent, Harry Potter–like lightning bolt of bloodshottery that appeared somewhere amid the years of sleepless nights, which had only ended the month prior. I didn't want to be therapized by Princess Aurora when I looked more like Snow White's haggard cousin.

I came to a picture of an earthy, make-up-less woman with round glasses and a scarf that looked like it was purchased in an actual rural village instead of an Anthropologie. Her name was Mary and her bio mentioned her passion for travel and finding commonalities with mothers she'd worked with across the globe. I wondered, what might mothers in other countries know that I didn't? Wasn't it true that they weren't expected to play with their kids 24-7 like we were? And wasn't it true that French kids sat obediently at the table for three meals a day without any whining or snack requests? Sure, they also drank wine at age five.

I kept reading.

Mary also had two kids, a boy and a girl, just like me. Mary's quote read: "Mothers everywhere have a universal need to be mothered themselves—for someone to hold space for their experiences, challenges, and emotions, just as they do for their own children."

My shoulders dropped and I sat back in my chair, letting out a loud exhale from deep down. *I still needed what Marnie could never give me. Dammit.* I felt understood in a way that I hadn't in eight years, by the bio of an internet stranger. I was also pissed.

I didn't need to look at any other profiles. I knew I would be safe within Mother Roots's walls, specifically in the arms and at the bosom of Mother Mary, who would surely wipe my tears away with her long mousy hair. Mary was going to impart wisdom from the ages into my fractured soul. I couldn't wait to tell her everything. I knew I had to act now, while I had a kid-free moment to make a coherent phone call and before I talked myself out of it. Something had to change and this would be the kickoff.

I abruptly dialed Mother Roots's phone number, my heart racing.

Then I hung up.

What am I doing? We don't have money for this. Maybe it's just been a bad day. Week. Month. Years. Shit.

I called again. They picked up.

"I uh, I wanted to book a session with Mary. I don't know if there's an initial consultation or whatever. I don't even know what I really need. I love my kids, of course, but I guess I just need to know if there's something wrong with me." I was saying too much.

The sprightly voice piped up, "We get this kind of call every day. You are not alone."

"Okay, good." I was genuinely relieved.

"You and your therapist will have an initial session and from there, you two make a plan of intention together. It's very much a partnership."

"I was on your website and Mary looked like a great fit for me."

"Mary is lovely. And as such, she has quite a full clientele. She's booking a month out right now."

The losing jingle from *The Price Is Right* played in my head. Mary was the key to my sanity, and waiting thirty days to receive the secret to mastering motherhood felt unbearable.

"I was really hoping to get in sooner now that I found the balls to make the call," I said, cringing at the fact that I'd just said "balls" out loud. Was this person going to write that down in my chart? "Has morals loose enough to say 'balls' to strangers," it would read.

Luckily, the voice didn't waver. "It's hard to wait once you're ready. How about I book your consult appointment with Mary for a month out and then also add you to a cancellation list? We'll call you if something opens up with her."

"Yes, please."

I finally had some hope, mixed with impatience at having to wait an entire month to be tucked under Mother Mary's warm wings. As quick as I hung up my phone, it buzzed. It was a text from Aaron.

Hey A.B.

Hey.

I wasn't sure where we stood after a morning of tiptoeing around the ruins of the previous night.

I'm sorry about last night.

The Aaron I married had surfaced.

Me too.

I know it's hard being with the
kids non-stop.

He couldn't possibly know, but I appreciated the gesture.

Things may be looking up
because I booked an
appointment with a
therapist. 😳

My phone ringer blared. Aaron was calling. I picked up.

"You're seeing a therapist? Why?"

"Because I feel like I'm going to snap. I'm not doing this motherhood thing right."

"Wait, what? But you're a kick-ass mother."

"Thanks Babe, but I'm not doubting what kind of a mother I am to our kids. I'm doubting what being that kind of mother is doing to *me*."

He was silent. I could tell that he didn't understand how those things could be separate. "Oh. Is this like that post-partum depression thing they talked about in childbirth class?"

"I'm not sure what it is. But it shouldn't feel this hard."

"What if you go to the spa and get away for a few hours? Maybe that would help. My boss's wife does that sometimes."

"Aaron, I need answers, not a fucking facial."

"I just don't see you as needing therapy. You are such a good mom. It feels like you're overreacting. Did something happen today?"

I held the phone away from my face and burst into tears, silently. Aaron would never understand how my inner life and my outer mask could be so contradictory. He only took things for face value, and there were so many hidden parts to mothering. Since the minute Elliot entered the world, there was a conveyor belt of thoughts constantly running in the back of my mind, preparing for whatever might come next—the diaper blowout, the spit-up massacre, the inconsolable crying complete with hours of bouncing on a giant ball that took up the entire living room. As the kids got older, the internal mother machine never stopped, the fuel just changed from anticipating baby needs to toddler needs, then to big kid needs—not to mention husband needs. And then the outside pressures —"Don't be a helicopter mom, but also, we'll call CPS on you if you try to teach your kids any independence." Motherhood was far too nuanced for the English language. There were no words to explain it to Aaron. What was the word for wanting so badly to be a mother, then the reality being so much more intense and constant than you ever imagined? What's the word for "no pause button to catch your breath for eighteen years?" The Germans surely had a word for it. They had words for all the most fucktangular situations, like *schadenfreude, mittelschmerz,* and *torschlusspanik.*

I wiped my eyes and steadied my voice. "I'm going to see this therapist, even if I have to pay for it out of the money from my grandma."

"A.B., you know I'll support you in whatever you want to do. We can pay for it. I just don't want you to feel like you're broken or something. You are seriously such a great mother."

I rubbed my temple with my thumb. It was all too confusing. Aaron was checking all the supportive boxes, but I wanted him to really hear me rather than cheerlead me into doing more of what was breaking me.

"Thanks," I forced.

"And good news, I won't be home as late tonight, just normal late, only an hour or so."

I breathed in deeply, but didn't exhale. No one was going to save me. Again. Always. Not Danielle, definitely not Marnie, and not even Aaron. No one was going to mother me. Except for Mother Mary, in thirty painstaking days.

CHAPTER SEVEN

Reclaiming My Time

*T*wo weeks inched by like watching a child's botched bangs grow back. I hadn't realized how much I craved help until I was forced to wait for it. I mentioned my therapy appointment to Danielle and her response was, "Take that money and hire Tanya with it instead." I didn't say anything to Marnie about it.

It was a Tuesday afternoon when my phone rang. I usually never answered an unrecognizable number, but maybe this was my salvation.

"Hello?"

Violet looked up from the family of anthropomorphic bunnies she'd been dressing and undressing two seconds earlier, and ran over to me, repeating her life's mantra.

"Mama, I needs something eat . . ."

I instinctively turned away from her request, put my finger in one ear and closed my eyes, tuning everything out so I could hear the voice on the phone. "Is this April?" it asked.

"Yes."

"This is Jackie from . . ."

"I NEEDS SOMETHING EAT!" Violet's screams dominated the air waves. I could hear nothing on the other end of the phone. I bared my teeth and desperately motioned with my whole arm for her to go back to what she was doing over by The Bunningtons, like I was in an angry game of charades. But the exaggerated motions only made her yell louder.

"I'm so sorry, can you hold on just a moment, please?" I begged.

I bolted to the snack cabinet, grabbed all the snack boxes, and splayed them out on the floor, willing to let Violet have free reign of the Goldfish, pretzel, and Pirate's Booty smorgasbord. It did not appease her. She was out for blood—mine. I was left with no choice but to do what all mothers everywhere are forced to do when they absolutely must take an important phone call. I cupped the lower part of my phone to muffle Violet's protest and zoomed upstairs to my closet, like I had a mushroom speed boost on Mario Kart.

"No Mama, waaaaaaaaait," Violet pleaded as I flew past her.

"I'm so sorry for that," I said to the voice on the phone, rounding the corner into my bedroom and then into the closet. I shut the closet door and quickly pressed the lock button, an unintentional gift from the home owner before us. They must've had children.

"Are you still there?" I tried to catch my breath and hoped I wasn't about to be congratulated on the timeshare I'd just won.

"Yes. This is Jackie from Mother Roots."

I smiled into the phone. Violet was now on the other side of the door, crying and pounding her fists. BOOM. BOOM. Determined, I walked straight into a rack of Aaron's hanging suit jackets and slid them closer to my ears. I was now soundproof.

"We had a last-minute opening at three this afternoon. It's short notice, but would you like to take it?" If only they could see me burrowed in my husband's suits with a tiny hurricane on the other side of the door, then they would know that the answer was *hell to the yes.*

"I would love to take it."

I was buzzing, and apparently out of my mind because I had forgotten that I needed childcare before saying yes to anything in my life. Three p.m. was only two hours away. I peeked my head out from the wall of wool surrounding me. There was a strange lack of sound. The ruckus against the door in all forms had stopped. I relished the moment of silence, knowing it wouldn't last, and sat down on a pile of dirty laundry. I quickly S.O.S. texted my next-door neighbor, Chloe.

I moved on to Aaron's mom, Lucinda, who lived about twenty minutes away, forging a back-up plan. Someone *had* to help me. I switched back and forth between Chloe and Lucinda's text screens, hoping to see response dots pop up, but there was no sign from either of them.

I panicked, knowing that I would have to do the last thing I wanted to do. I would have to ask Aaron to come home early to watch the kids. I hated involving him and the wife guilt it would induce, but missing this opportunity with Mother Mary just wasn't an option.

I began my campaign.

> Heyyyyy. That therapist's office called and they have an opening for me today at 3pm. I tried Chloe and your mom to

see if they could watch
the kids, but no word
back. I MUST go to that
appointment. Is there any
way you could work from
home so I could go?

I felt sick as I pressed send. It had been hard enough to convince him that this was necessary for my mental health, and now here I was groveling like an underling, hoping I would be granted permission for self-care. Exactly how were moms supposed to partake in self-care when it usually hinged on begging other people for help? Isn't that technically not "self" care?

The response dots appeared.

Yeah, I can leave in ten.

Moments like this reminded me why I married Aaron. I knew plenty of my friends' husbands wouldn't say yes. And yet, beneath my gratitude, there was irritation. It wasn't directed personally at Aaron, but at the way motherhood turns even the nicest husbands into overlords. My former independent self was turning over in her grave.

Aaron messaged back the emoji of the smile with the hearts for eyes, which abated my inner dialogue. And then he sent the peach, which looked like a big round ass. I responded with the eggplant, which looked like a penis. He messaged back the double cherries. We were eighth graders at our core.

I remembered I was sitting on a heap of dirty laundry and locked in a closet when I heard a rip outside the door that sounded like paper tearing. I hoped Violet wasn't shredding cash from my wallet again. I burst out of the cave of clothing to find her surrounded by opened maxi pads with their stickies peeled off. About ten were stuck to the bathroom wall and she was flapping the absorbent wings as if they were butterflies.

"Mama, I stick!" Violet pointed proudly at the decorated wall. Oddly, the maxi-pad mural didn't phase me. *I'm outta here in two short hours.*

"Wow, you figured out how to open those. Smart girl."

Violet grinned, puffing out her chest. I let the engrossed artist continue her work, and sat down on the edge of the bed, finally feeling the excitement of what was to come in a few hours at Mother Roots. And then came the nausea. My stomach fluttered. I'd assumed Mother Mary was warm-hearted and forgiving, but maybe I was wrong. It hit me that I didn't actually know much about her. And me—where would I even begin in my story? It would take weeks to tell it all. But just as quickly as my worry came on, it dissipated when I remembered that I would be getting kid-free time.

Violet started yawning amid a sea of pad wrappers. It was thirty minutes past her usual nap time. I hoped I hadn't missed the precious "sleep window." I had stockpiled every book on infant and toddler sleep, and granted, my mind was about as sharp as a Boppy pillow when I read them, but one thing that all the books talked about was this elusive "golden window" when putting babies and toddlers to sleep. It was some magical timeframe that you had to adhere to or the nap would be ruined and it would be the mother's fault for not recognizing the signs earlier. The child had to be sleepy, but not too sleepy. You had to sense this window before your child showed any signs of it, or else it was too late. Your kid is yawning? Too late! It wasn't enough that mothers had to be cooks, drivers, doctors, and playmates, they also needed to be psychics if they wanted their kids to sleep, and that still wasn't a guarantee.

I swept Violet up from the pile of green wrappings and snuggled her close. She welcomed it. "I love you big," I whispered into her tiny ear, setting her down softly inside the crib. As I brought Purple Blanket up to tuck her in, I heard a ruffle duffle. A maxi-pad was stuck to her back. It was an extra-long nighttime one and covered the entire length of her torso. I laughed quietly to myself, then reached for the pad to slowly pull it off, in hopes she wouldn't notice. But she did.

"No, Mama, I needs sticker."

"Fine, it's all yours," I said and handed the maxi-pad to her. She took it in her hands and hugged it close, like it was a treasured part of the crib crew. I blew a kiss and crept out of the room.

It was already 1:45 p.m. Elliot would be coming home from school shortly. I glanced down and realized that I looked like a street person. Everything—including my wardrobe, hair, and makeup—could be used for or against me today. I wanted to look nice, but not too nice. I wanted to be my real self, but not actually wear what my real self was wearing. Even Mother Mary wouldn't be nurturing enough to look past someone who literally couldn't get dressed before going out in public.

I scanned my closet, looking for my go-to "I'm a functional adult" shirt. It was an India-inspired lilac tunic with an Americanized spin (light distressing). Mother Mary would love it. I slipped it on along with jean capris, grey Toms, a quick pass of mascara, and hoop earrings. You can't be clinically depressed if you're wearing hoop earrings.

On my way out of the bedroom, a shimmer across the room caught my eye. It was the afternoon light hitting the shiny, sharp needle in my sewing machine, which was dusty and sitting in the corner, in a perpetual time-out. We hadn't spent time together in ages. I plucked a tissue from the box on my bedside table and ran it across the body of the sewing machine, freeing it from the fuzz.

Downstairs, I flicked on the monitor and there was Violet, sitting straight up and swimming her Ariel doll in the air instead of sleeping. I'd missed the fucking window. But her lack of nap would be Aaron's cross to bear. At least for a bit.

It was ten minutes before I needed to leave and Aaron still wasn't home, nor was Elliot, until the sound of the garage door hummed. Elliot burst through the door, already halfway through taking off his pants. "Mom, Jackson just told me about the coolest thing in Five Nights at Freddy's—there's a golden Freddy and he only comes up sometimes but when he does it's really special and it means that you unlocked something. But Chica is my favorite because she looks like an evil rubber duck but I think she's really a chicken . . ."

The will to live drained from my body as he kept talking about a world that I had zero interest in. I didn't know if one could die from listening to their kid talk about video games, but it felt possible. I tried to stay present and listen to the run-on sentences about a scary-ass animatronic bear and chicken/duck that had been giving him nightmares, but what I really wanted to do was shout, "Reclaiming my time. Reclaiming my time." I focused on his eager eyes, which pulled me back into the moment as he finished.

"Sounds cool, El," I managed.

"Violet?" he asked, looking down and pointing at the failed snack bribes on the floor.

"Yep."

"Are you going somewhere?" he asked me. Maybe my functional adult shirt tipped him off.

"Yes, I have a meeting."

"A meeting? But you don't have a job."

Just great. The people I worked for considered me unemployed.

Instead of educating him on the ignorance of his words, I looked at the clock again for the twelfth time. Five minutes past when I needed to leave. Aaron was making me sweat it out. Then I heard the telltale hum of his Prius pulling in.

"Love you," I yelled to Elliot as I bolted out the door, purse in hand, blowing him a kiss. He blew one back.

"Sorry. Have to hurry. Late!" I said to Aaron as I opened my van door and quickly started the engine.

"What time will you be home?" he shouted through the passenger window. *Wouldn't you like to know? Maybe Mother Mary and I will grab some Thai food after our session and discuss the international human-rights struggle.*

"I don't know," I mouthed through the window, liberated to be the keeper of time, for once. Aaron nodded with a hint of submission I recognized all too well, and then he walked into the house.

I was alone. In a minivan. The world was my oyster. There were socks, bowls, books, sticks, and snack wrappers everywhere behind me. That limo-like partition couldn't come soon enough.

As I pulled out of our street, I saw one of my neighbors, Val, picking up strewn pieces of sidewalk chalk while chasing her naked toddler out of the street. *So long, suckers.*

I attended to the first order of business as a white suburban mom with freedom—putting on old-school hip-hop, a music that was not made for us, but made me feel free. Childless even. I cranked the volume to a deafening level and the painkilling backbeat of Ice Cube's "Today Was a Good Day" poured through my garbage can on wheels. The outside world was bright, so I slid my Target sunglasses on. Soon I would be in the shelter of Mother Mary's loving arms, burrowing my head in an authentic scarf from the holy city of Tiberias.

CHAPTER EIGHT

Mom Vomit

The waiting area of Mother Roots was a shabby-chic sanctuary. There were overstuffed, inviting armchairs and perfectly mismatched mugs for complimentary tea and cucumber water.

Immediately upon walking in the door, my eyes fixated on an immense mural of the deeply rooted, leaf-changing tree from their website. The trunk and branches looked like they were cross-sectioned off a real tree. The thick roots were made from some sort of tightly twisted rope and were embedded in dirt behind glass, like in an ant farm. The leaves were shiny, colored glass pieces with delicate veining. I moved close to the wall to examine it more carefully. The tree was exquisite—a genuine work of art.

"Hello there," a small voice called from across the room. As I moved toward the check-in desk, the tree's leaves changed color in unison with my step. I back-stepped. The glass was a different color from each angle. I couldn't take my eyes off of it.

"I see you're hypnotized by our tree," the receptionist said. I nodded. Her nametag read "Jackie."

Like her phone persona, Jackie was a sunny woman. With tiny eyes and a pointy nose, she looked a bit like a mole from a storybook. She wore a dress that appeared to be a giant flap of corduroy material that had a hole cut for her head in the middle.

"Just gorgeous," I said, still gawking at the tree.

"Mary, one of our therapists here, dabbles in sculpture." Mother Mary was already batting a thousand. "You must be April."

I nodded. "Thank you so much for fitting me in."

Jackie smiled bigger than necessary, making her cheeks grow a size larger. "Here is a form and questionnaire to help us help you best."

I sat down and soaked in my solitude. It reminded me of how I didn't see the night sky for a year after my kids were born, constantly staying inside after dark, working hard for their sleep. Standing outside in the crisp night air and seeing the moon for the first time in twelve months felt like a revelation, just like sitting in this spotless chair, sipping on cucumber water, and gazing at actual art, with zero chance a child would ruin the moment. I turned off my phone ringer just to be sure and when I did, I noticed a small adhesive backing from the maxi-pads clinging to my sleeve. I looked around to see if anyone saw (they hadn't), crumpled it, and tossed it into my purse. The sound of a babbling brook trickled somewhere in the room, hidden.

Clipboard on my lap, I blazed through the boiler-plate questions, halting at "Occupation." There were so many things I used to do—the clothing line, assisting the city's best caterer with red-carpet events, teaching dance classes at the local rec center, showering without an audience.

When Elliot first went to preschool, I restarted my clothing line part-time, focusing on children's designs. It was serendipitous that my first-ever mommy friend, Lizzy, also sewed. I hired her, and together we learned how to mother while also making baby and kids' apparel with appliques made from vintage t-shirts we'd score at local thrift shops. We called each piece a "work of art" because no two were alike. There were shirts with appliqued octopi, elephants, turtles, cars, hearts, cats, horses, robots, or any other design a kid could beg for. It was almost hard to believe how entrepreneurial and motivated I was as a new mom. Naïve too.

My Russian great-grandmother taught me to sew when I was a child. Great Grandma Ruby was fiery and lived to be 104 years old. She was also an enigma—skilled at being a devoted mother of five and also an activist on the front lines of the women's suffrage movement. She sewed protest banners. One of my biggest heartaches was Great Grandma Ruby passing before I knew to ask her how she juggled all the various pieces of herself. I often had dreams where she and I were sewing together—her hands guiding mine as I fed the cloth toward the needle and thread. But every time I'd take the finished fabric out and tug at stitches, they would rip apart.

I named my clothing company Ruby Riot, in honor of her. It was on its way to being successful, getting picked up in a few Los Angeles boutiques, and on the backs of two celebrity children. But everything had stalled out after Violet was born, despite my intentions of keeping up with orders from a handful of regular customers and friends. The demands of two kids at two different stages made juggling one more ball impossible. My once-organized fabrics and threads were now stuffed haphazardly into bins in the garage, under the Easter baskets.

I stared at the intake form on my lap. I couldn't bring myself to answer the occupation question with "none" since I managed every last detail in our household, from scheduling the plumber to the whereabouts of every toy we owned, and for no pay. So instead I wrote, "CEO" and flipped the page.

The first question read: "What are you hoping for today?" *A diagnosis that could garner me two weeks solo in a quiet hospital with room service sounded ideal. Hmm, maybe I shouldn't have worn the earrings.* Instead I wrote: "I'd like to know if what I'm feeling as a mother is normal or not. I'd also like to learn how to make it feel easier."

Next was a section that asked me to check 'yes' or 'no' if I'd ever experienced any of the following: Extreme depressed mood, rapid speech, sleep disturbances, unexplained losses of time, unexplained memory lapses, frequent body complaints, eating disorder.

I sneered out loud while reading these. Jackie glanced my way, so I curbed my laughter with a fake cough and looked back down at the page. If I was being honest, I could answer yes to every single one of these things, but I'd need at least a paragraph of explanation for each. Extreme depressed mood? Like you get when you've been with kids for twelve hours straight and your husband tells you he has to work late, again? Sleep disturbances—really? Wasn't this the biological essence of babies? Unexplained losses of time? Like when you forget to move the clothes from the washer to the dryer over and over again for an entire week?

My amusement turned into frustration. The "red flag" items listed on this form were an inherent part of motherhood. It felt like a trap. I didn't want Mother Mary to misdiagnose me just because I checked some boxes on a form, so I checked "no" to all of them.

I hesitated at the next question: "Have you ever had suicidal thoughts?" Here was the big one. The glaring, cardinal flag. The truth was, any parent who had gone long periods of time without sufficient sleep (all parents) would tell you that at some point—even if for a microsecond—they had to acknowledge that the only way they could get immediate, uninterrupted sleep was to be dead. And for that split second, death sounded really great. But that for sure wasn't the same as driving your van into the ocean, so I checked the 'no' box, finished up, and handed the forms to a jolly Jackie.

"Come with me," she said, getting up from behind the desk.

The halls were adorned with *National Geographic*–type photos of mothers and children of different ethnicities. It stuck out to me that not all the mothers were smiling. Many looked desperate. Some had their tube-like breasts exposed with babies suckling. There was something delightfully disarming about walking through a hall of mothers baring it all, not smiling for the camera. It was the opposite of Facebook.

As I followed a shuffling Jackie, I spied the photos of the counselors from the Mother Roots website. There was Mother Mary, exuding wisdom and tenderness. And there was the headshot of the perfectly-coiffed blonde with model hair. *Barf.*

Jackie stopped and peeked her little head into one of the offices, setting my paperwork down inside the room. "I've got April for you."

I could smell an earthy, slightly sweet fragrance coming from the room. Maybe it was a flower essence straight from a field in Iceland from one of Mary's visits. Maybe we would have our session on floor pillows, like the Japanese. Mary was so worldly.

Out from the office walked the flawless blonde. The record inside my head scratched and I felt like I was going to heave. Jackie spoke. "April, this is June," and then she stopped, turning red as a ripe radish. "Oh my. April and June," she said looking back and forth at us. "We've left out May. Someone find May!" she joked, while emphatically looking around the hallway like a jackass telling a bad joke that people had been subjected to their entire life.

June reached her hand out to shake mine, cutting off Jackie's performance. "Hi, April, I'm so happy you're here. It's a pleasure to meet you."

I limply shook her hand and forced a meager shock-induced smile. Everything was crumbling—there would be no tenderness, no burrowing in an understanding bosom, no pearls of wisdom from around the globe, no safe space for me to speak my truth. Instead, there would be judgment from someone with the time to precisely apply bronzer, who would surely hear one word out of my mouth and give me the verdict of severe and incurable depression, or worse. I felt the blood drain out of my head and drop to the bottom of my feet as I suddenly realized I didn't want to be looked at under a microscope, namely by this woman. I needed to find a way out. What would Marnie do? Marnie would point out the fact that an error had occurred and that she was very disappointed and what could they do to accommodate her? And Marnie would not worry about having any tact while doing it.

My heart was racing, telling me to do something instead of freezing. "Hi, umm, I was expecting Mary. That's who I was originally booked with, or so I thought."

"Was that on the notes?" Jackie asked. "I thought you were on the list for the next available counselor. I'm sorry, let me double check," she said as she scampered off down the hall. The mole had ruined everything.

It was just June and I standing there in the hallway. She raised her eyebrows and said, "The month jokes never get old, do they?" I let out a sigh of relief that sarcasm had just entered the picture. "I'm sorry you were expecting Mary and we screwed things up. Do you want to reschedule? You won't hurt my feelings if you prefer to do that."

Yes, I wanted to reschedule. But Aaron had come home early for me and I had gotten my hopes up for some kind of help today. June stood there, kindly waiting for my answer, with a welcoming-enough smile, but looking like she was a cast member from *Real Housewives of Orange County*. I cleared my voice, let go of what I thought this would be like and nicely lied. "It's fine." Apparently I was believing my own bullshit lie because I felt the blood pumping back up to my face, the nausea subsiding. Marnie would've been at the front desk, deep in Jackie's grill, taking DNA samples, pinpointing exactly where the error occurred, and asking for a discount because of the inconvenience. But I recalibrated myself and followed June into her office.

June's office was just as organized and curated as she was, which wasn't as off-putting as I expected because it felt so damn calming to be among order. Of course, there was a color scheme—teal, coral, and grey, with pops of bright yellow in the throw pillows. Mental illness meets beachy. There was an aqua-colored, knitted blanket folded up nicely on the side of the couch. I wondered what kind of scenario would have me—or anyone—cuddled up under a blanket on this couch. Maybe a past-life regression? The couch looked like the material of a grey business suit, not very different than the ones I had shoved my face into earlier that day in the closet, and there was a side bookcase made from what appeared to be weathered ship planks. This must be how people decorated when they weren't making decisions amid a toddler meltdown at Ikea.

"Have a seat." June motioned toward the couch, sitting herself down in a cream linen armchair with colorful, upholstered buttons along the back. I looked around, avoiding direct eye contact and analyzing everything within the walls. My feet dangled from the couch, like a little girl's, and when I noticed it, I quickly sat forward, feet on the floor, and began to sweat. June leaned over and put my paperwork on her desk. "I kind of hate these things. Let's move beyond the boxes and talk about *you*. I see that you'd like some guidance about what is normal and how to make things easier. Where would you like to begin?"

I looked at her and took a breath, pausing for a moment. She had not crossed over into the fake eyelash territory. There was hope.

"I guess I'll start with the fact that this whole motherhood setup is hard for me. I feel like I'm in survival mode most every day because it's all so constant. I have two kids. Someone's always hungry, tired, cranky, growing out of shoes, nails need trimming again, slept too much, didn't sleep enough. And there's so much screaming and crying. I feel like I'm parenting with a gun to my head, trying to do whatever it takes to appease the shooter." Then I clarified, "My kids are the shooter."

She gave me a quick nod. I kept going.

"I am interrupted during every task and pulled in different directions by whoever needs me that minute. It's like I'm on a short leash and my family are the ones holding it. I don't feel depressed, or whatever I think depressed is supposed to feel. But I also don't enjoy being with my beautiful and needy children—namely my toddler—for thirteen hours straight every single day for years on end while my husband has a career and gets to shit alone in a building with only adults. Soooo, I guess I just want to know if what I'm feeling is normal or if I'm a whiny, ungrateful bitch who should just make peace with motherhood and be happy."

I took a much-needed breath. I knew I had been talking rapidly—one of the red flag checkboxes on the questionnaire. *Shit.*

June leaned her head back a bit, as if she was trying to get a higher view of me. She appeared to be collecting her thoughts before speaking. Either that or she was about to bolt.

"First, what I hear you saying is that you feel overwhelmed with the day-to-day duties of motherhood, especially with your toddler. It sounds like you are multitasking more than you want to be. I also hear a possible agreement you have about being able to handle it more easily, that there's something wrong with you if you aren't able to. That's the first part of what I'm hearing, correct?"

She had just magically poured my verbal vomit through a sieve.

"Yes, that's exactly it," I said. I felt a fire inside me. "The fun, easy moments exist, but they aren't the bulk of it. How I thought being a mom would feel and how it actually feels are often two different things. Should it be that way?"

"Different stages have different challenges." She looked down at my form, searching. "Remind me again how old your children are?"

"Violet is two and Elliot is eight."

June nodded her head like something new clicked. "I don't know if you remember with your first, but life with a two-year-old is one of the most challenging phases of motherhood. Two and I'm sorry to say, three, are the times when many children are their most difficult. Their needs and desires blur together, everything feels immediate, and they will do whatever it takes to get those things. The role of constant caretaker to a person who can't be reasoned with is a somewhat impossible spot to be in. As you well know," she said, softly motioning her open hand toward me. "It doesn't make you ungrateful to need a break from that role."

I felt like I'd just taken off a wet coat. My shoulders released. I wished Aaron had been there to hear June's words. They were different coming out of a professional's mouth than they would be coming out of a friend's.

"But people—other moms—come up to me all the time and say things like, 'I would give anything to have mine that little again,' and it makes me feel like I should just be loving every minute of it. And I want to say to these moms, 'If you would give anything to have little ones again, then why aren't you having more kids? If it's so fucking fun, then why did your husband get a vasectomy?'"

A tiny smile snuck up on June's face. I felt relief that an f-bomb seemed to be welcomed. I would've had to leave otherwise.

"So you are feeling judged for not finding it entirely easy?"

"In a way, yes."

"Is it judgment from others or from yourself?"

I tilted my head to the side and looked up, as if the answer was stuck in the corner of the room. But I didn't know. No one had directly told me that I had to love all of motherhood, but on the other hand, no one had told me that it was okay not to, specifically the memes about how many summers we have left with our kids, so we better soak up *all* the fucking fun while we can.

"Don't worry if you don't know yet. We're just scratching the surface today. What did you think motherhood would be like?"

"I thought it would be amusement parks and camping trips and building couch forts. All smiles. But those things are so much harder with a toddler, to the point where it's near torture for me to manage just going out to eat as a family. I love my little girl, but right now she adds this wild-card layer to our family and we all—well, mostly me —have to be ready to dodge her toddler bullshit at any moment. If we make plans and she doesn't nap, we'll have to cancel because no one wants to wrangle a cranky toddler in a booth for an hour while they try to eat. I didn't expect it all to feel so fragile. I know I should know this, she's my second kid. But their age gap is so big that I've seriously forgotten everything."

"I don't blame you for not wanting to herd a toddler while out to dinner," June said. "And at least you know your boundaries and will cancel a dinner if it makes the night more tolerable for you and your family."

That was one way to look at it. I guess my choice to cancel—or not even make plans—always felt like a weakness, but maybe it helped keep my head above water. I was in survival mode with a two-year-old, but I also *was* surviving, albeit barely.

"I just want my old life back." The second I said it, I wished I hadn't. The words escaped my mouth before I could put a more grateful spin on them so I didn't seem like a monster who didn't love her kids. I *did* love my kids. I never questioned that part. But June didn't flinch.

I looked down at the floor and then back up at her. Something new was making its way to my surface. She waited.

"I guess I signed up for a job that I really knew nothing about. And I assumed that I would love it so much that I could take the twenty-four-hour, seven-days-a-week shift, but maybe I just wasn't a good candidate for the job." My voice cracked and my throat ached admitting that. Then the tears came. June subtly slid the tissue box next to me on the couch.

"None of us are necessarily good candidates, April. Nobody can do that job without falling apart, with those kinds of hours and demands. And nobody should."

I nodded, dabbing my tears before too much mascara damage could be done.

Switching the cross of her legs, June continued, "Maybe you're realizing that you need to fit in more breaks for yourself. Or perhaps being a stay-at-home mom *isn't* for you. It's not for everyone. If you tease out the self-judgment there, could it be possible that you might thrive having more of a balance, like you mentioned your husband has?"

June made it sound so easy, as if the self-judgment could be neatly boxed up and shipped away. She leaned forward and spoke quietly, almost in a whisper. "Could it be that what you feel like you *should* be doing and what you are capable of doing might be two different things? And might that be okay?"

That statement pinged somewhere deep in my core. I didn't want it to be true, but it was. "How do I ever rectify any of this? It's like I'm in a prison of my own doing—I don't want to be with them, but I also don't want to be without them." I finally saw the lure of the knitted blanket on the couch. I wanted to crawl under it and never come out. This whole matter was too tangled and too contradictory. There were no adequate words, only tears.

June waited patiently while the emotion washed over me, and then steered the ship forward. "I hear you saying that you are the main caretaker, in excess. How does your husband fit into this picture? Does he help you?"

Just when things couldn't possibly feel worse, now I was adding "guilt for painting my husband as a deadbeat dad" to the mix.

"Oh no, my husband, Aaron, he's a great dad. He has Nerf gun wars with Elliot and stuffed animal tea parties with Violet. They all watch *Star Trek* together. The kids adore him. He's a fun dad." I found myself struggling to come up with examples of how Aaron helped *me*.

"In addition to him, do you have a family member, a friend or a babysitter that you can call on to help you out?"

"My mom lives out of state, but sometimes my mother-in-law helps. My next-door neighbor and I trade kids sometimes. But in terms of having an outside babysitter we pay for, I've never used one."

June's eyebrows raised. I finally realized just how crazy I sounded. Again, it was really different having a trained professional react to your parenting choices than your friend who also has flaws.

"I know, I know. My friend always tells me I need to get a babysitter, that it's the best thing ever."

June made a note on the paper. *Shit, she's probably writing "Diagnosis: insanity."*

"Let's talk about your alone time, April. Does this exist?"

"Does sleeping count?"

"It does not."

"So then basically never. Probably just doctor's appointments, Target runs when Aaron can watch the kids after work, Elliot's teacher conferences, and stuff like that. I recently got a few cavities filled and had about three hours of alone time. And right now I am experiencing 'alone time' here with you."

"Did you just refer to getting cavities filled as 'alone time'?"

"Yes. Yes, I did. Even though my teeth were being drilled into, there was no whining, no people climbing on me, no requests for food. Alone time. Autonomy. Sort of."

June laughed with a smidgen of sorrow and then, with a burst of new energy, sat up straight in her chair. "Okay, let's say money wasn't an object and a magical Mary Poppins appeared who was a trustworthy babysitter that your kids liked. What would you do?"

"Oh wow." I gladly dove headfirst into this alternate reality. "I would for sure make Mary Poppins feed Violet all of her meals. I would go to Target alone, in the day time. I would buy organic strawberries every time. And those overpriced bath salts in the clear glass jars. I would hire a cook to make all our dinners and they would have to make one meal that worked for everyone's tastes, like I do every night. Oh, and a housecleaner. A pube-free bathroom floor. And a professional organizer too. The stacks of school papers and toys are closing in on me. I can't imagine what it would feel like to be de-cluttered and for everything to have its place, like it did when I grew up."

June had grabbed her pen and was taking notes as I went hog wild.

"And I would go to Nordstrom—not even Nordstrom Rack. I'd go legit Nordstrom and I'd actually try things on in the store, alone, instead of just buying, trying on at home and returning." And then I remembered. "I could even get back into sewing. Having a Mary Poppins would mean I'd get to focus on one project for hours. Without interruption, right?"

June nodded yes and scribbled something on her paper.

"I could do anything without interruption. I could maybe dance again."

"Super." June stopped me. "There is so much here for us to work with. Let's take a few of these pieces and move toward something actionable today."

"But how does any of this dream life happen without the endless money and enslavement of a Mary Poppins?" It was like I had woken up from the world's best dream, that moment right before Justin Timberlake and I finally consummate our love.

"First, we have to think without any restrictions so that we can tap into what it is we specifically want."

I was beginning to feel hopeful.

June looked at her paper. "Things I heard you say: you want help with harder tasks with Violet, specifically feeding her meals. You'd like more alone time, even if you're running errands for your family. You'd like help with making dinners that please everyone. You'd like to get some special clothing pieces from somewhere nice. You'd like to have a clean, organized home. And the one that seemed to hold the most oomph with you was that you'd like to get back into sewing."

It was as if Santa were here reading my Christmas list back to me.

"Yeah, just all that, no big deal," I shrugged.

"Let's pick two and focus on those for right now. Start small. I have something that might help you with the organization and de-cluttering piece. Now, which other item would you like to tackle?"

I tried to choose something more practical, but I couldn't hide from myself or June. "Sewing. But I don't know how to get the time."

"Let's not worry about the 'how.' That will come, and it is your job to seek it out," she said with a wink that wrinkled a long thin scar on her right temple. "Before I see you again, I want you to take one step to find time to sew alone."

I groaned. "This means I have to get a babysitter, right?"

"That's entirely up to you. You will know what you need to do. In regards to organization, there is a book I'm going to loan you called *The Life-Changing Magic of Tidying Up* by Marie Kondo." I'd heard of it, and the title alone was orgasmic. I wasn't confident about finding time to read anything other than *Goodnight Moon*, but this felt vital.

"What about a next session together? Next week?" June inquired.

"What do you think I need?" My worry about a diagnosis, which had been dormant all session, suddenly crept back up to the surface. June put her paper and pen down.

"You are really open, April, and that is half the battle. You articulate what you feel, which means we can help you move forward more quickly, and hopefully see some positive changes sooner rather than later. You just rattled off a huge list of things you want. That can take months for some people." I felt like a dog being patted on the head until its tongue dropped out of its mouth. I tightened my jaw to make sure my ego wasn't drooling.

"And what you asked in the beginning, about what you're feeling being normal or not . . ." She paused before continuing. *Why was she stopping? Stop stopping.* "It *is* normal for moms to forget how to take care of themselves. They're so busy trying to get it right by doing for every-one else that they forget about their own needs. Your hap-piness is critical to the health of your entire family unit." I almost didn't hear anything after the "*is* normal" part, ex-cept I for sure noticed she said the word "unit." #eighth-grader4life.

It turned out that I wasn't broken, after all. Maybe I would stop badgering myself now.

June touched my arm. "That's where we're going to start—with helping you tend to yourself. It's not something most of us mothers instinctively know how to do."

But Danielle sure did. *Apparently the badgering-myself thing hadn't just fixed itself in the past ten seconds. Strange.*

"So you're saying that 'me time' shouldn't have to in-volve a needle in my gums or a speculum in my lady bits?" I joked.

"Yes, precisely. Let's meet next week so we can build off of this strong start." I wished I could sleep on June's couch, nuzzled under the teal blanket until next time.

"Stop by Jackie's desk on the way out and she'll get you scheduled." The mole. I had forgotten all about Jackie's grave mistake.

After all I'd shared with June, I felt inclined to hug her, but that felt too needy, so instead I opted for an awkward wave like Forrest Gump. As I walked down the hall and passed her picture, I felt a stab of guilt. I saw a different woman in that picture this time—one that was caring and down-to-earth. I told myself that in the future, I would try not to be such a judgmental jerkhole.

CHAPTER NINE

As in Birth, in Life

*D*riving home, the pink and orange cotton-candy clouds reached right down to touch the familiar mini-malls and neighborhoods as I mentally replayed pieces from my session with June. Words and images softly floated in and out. I felt peaceful, satisfied, like I'd just gotten a massage. I guess I had, in a way. I felt hopeful that June's wisdom and my homework assignments would spark something new in my life. I wanted this buzz to last forever.

I turned onto our street, stopping while the neighbor kids hurried to move their scooters out of my way. I smiled and waved at them, realizing that for the past two hours, I hadn't even checked my phone to see if anyone needed me. I had truly been off my leash.

I paused at the door before entering. What was this strange feeling of eagerness to return to my family? I didn't know, but it was how I wanted motherhood to feel, always.

I opened the door, stepped over Elliot's pants, and looked to see Aaron sitting on the couch, eyes down, and typing furiously on his laptop. Elliot was sitting nearby on an armchair, in a deep iPad coma, full slouch. Violet was watching *Alice in Wonderland*, yet again. She looked up from her movie, noticing me. "Mama, I needs something eat."

In that one moment, I felt all of my openness and eagerness implode. Hope turned to stifled rage—specifically at Aaron, who had seemingly not tended to the kids, but had left it for me to do immediately upon my return. If I had to make up for whatever time was allowed to me, did that alone time even exist?

I headed straight into the kitchen, purse still on my shoulder, to get Violet a bowl of pretzels so I didn't have to hear the words "something" and "eat" again. Aaron barely looked up from his computer when I handed her the bowl. She was sitting right next to him on the couch.

"She wasn't hungry before," he muttered.

I focused my attention on Violet instead of Aaron's lousy excuse, and felt the front of her diaper to see if it needed to be changed. It was squishy and filled to the gills, probably holding about three gallons of pee.

"No, Mama, no!" she whined, knowing a diaper change was imminent. She crawled over Aaron to the corner of the couch and snuggled into his side, as to say, "Checkmate, bitch." I saw a flicker of white on her back, and as her little body curled into him harder, it became clear that the maxi pad from earlier was stuck to her back again.

In birthing class, we had learned pain-coping techniques for labor in which you breathe in and out easily and naturally, while allowing all of your senses to notice what they're picking up on. If you're nailing it, you even start to become curious about what's going on around you rather than hoping everything will shut the fuck up. My childbirth teacher had explained that in labor, this could be

helpful—say, if you're in the middle of an intense contrac-
tion and a nurse wants to ask you what your highest level
of education is for her intake form. Instead of saying, "I
wish this twat understood that you don't ask a laboring
woman questions during contractions," you would simply
acknowledge what was happening, sans any shitty judgment. You would say to yourself, in your head, "I hear a
voice talking to me." The idea was that in moments where
you cannot change what is happening around you, it is
sometimes easier to take them in fully—the sounds, the
sights, the smells, the physical feelings, the tastes—rather
than try to unsuccessfully tune them out, resist them, or
wish they were different. I didn't realize that I'd end up
using this practice more for diaper-change protests and
eyeball-poking rather than for birth itself.

The tension in that tiny corner of the couch grew
thick as Violet burrowed in even deeper, now bucking her
legs furiously to keep me at bay. Aaron leaned out, trying
not to get hit by her feet, but still typing away, making no
eye contact with either of us. I breathed in.

I hear the sounds of typing.

Then I breathed out. I breathed back in again.

I see Violet kicking.

I breathed out another audible breath, and in again.

I see a maxi-pad on a person.

I breathed out.

It was working. I felt calm enough to form a more
compassionate plan for how to get Violet out of the couch
corner rather than pulling her out by her ankles. I
breathed in and out again deeply as I moved toward her.

Aaron, visibly annoyed with Violet and me, was not
practicing Zen breathing but, instead, the art of subtle eye

rolling. He closed his computer in a huff and fled the scene, heading upstairs to finish working. My cool-headedness immediately shifted to jealousy with a heavy sprinkling of resentment at all the times I'd wanted to flee the scene when Violet started kicking and shit got hard.

Violet laughed her head off at me trying to wrangle her. She stood up and ran along the couch until I softly tackled her before she knocked the lamp off the end table that her wobbly, cackling body was headed straight for. She giggled wildly at it all, which flipped my switch back closer to calm. There was no ignoring those guttural, toddler laughs. They were the antidote to everything. I pretended to eat her belly which made her laugh so deeply that her chipmunk cheeks shook. Her pure joy melted me until I noticed the zombie in the armchair, holding the iPad.

"Hey El, has your timer gone off?" He was allotted an hour of screen time per day, which vacillated widely depending on my level of doneness.

In contrast, I had grown up with zero time limits for watching TV and playing video games. Zero. Marnie and Wayne parented in the golden era, before the all-knowing internet had ruined everything with its studies and parental guidelines. My childhood summers consisted of waking up, browsing through the *TV Guide*, and highlighting which shows would help me pass every hour of the day until my parents got home around sunset. *Price Is Right*, then *Love Connection*, and next was *Press Your Luck*, and so on. Game shows were the closest thing to reality TV, back then. But with screens everywhere these days, I felt irresponsible if I didn't at least try to put some sort of limit on how much my kids came into contact with. Steve Jobs himself hadn't even let his kids play with screens, or so the Interwebs said.

"El, are you listening to me?"

"Uh huh."

I pulled his chin up to look at me. "Hi, remember me, your mom? Did your timer go off while I was gone?"

"Yeah, but Dad said I could keep playing," he explained as his gaze dropped again.

"No more."

"But Mom, I'm on this level that I've never seen before and I've never done this good and I can't save it." I actually understood his pleading. Beating "The Legend of Zelda" had taken massive effort by way of dedication and research in *Nintendo Power* magazine when I was a kid. And yet, WWSJD here? (What Would Steve Jobs Do?)

"You're done. But you can go outside and play with your friends for a bit until dinner, since you got your homework done."

He smiled half-heartedly, his eyes squinting, like he was waiting for a lashing. My head rolled to the side. "You didn't do your homework? You were getting your binder out when I left. What happened?"

"Dad said that I could play my game first and do homework later."

I breathed through my nose like a bull. "No playing outside, Elliot. Homework, now." I walked into the kitchen because someone had to make dinner. I hated myself for playing the role of subservient housewife, but my other option was hangry kids.

⚬

Four steaming bowls of rice, beans, and the preferred top-
pings for each person sat on the table, awaiting eaters.
Where was my fucking Mary Poppins? Until I became a
mother myself, I didn't realize what a loving gesture providing a meal for someone really was. I missed Marnie's
fried chicken and homemade vegetable soup with ham-
burger meat.

"El, will you go tell Dad dinner's ready?" I asked my
little messenger. It was sometimes too humiliating to stand
before your husband and kindly let him know that his warm
meal awaited downstairs at his earliest convenience, Sire.

On his way downstairs and back to the table, Elliot
shouted, "Dad said he has to work longer since he had to
come home early today."

Elliot had no idea the gravity of what he'd just said as
he dug into his dinner. I purposefully bit down hard on the
side of my tongue to trap the words that wanted to be
screamed. I sat there staring at Aaron's beautifully presented burrito bowl—the thoughtful lack of sour cream
that he hated, and the addition of his favorite hot sauce—
waiting there, uneaten. My hunger got to me. I eased up
on my tongue and began to eat food instead of feelings.

Ten minutes later, Aaron sauntered downstairs in his
usual jovial manner, not letting the tension of the day take
hold. I was already doing dishes.

"Dada!" Violet squealed, getting out of her seat and
running to him like he was returning home after deploy-
ment. "I wanna paint more toes pink."

I could barely meet him with anything but a passive
gaze. He must've noticed because he put his hand on my
arm as he walked by and said, "Stop with the dishes. I'll do
them after dinner."

I was prepared to explode on him but this was the thing—he was the one who worked to provide for us *and* he'd come home early today as a favor to me. And now he was offering me what felt like another favor that most other husbands wouldn't, washing the dishes. I knew there was something fucked up here, but I couldn't pinpoint it. Sarcasm was all I could turn to. "Your royal dinner is cold," I mumbled, wiping off my wet hands.

Aaron sat down at the table, unaffected by my words. Maybe I hadn't spoken them loud enough. Maybe it was for the best.

The kids sat on the couch, looking at a *Star Wars* sticker book together. Their bellies were full, they were cooperating, and not staring at a screen. It was a momentary miracle. I put on the tea kettle and stood over it, watching the blue flame tickle the sides, to avoid Aaron.

"So how was the meeting thingy today? Was that Mary lady as nice as you'd hoped?" he asked while jamming his fork into rice.

"Um, it was good." Being measured took more energy than I had, so I caved. "But I didn't get to meet with Mary. I got booked with another lady." I tidied the table. Cleaning was my go-to for spousal anger diversion.

"What did you guys talk about?"

I hesitated. This suddenly felt very personal, even too personal to tell Aaron, especially in this moment. But dammit, I needed his help. "We talked about how I need more time alone, other than when I get dental work or a pap smear." He gave a small laugh, mouth full. "Then she asked me what I would do if I had endless money and a trustworthy babysitter, and I went into this fantasy spiral where I was shopping at Nordstrom and we had a housecleaner and I was sewing again." I was finally starting to let go of the day's crimes against humanity.

"Weird. How would that help? We don't have endless money."

Never mind. I hate you again.

"Yeah, I know that, Aaron. But it helped me. So we picked a few of the things to start with and I'm going to find a way to make them happen. That's my homework." He looked confused. "I really miss sewing. I miss being creative and getting to do my thing, alone." He took a slug of his beer. "How can you help me get time to sew?"

He considered this as he sipped. "I can put both kids to bed a couple nights."

"Shit, Aaron, I don't want to sew after the kids go to bed when I'm exhausted. I want a break during the day. Like instead of being with the kids non-stop." This should've been obvious. If I had wanted to sew after the kids went to bed, I would've done so a long time ago and wouldn't be asking for his goddamn help to make it happen.

"Okay, okay, so you mean like on the weekend or something?"

"Whatever gets me four hours to myself, during the day."

"Hmm, I could take the kids to the museum this Saturday," he said with a mid-bite smile. He loved museums.

Thank you, Aaron, and also, fuck you. For holding the cards. For making me ask. I was so tired of permission. So tired of needing him to approve my freedom, my time to breathe, to be human.

"Okay, thanks," I muttered, wondering which one of us I hated more.

For once, the kids' sudden arguing was a welcome excuse to eject myself from the twisted conversation with Aaron. "Violet, that one's mine," Elliot whined, holding a giant Death Star sticker above his head. She appeared to be preparing for a body slam. I jumped up to referee just as she launched. Violet would be no one's bitch. She just didn't yet know that you can't kick someone squarely in the head to assert your power. And so there was Elliot, a tall third-grader brought to his knees—and to tears—by a two-year-old's foot to the temple. I deeply understood his pain and hugged him tight, while Violet retreated to Aaron.

"I'm sorry she kicked you, buddy. Those small feet hurt. I know." Elliot nodded, sniffling his tears away. Aaron was having a serious talk with Violet, the way only a father with a beard can.

Elliot's tears were the cue for the commencement of the bedtime pageant of everlasting negotiation and naked toddler screeching. I headed upstairs with Violet while saying for the hundredth time that feet are not for kicking, whilst being kicked. I could hear the clanking of Aaron making good on his offer to do the dishes.

The night sky darkened, flecked by bright bathroom windows throughout the neighborhood, as Elliot and every other kid half-assedly brushed their teeth before bed. Aaron followed him into his room and shut the door, hunkering down for the long haul, likely knowing that he would probably doze off in there with him. Aaron and I often discussed how there was probably a better, healthier way to have Elliot go to bed (alone), but neither of us ever had the energy to change course and manage the subsequent backlash. And sometimes it was nice to just lie down.

After some glider snuggles, kisses, and two songs, Violet the squirrely savage finally quieted down and let the sleepiness take hold. I triumphantly made it to the other side of the door without suffering any final slings or arrows. Surfacing from the smoke of bedtime was like being high. Total relief.

I tiptoed downstairs and headed directly to the snack cabinet to eat all the things I couldn't eat in peace that day, such as a handful of Junior Mints I'd been craving for five hours. Next, I wanted to do a belly flop onto the couch, but toys were strewn everywhere and I needed at least some of the day's chaos to be turned into order before it would all be undone again in the morning. I knelt down in the family room and began sorting the MagnaTiles and puzzles into the appropriate bins, berating myself for forgetting to have the kids do their own tidying. Around the room were balls of tightly-wrapped diapers that hadn't made it to the trash yet, hidden like little explosives. As I shuttled them into the kitchen, I noticed that despite Aaron's kind offer, the dish pile had strangely gotten bigger, rather than smaller. I closed my eyes hard. *For fuck's sake.* His version of doing the dishes for me had been rinsing them out and stacking them on top of the existing pile that would still be waiting for me to load into the dishwasher the next morning. I mean, he saved me a ten-second rinsing, but ultimately he hadn't done the dishes, just postponed my doing them. A fucking bait and switch.

I was too fried to feel anything anymore, so I chose to ignore the dish mound and crouched back down to tackle the most loathsome layer of the toy debris, which consisted of the never-ending trinkets from birthday parties, dollar-store garbage, and Grandma-given junk that all lived in the Big Bin of Pointless Crap.

I suddenly remembered the book June had given me. It

was still in my purse, which was really just an adult, travel-sized version of the Bin of Pointless Crap. I sat down on the couch with the book in my hands, running my fingers over the smooth hardcover. *The Life-Changing Magic of Tidying Up: The Japanese Art of Decluttering and Organizing*, by Marie Kondo. Maybe this book would change everything in my life. Make motherhood easy. The cover showed a water-colored Japanese-style sky to instill maximum tranquility. It was the teensiest bit smaller than most books—journal-sized—mindfully taking up less space, doing its job from the get-go. Just merely holding the book gave me the feeling that I'd already made progress.

I skimmed the crisp pages and hypnotic chapter titles, looking for something that nodded to the piles of junk that kids accumulate, which sat directly in front of me. That's what I really wanted to know—how does one tidy with children in the mix? Isn't that like shoveling while it's snowing? Brushing your teeth while eating Oreos? There had to be something about mountains of stuffed animals or the influx of Oriental Trading Company sewage. But there was no mention of children or tchotchkes anywhere. I kept skimming and stopped dead in my tracks when I read the advice to place every single clothing item you and your family own onto the floor, in one giant heap, then hug each thing and ask yourself if it "sparks joy." First of all, if I placed every single piece of my family's clothing on the floor, I would have to step around it for the next ten years. This was pretty much already happening with the clean clothes that never got put away. Second, if this book came with a nanny and an inheritance to buy only joyful things, then sure, there were probably some life-changing concepts in there. But my time would be better spent actually cleaning rather than reading a book about how to do it right. Thirdly, I am not hugging and then having a conversation with my period panties about their value. I'm just not.

I texted Danielle and asked her if she knew about this book, and if so, was any of it was useful.

> Never heard of it. Sounds
> like some white people shit.

She wasn't wrong.

I picked up my phone and Googled, "Did Marie Kondo have kids when she wrote her book?" Google's answer was: of course not. I shut the book. I knew I would want to do the things Ms. Kondo suggested to achieve decluttered ecstasy, but none of them could be done with small children. June had recommended it, but why would she blueball a frazzled mother of two with home-organization porn?

I put the book on the table and bent down again, leaning over the Big Bin of Pointless Crap. I did a quick liquidation of the next most obviously worthless items, such as a deflated latex balloon, an unfixable wind-up toy, an old toothbrush, and a toxic Mardi Gras necklace. The small purging felt like a spiritual cleanse.

Just then, a groggy Aaron walked down the stairs. He rubbed his eyes and squinted, adjusting to the light of the world outside Elliot's cave. He was wearing his thin comfy pants that outlined his package.

"Hey," he said, heading straight for the snack cabinet.

"Hey."

"I looked up the museum hours and they open at ten on Saturday morning, so we can get out of your hair then, if you want."

"Oh my God, yes."

"And we can get lunch on the way home too," he added, sitting down on the couch with a bowl of popcorn. Sometimes marriage felt like a constant ping-pong match between resentments and redemptions.

I scooched into the crook of his arm, between he and the popcorn bowl. "Thank you," I said, stopping and looking up into his emerald green eyes. And then I kissed him.

"Wow, so all I have to do is mention taking the kids somewhere and I get that?" he asked whilst shoving handfuls of popcorn into his mouth. It shouldn't have taken him eight years to figure this out.

"Yep. But the lunch offer was really the clincher."

"In that case, consider every Saturday yours—and the children fed."

I kissed him again, popcorn mouth and all. His soft lips reminded me of how our love started, in my dorm room on that cold night when someone threw a beer bottle through the closed window while we made out. Amid the shattered window glass, we found the beer bottle standing straight up on the floor, unbroken, as if someone had intentionally set it there. Aaron wouldn't let me set foot on the floor until he had found and removed every last glass shard.

When I pulled away from him, I noticed white popcorn flecks in his beard. He held still as I picked them out, like an ape. I wondered what Marie Kondo would say about that. She probably had a pocket Dustbuster for moments just like these and wasn't above vacuuming a grown man's beard before a kiss, or pubes before intercourse.

CHAPTER TEN

The Life-Changing Magic of Alone Time

*O*n just two days, I had a hot date with myself. And an old fling—my sewing machine. I sat at the kitchen table, daydreaming about what project would win my attention first, while Violet watched *Sofia the First* nearby on the couch. One single session of feeling seen, heard, and validated by June had freed me. My inner cassette tape of wonders, worries, and resentments had mostly gone from a fast-talking, high-pitched chipmunk voice down to a deep, slow, witness-protection voice. Clearing up some of that head space made room for patience and pleasure.

My email dinged. It was a message from my birth doula-turned-friend, Martha. She was at least twenty-five years my senior, and had silver hair, like all fantastical creatures do. Martha rubbed my hips during back labor with Elliot, and she held Violet on top of my chest for skin-to-skin contact in the operating room as I was stitched back together. Unexpectedly, I watched the entire thing in the OR lamp's reflection above myself in horror. It was like being in a *Saw* movie. The birth books hadn't mentioned that part.

Martha was by my side, vagina, and breasts during the two most vulnerable and meaningful moments of my life. She mothered me in those early days, and for some reason that I didn't fully comprehend, she continued to show up for me, as if I offered anything. She always seemed to be tapped into something bigger. Like a fairy godmother, she could sense when she was needed, so it was not surprising to find her divinely-timed email in my inbox as the birds chirped outside my window.

Martha Blackman
To: April Stewart
Hello

Good morning, my dear. I have an exciting opportunity for you that I wanted to discuss. Can you steal away from the littles to chat on the phone either tonight or tomorrow?

Sending love,
Martha

I sat up straight in my chair, excited and puzzled. This sounded different than our usual emails about life, kids, and birth. I immediately let her know.

Suddenly Elliot barged through the door, slinging his backpack off and waving a yellow paper. "Mom, I'm gonna do the science fair!"

"Fun!"

"It's gonna have all the planets and a supernova and maybe somehow show the multiverse." He made grand sweeping motions with his hands.

"Sounds like a big project. When is it due?"

"Tomorrow."

My head fell back in despair, as if my neck muscles had been severed in one clean slice. I had not intended a trip to the craft store, nor paper-mâchéing a multiverse before dinner, but I should've known this was coming for me, like an envelope of anthrax in the mail, as we neared summer break. It was as if the teachers purposefully withheld all the most intricate, and also unnecessary, projects until us moms were at our most vulnerable—having just barely survived one week of constant kid togetherness for spring break, and now hopelessly looking down the barrel of ten weeks of summer. I imagined the school's barrage of last-minute projects as retribution for the year of parental sins such as sending nut butter sandwiches for snack time, vehemently refusing to volunteer at the carnival churro booth, or your kid being a total shitbag in class every single day of the year. But before I answered Elliot in frustration, June's voice chimed in, reminding me to tend to myself. My muscles re-engaged as I brought my head back into a neutral position.

"I'm sure your dad would love to figure that out with you when he gets home."

Aaron pulled in the garage as the street lights blinked on. He had no idea what was waiting for him. Before he was fully in the door, Elliot was all over him like slime on your rug.

"Dad, you and me get to make a whole solar system tonight with a black hole and can I use the glue gun, pleeeease?" I pretended to be distracted by Violet in the other room, as to not get sucked into any of the black-hole discussion. Aaron could figure it out, just like I'd had to all these years.

"Can I eat dinner first?" he begged.

One bowl of leftovers later, Aaron sat at the kitchen table helping Elliot cut, color, and glue planet printouts onto the back of an old poster board from last year's project. A little glitter and some labeling, and it was done. Elliot's last-minute science fair decision had surprisingly made the entire process less stressful than if we'd had an entire month to prepare. No life-size, spray-painted, delicately hanging, to-scale model of the solar system here. Nope. Just a half-baked but good-enough planet poster, with which he was thrilled. No capital Q's either. Aaron was such a lucky bastard.

When both kids were finally asleep and alone in their beds, I whisked away upstairs to call Martha, cup of tea in hand. Aaron gave me a glittery thumbs-up as he blissfully started episode six of another captivating murder documentary on Netflix—post-dinner chips and salsa on deck.

It was the time of the day when my bra had to go, even if it made my petite silhouette look boyish in the mirror. I propped up the pillows in my bed, got my legs under the covers, and dialed Martha. One of my core life philosophies was "Everything's better while lying in bed." Old age and the prepared meals of a retirement home couldn't come soon enough for me.

Martha answered in an almost meditative tone. Her slow, soothing voice always brought me back to my labors. "April, it finally dawned on me today why I've been busy with at least five births a month the past handful of years and it's finally slowing down. Do you have any inkling of why?" I didn't know. "The birth of a book franchise called *Fifty Shades of Grey*. Lots of sex and lots of babies. I am one tired doula."

I hadn't read the book myself, because that would require free time, but I knew what Martha was talking about. "And you made it to all of those births?" I asked.

"Somehow I did. I have no fucking idea how," she said, cackling. One of my favorite things about her was that age didn't squash her ability to drop obscenities. "What are you guys up to over there?"

"Just recoiling from Aaron's touch and seeing a therapist," I joked, but not really.

"What is *that* about?"

I retold the story of recoil.

"Been there. Plain and simple, you were touched out," she said.

Martha had been married for forty-five years, had six grown kids of her own and ten grandbabies. She often spoke about the ups and downs of married life and parenting from an eagle's view, seeing everything as part of a whole, and noticing what was truly important and what wasn't. It was the opposite of how I saw things from behind my in-the-trenches, mud-splattered goggles.

"Martha, how do I do it? How do I fulfill everyone's needs and not lose my sanity?" I asked. I was on a never-ending quest for the answers to my burning questions and I'm sure I annoyed the shit out of people. They all pretended not to hate me because of it.

"You don't do it, really. There is no fulfilling everyone's needs. You know none of us get through this thing without fucking up our kids, right?"

I didn't know that. Embarrassed, I said nothing.

"And it's never the thing you think," she continued, chuckling. "You focus so hard on not messing up one thing, you completely miss another. We all do. But you get through it and hopefully there are some sweet spots along the way for everyone."

"That's bleak, Martha."

"Well, hopefully you don't miss the big stuff, but maybe you do. You won't know until it's too late anyway."

She was laughing again while I was basically hyperventilating. I refused to miss the big stuff. Also, I wanted to be at the stage where I could have a good ole guffaw about my parenting missteps. I wasn't there yet. Would I ever be there?

"What about husbands?"

"Do you know what Aaron's sweet spots are, like little things you could do to let him know you're still connected, that are meaningful to him personally, and don't cost you your sanity?"

I hated that we were focusing on Aaron's needs, but I was the one that asked her the question. "His are mostly sexual. I am barely in one piece when I crawl into bed at night and I simply don't have any energy to put out."

"I remember feeling like that. There was no way sex was going to happen. Can you maybe scale it down a bit. What if it wasn't full-on sex?"

"Are we talking blow jobs here?"

"Well, whatever somewhat satisfies his need for connection but is doable for you. Maybe that's a blow job, maybe it's a hand job, or something else altogether. I bet he'd rather get a few hand jobs from you than nothing." The fact that Martha looked at babies coming out of vaginas for a living meant that we could also talk frankly about hand jobs—hand jobs I didn't want to have to give.

"I for sure can't do regular blow jobs," I admitted, wincing.

"Then don't. But in marriage, you have to find each other's currency and make little deposits into your accounts. You can't give them a big lump sum all the time, so you throw 'em some chump change when you can," she explained. *Really Martha, when I'm at my lowest I need to be giving my husband more blow jobs?* "So, what is *your* currency, my dear—what is *your* sweet spot?" *Okay, better.*

"Not sex, I can tell you that. Sleeping in. Sleeping in is my sex."

"You need to tell him that. And maybe these little efforts will keep that spark going. I don't envy you though. Your generation has it way harder than mine did."

I believed her—God, I believed her. I never once saw Marnie wipe a cart handle with an antibacterial wipe nor read a food label—things I did multiple times a day as a mother. But I wanted to know what Martha saw through her lens, so I asked her.

"I was young when I became a mom. I didn't even know who I was yet. Today's moms have entire careers and lives before kids. You all are trying to be more than we ever were," she said.

"Including thoughtful wives," I added.

"It ain't easy, that's for sure. I wish I could tell you to just ignore your marriage in these hard years with little ones. But if left unattended, that spark can die out."

It felt like someone had sucked the air out of the room. Her words scared me, because I knew she was right. I took another sip of tea, gripping the cup handle for dear life.

"So what's this about a therapist?" she asked.

I didn't want Martha to counsel me for our entire conversation. I now had June for that. "Long story, but first, I'm dying to hear about this *opportunity*."

"Oh yes. That." Her voice quickened. "I have a friend of a friend who owns the cutest little boutique in Costa Mesa. Both of them were at my house for dinner last night and saw Danny in the octopus shirt you made for him a while back. The store owner fell in love with it and wants to carry your stuff in her store. Do you have time to put together some things for her—she said maybe ten shirts or so?"

I set my tea cup down on the nightstand and sat forward, smiling in disbelief.

"Do you even have the time for it right now? I don't want to pressure you. I just know that my friend was impressed with your . . ."

"No, Martha, this opportunity could not have come at a better time," I interrupted. "Thank you for pimping me out."

"It wasn't me, my dear. You're the one who gave Danny that adorable shirt. I will email your information to the boutique owner. Her name is CeCe. Let me warn you, she's out there. Oh wait, Rick's motioning something at me and it looks urgent."

"Let me guess, it looks like his hand is gripping something and he's moving it in and out of his mouth?" I played. Martha cackled so hard she coughed.

"Oh Lord," she said, catching her breath, "He knows better than to get me off the phone to give him a blow job. Or does he? We shall find out."

I sat smiling in bed alone, like an idiot. I had been given value, outside of being "just" a mom. My hands were needed in this world for something other than ass wiping. My mind wandered, imagining my designs popping up in a variety of local stores, remembering what that felt like before. But before, I wasn't trying to juggle two kids while doing it. Was this even possible now? My brain was trying to get ahead of itself and strangle all my fun. *Back the fuck up, April. It's just ten shirts. You're not some working mom all of a sudden.*

I took a final gulp of tea and raced downstairs to tell Aaron the joyous news about having value again. He didn't blink as I galloped down the stairs. He was too gripped by grisly footage and a new twist in the case.

"Guess what?" I asked. He didn't break. "Hey guy, over here," I said, like I had to do with Elliot and his iPad. It broke his trance.

"Martha just told me that someone she knows who owns a boutique wants to carry my shirts!" I was sqeeeeing.

"Whoa, awesome, A.B.!" he said. "Where? How?" After I told him, the magnetism of the tampered-with evidence pulled him right back to the TV. Of course he had no idea of the significance of this news. As a working man in the world, he had never lost his value. But I was so proud that *my* art, *my* octopus t-shirt had created a legitimate opportunity, that I refused to be bothered by his lackluster response. I left him to his manslaughter and went back upstairs.

༄

When Saturday came, I could hardly contain myself. Four hours of impending freedom were going to feel like a defibrillator. An email from the store owner, CeCe, helped. It read somewhat like a telegram.

CeCe D'Ambrosia
To: April Stewart
No Subject

I adore your designs. I think my customers will too.
Please bring me ten shirts. A variety of sizes and
styles. That octopus stole my heart. Make sure you
put a few in there. I will pay you. Can you drop them
off within two weeks? Love and light, CeCe

I fired an enthusiastic email right back, before I could
overthink the logistics.

Violet whined, writhed, and tried to run away as I attempted to pull a shirt over her head to ready her for a
trip to the museum with Dad. But her animosity didn't
break me this time since my shift would be ending so soon.
I was getting first-hand intel as to why Aaron had so much
more patience than I did. Anyone could be patient for the
twenty minutes before freedom.

"I think we're ready to go," he said.

I pointed to the kids' feet. They had no shoes on.

"Oh. Right. Let's get shoes on, guys."

Elliot quickly grabbed his nearly too-small sneakers
and Violet put on her red and black polka-dotted rain
boots that looked like ladybugs. Aaron looked pleased.

"She can't wear those," I said.

"Why not? She wants to."

"Because she likes them at first and then she takes
them off because her feet get sweaty." She was jumping
with joy in her clunky boots.

"They're fine. I got this," he said, looking at a happy
Violet.

"Never mind then," I said, holding my hands up and stepping away. He was going to find out for himself, especially since he unknowingly packed Violet's leaky water bottle.

I stood in the doorway, blowing kisses to the kids who were buckled in the car, all smiles. Violet had not only been compliant, but helpful enough to put her arms through the straps for Aaron. I shook my head. *The fruit of my goddamn loins and their ability to betray me.*

The house was empty for the first time in three centuries. I felt like doing snow angels in the crumbs on the filthy floor. Anything was possible right now. I could do any of the kid-free things I'd always wanted to do, like take pictures of all of my outfits and make a visual index for the days when I forgot what I had to wear, learn a sick online dance routine to "Bitch Betta Have My Money," or spoon with all my belongings and wait for them to tell me their life story. But today I was promised to my sewing machine—and I had an order to fill, money to be made, value to be had.

My first stop (after sitting on the toilet alone) was to dig up the bin of forgotten fabrics in the garage. I unearthed it from the bottom of a sky-high stack of boxes and lugged it upstairs, breaking a sweat from all the unstacking, then the restacking, while cursing about the prevalence of bikes and scooters underfoot—which felt like I was channeling my dad circa 1984.

Once upstairs, I opened the lid to the bin and the smell of used shirts wafted out, carrying me back to a different life. The bowling-shoe-spray-like odor conjured up the memory of asking the Goodwill manager if they sprayed all the donated clothing with a certain kind of disinfectant before selling them. To my surprise and disgust, the manager said no, they do absolutely nothing with them, and then added that most came from post-death estate removals. Gulp.

I rummaged through the death-riddled shirts, taking inventory. At the very bottom of the fabric bin was a plastic container with colorful threads and matching bobbins that Violet would surely love to sort the shit out of. Tucked to the side of the spools was a bag of leftover tags with the "Ruby Riot" logo on them.

I approached the small work table in the corner, plugged in my sewing machine, and carefully placed the foot pedal on the floor in front of me. I flipped the power switch on and the light awoke, still working and illuminating the needle, the star of a show. Sitting down, I put my hands next to the sewing machine, and then I hugged it. It was sparking goddamn joy. *Curse you, Marie Kondo!* I grabbed the closest fabric scrap from the bin. Lifting the lever, I slid the scrap under the presser foot and pushed the lever down, the metal foot landing softly on the fabric. The ball of my right foot pressed against the pedal on the floor and the rhythmic hum of the machine began. How I'd missed that sound. With a heavier press of my foot, the needle started bobbing up and down.

I was sewing again.

I pulled the fabric out and tugged at the seams to test the stitches. Solid.

Luckily, I had leftover blank-shirt inventory in toddler sizes, in a tri-blend grey color. Creative juices coursed through my body as I contemplated which other designs to include in addition to heart-stealing octopi. The whale was a favorite, but perhaps too many sea creatures wouldn't be varied enough. The elephant and its cutely curved trunk could be great, but perhaps not in this atrocious political climate. Maybe the squirrel was a safe bet. And the guitar. I made a visual plan and then hunted with my fingers through the mish mash of t-shirt fabrics, holding them up against the grey shirts to see what would look best—which pattern was more squirrelish and which was more metal for a guitar? Then, with a thin Sharpie, I traced the sturdy shape stencils I'd made years ago onto the most interesting sections of the t-shirt fabric, and cut them out with my special magenta-handled fabric scissors. I was known to murder the man who used them to cut paper. A quick and light adhesive spray on the back of the appliques, and they were ready to meet their destiny with the needle. I got completely lost in my work—in the flow—so I was startled when my phone dinged with a text from Aaron.

> On our way home. Should be
> back in about 30 minutes.

How had it been four hours already? It couldn't be possible. I hadn't looked up from my project the entire time. There had been no interruptions. I felt a mix of feelings—content and thankful, yet already longing for the next time. This wasn't enough. Would anything ever be enough? I didn't know when I would get to sew again, but I knew that it would have to be soon because I had only finished three of CeCe's ten shirts.

I looked around at my corner of beautiful disarray. The contents of the fabric bin were scattered across the floor, there were cut thread ends here and there, a pile of fabric cut-outs, and stacks of shirts—some done and some not. I knew I had thirty minutes to put it all back together before Violet would be throwing it all into the air like confetti.

When everything was out of toddler reach, I went downstairs and opened up the fridge. My stomach was grumbling. I had chosen to forgo lunch in exchange for food for the soul. I spied the sea salt butterscotch caramels and quickly opened the bag, slightly shaking from the sudden lack of sustenance. I took out one of the shiny, round orbs, popped it in my mouth and stood there, savoring the rich, buttery flavor of about five more, until I heard the sound of the garage door, which meant my time was up.

Elliot barged through the door first. "Mom, we saw these huge dinosaur bones!" His story was hijacked by Violet's cries coming in behind. Aaron, looking like a soldier returning from combat, held her, until he aggressively handed her to me. I felt her damp shirt. Aaron shook his head and refused eye contact with anyone. There was something so satisfying in seeing an endlessly-patient-with-kids Aaron undone.

Elliot, the messenger, spoke. "Violet spilled her water all over herself in the car on the way there. She's been wet the whole time. And crying."

I couldn't bear to look in Aaron's direction. He seemed mad and embarrassed, banging around the kitchen. I had been there before, only for the past eight years. The God-forsaken Ariel water bottle leaked everywhere when turned over, which was why it existed in the back of the cupboard. Discarding anything with Ariel on it was not an option.

"Let's get you some dry clothes," I said, turning to take Violet upstairs.

"No!" she wailed, kicking to get down. Amidst the thrusting of legs, I saw something black. I grabbed one and firmly held it for inspection. Her feet were bare and dark black, as if she'd stepped in charcoal.

"I no wear my way-dee-bug boots, Mama," she admitted. I looked at Aaron, who finally broke his vow of huffy silence to take a stab at justification.

"She was wet and crying and wouldn't fucking wear her boots and I tried to carry her, but she wouldn't let me so she walked through the entire museum barefoot. I didn't have a choice." We both ignored the presence of profanity amongst children because Aaron was too upset. I deeply empathized with him while also appreciating the real-life education he was getting in toddler-ology. Maybe now he would understand why I couldn't just "relax" and why I constantly carried a bag with an extra pair of clothes and shoes and endless wipes and Advil. The rules and strategies I put into place weren't me being a buzzkill, it was just the way things had to be so that everyone could get through this day and the next and the next in one goddamn, dry, shoe-wearing piece. I recognized myself in his exasperation and resisted the urge to smirk like an asshole, albeit a right one. Instead, I changed Violet into a clean shirt, set her on the kitchen counter and went to scrubbing the museum off of her. It tickled and she giggled uncontrollably, easing some of the tension.

"Oh and we didn't have lunch yet. I'm starving," Elliot called from the other room, sitting pants-less on the couch.

"I needs something eat."

My throat burned in frustration. I had fallen for Aaron's bait-and-switch promise yet again. Today's episode: lunch. My disappointment must've shown.

"Violet was too upset to stop anywhere. She was filthy and wet. I had to get her home," Aaron said.

There was nothing I could say that would change anything, or that I wouldn't regret. Here they were, home and hungry, myself included. I had counted on the respite of having one less meal to make that day and nothing was going to get in the way of it, dammit. All I said was, "Everyone get back in the car right now, we're going out to lunch because I'm not making it today." And everyone obeyed.

CHAPTER ELEVEN

Seeds

*F*uck yeah, today was June day. I was eager to tell her what had happened in the short time since our last visit. And I had made sure to schedule our session on a day that Aaron's mom, Lucinda, could babysit, so as to avoid unnecessary marital turmoil.

The kids went bonkers when she knocked on the door, as usual. They loved their "Lucindy"—a name Elliot had given her when he was small. Violet simply called her "Lu."

If Aaron was the world's most optimistic man, Lucinda was the world's most optimistic woman. She had a twinkle in her eye and was good luck in human form, mostly. When together, their positivity infinitely multiplied to the point that their zest for life was off the fucking charts. This was typically a fortunate trait to have in family members—especially in a mother-in-law who saw the best in me. But it proved to be challenging on days such as Christmas, when I wanted to crawl under the tree skirt and die from my sheer exhaustion at having planned all the festivities—including every single present (and homemade Chex Mix)—and Aaron and Lucinda wanted to smile at each other all day long and exclaim, "Isn't this fun?!" back and forth on repeat. The only thing that stood in the way of my throat-punching them every December 25th was that I knew their way of being with each other stemmed from truly terrifying times together when Aaron was young and his dad was going through the kind of severe and sometimes violent mental breakdown that causes one to take a baseball bat to the neighbor's car. Aaron and his mom had always been there for each other amidst the fright, eventually leaving it, and then somehow rebuilding a stable life at his grandma's house. So to them, the world *was* rose-colored and their love for each other was one of the purest things I had ever seen. My low-grade envy of their connection almost made me wish my dad had been that level of crazy too, so Marnie and I could've bonded over it.

Unsurprisingly, Lucinda was the quintessential fun grandma who said yes to everything—including sugar in all forms (even cubed). When she came to babysit, I had to let go of any rules being enforced, but she was so damn fun it didn't matter. Mostly. Not to mention that it's hard to complain about someone's job performance when they are volunteering.

"My little sweethearts!" Lucinda said as I opened the front door for her. She was already digging in her purse for treats. Elliot and Violet ran to her, their hearts and palms open. She gave them each a kiss and hug, and a large pack of Skittles. I pretended not to care.

"Thank you for helping me out today."

"I'm happy to. And don't you look so cute." I smiled, looking down at my burgundy blouse with the sophisticated buttons and ruched cap sleeves. I hadn't worn it in years. Elliot picked a Skittle out of his pack and handed it to Lucinda.

"Lu, we play monsser?" Violet asked with her mouth

full, tasting the rainbow. Lucinda looked at me for translation.

"I think she wants you to play *monster*."

"Yes, of course." Lucinda dropped her purse right to the ground, put her arms up above her head, and stomped around, chasing a bonkers Violet. Elliot joined in too. I slowly backed out of the room, grabbed my keys, and bolted.

"How are things?" June said, taking a seat in her own chair as I sat down on the now familiar couch. She wore a gauzy navy shirt with pink mandala patterns on it, white capri leggings, and leather gladiator sandals with the one strap that separated the big toe and second toe—a sort of thong underwear, but on a foot.

I updated her, and she smiled, as if she had expected this news. "And how did this make you feel—getting time to sew, and the order?"

"I felt ecstatic. Kind of like finding out I was pregnant with Elliot and Violet." *Totally unlike if I found out I was pregnant now.* "I wish it could be a regular thing, but . . ."

"But what? What are you telling yourself about it?"

I thought for a moment. My head slapped me from the inside, sternly telling me there was no way this could work. "I'm a stay-at-home mom. That's what I chose. We chose. What if it interfered with Aaron's work?"

"What does your heart say?"

I knew she was trying to get me to speak from a different place, outside of my skull. I closed my eyes and imagined what my heart looked like. Not an anatomically correct heart with valves and twisty purple veins, but a warm translucent red one with a miniature room inside where I could sit inside myself. It was peaceful in there.

"My heart wants me to be both a mom *and* a designer, but my stupid brain is telling me no fucking way."

"Our mind tries to keep us out of trouble, but sometimes it oversteps. What true words of warning do you think it's giving you, and what else can be tossed aside?"

That was a weird way to put it. How could I know which warnings were important or not—weren't they all? I shrugged.

June sat upright in her chair and planted both feet on the floor. "Are you willing to try something new with me?" she asked, eagerly. I hoped we were going to drop acid together.

"Yes."

"Okay then. I invite you to close your eyes or lower your gaze. Start to focus on your breathing. Not trying to force it in any way, but just become aware of the sound and feel of it coming in and out." This felt like childbirth class all over again. I tried to breathe deeply, like I imagined I *should* breathe. She must have noticed. "Let go of any ideas about doing it the right way. Your body knows exactly how to breathe. Yes, just like that." Her voice was slow and soft. "Bring this image of you being both a mom and a designer to mind. Let yourself play in the imagery of what it might look like."

Eyes closed, I imagined getting new orders, sewing often, and the freedom that would come with it—listening to an entire podcast in the car, alone, like Aaron did. I saw myself feeling capable and interacting with other interesting women. I saw the kids too, but at a distance.

June's words piped in the background. "Keeping with

your daydream, open up your concerned mind and ask it what it's most scared of, or wanting to protect."

I shut my eyes tighter. I was feeling for answers like a hand feeling for a light switch in the dark. The distant image of Elliot and Violet went blurry until they vanished completely.

Flick.

When I opened my eyes, June was attentively waiting. Quiet.

"My kids." I could barely utter the words. Tears were forming. Again. Always. My repressed emotions lived in my face, namely my tear ducts, just waiting to spill.

"What about them?" she asked calmly, leaning forward.

"Abandoning them. I don't want them grow up feeling like I was more interested in my own things than raising them."

"Do you know what that feels like, April, to grow up feeling like your mother was more interested in her own things than you?"

A sneak attack. I gasped for air, as if I had suddenly been dropped on a planet without oxygen. I think I nodded.

"What are you scared of?" she asked, her eyes fixed on mine, her voice grave.

I looked down at the floor. I couldn't say the words. I suddenly knew them, but I had never said them out loud. I didn't want to admit that I was paralyzed by the thought of Elliot and Violet feeling abandoned by me if I left them to pursue my own interests—like I felt by my own mother, who chose convenience and her own career over connection, and left me alone too often. I knew it wasn't really logical—plenty of my friends had outside interests or jobs and utilized babysitters with no blowback. Hiring a babysitter for a few hours or setting up consistent and loving childcare was different from expecting your kids to walk home to an empty house every day after elementary school, like I did. My brain could tell this difference, but my heart could not. Saved in my memory bank was Marnie dropping me off at a nautical-themed daycare called Little People's Landing when I was just a squirt. It was the Long John Silvers of childcare, and I remember being left to fend for myself with a bevy of other strange land lubbers, forced to eat everything off of my plate, including the milk that made my tummy upset. Looking back, maybe it was the loneliness I was reacting to and not the dairy.

"I'm terrified I will become my mother." The words sliced my throat open. "I wanted better for my kids."

June uncrossed her gladiator feet and reached her hand onto my knee. "You have given them that. You have worked so hard to create a deeply loving and respectful mother-child relationship, even though maybe you didn't grow up in one."

"It's a mountain I'm willing to die on, apparently." I pulled my lips in and smiled painfully. June handed me a box of tissues from her desk. I took a moment for mucosal management.

"What have you done differently than your mother?" The answer was just about everything. Although it wreaked havoc on my nervous system, my overly thoughtful nature was a guardrail for child neglect. "Because you have given your kids adequate love and attention, couldn't you take some time just for yourself and have that be okay—have it not scar them? The scar comes from not having the bond secured in the first place. It doesn't sound like your bond with your kids is in question at all."

She was right. And it hurt. And it gave me huge relief. And then it hurt again. Feeling profound pain at the passive hands of your own mother felt like it violated the very laws of nature and was the most disastrous twist of fate— one that I had been desperately trying to avoid with my own kids, but at my own expense. Sure, I wasn't a perfect mother by any means—and every day I edged closer to Marnie on the quirky scale—but I *had* built a strong foundation for us that could withstand a babysitter, of all fucking things. This simple acknowledgement unfroze me.

"Dammit, I wish I met you years ago. Why did I wait so long to take care of myself?" My question was maybe not for June.

"A million reasons. The stigma of therapy. Finances. Our healthcare system that doesn't have a safety net for moms. The struggle to see our value when there is no 'income' from our work as mothers. The feeling of being invisible, even to our spouse." Her voice wavered at the end. A first.

"Aaron had to be blind not to see that I was circling the drain."

June's fingers tapped on the chair's armrest like she was trying to resist saying something more. She looked down at the back of her hand. I wanted her to say whatever it was she was holding back.

Say it, June.

My ESP worked. "Our husbands will not save us. This is a hard lesson. We have to advocate for ourselves because no one . . ."

". . . else will." We finished the sentence together, mirroring each other.

"That's what led me here, to you," I said. June blinked

hard in agreement, opened her mouth to speak, and then closed it, brushing off the thighs of her white pants, nervously. I was in total support of this crack in her veneer, and also concerned about it. Her words had a palpable sense of desertion behind them and I was dying to know more. Maybe I had assumed too much about June and her curated outfits and office décor, and what I presumed to be a foolproof marriage. She re-centered herself, sitting up straight in her chair as she redirected course.

"How did you like the book I loaned you? Did you have a chance to read it?"

I pulled it out. "I hated it." June looked at me confused. "It's unrealistic. The crackpot lady who wrote this doesn't have kids. She talks about aiming for perfection. If I clean my floors, the second I put the broom away, one of my kids is immediately shoving veggie straws in their mouth like a wood chipper, spraying shards everywhere. Perfection is not possible."

"Okay."

"And this 'do it all in one go' thing, where you take every single item you own and put it in a pile like you're about to erect a tire fire in your house, is the worst idea I've ever heard. My life is measured in fifteen-minute increments and *Elmo's Worlds*. I don't have an entire day to do anything, much less have skin-to-skin contact with all my belongings."

She laughed out loud. "Duly noted."

At that, our time was up.

Saying goodbye was always odd, especially today, as we both stood there connected by the tiny seed June had dropped. A hand gesture, a limp handshake, or nothing at all felt insufficient after having bared my soul. *Thanks for watching me cry again today. Here's a creepy wave.* But a hug felt like an inappropriate next step, for some unspoken reason. Thankfully June eventually stuck out her hand and offered a warm smile before I fell on the ground seizing in awkwardness at how to exit appropriately.

CHAPTER TWELVE

Love and Light (and Lips)

*M*y last lingering hesitation about hiring a babysitter was laid to rest in June's office when she helped me realize the small detail that I was not my mother, and that we weren't even on the same track. Aaron's concerns about stranger danger were appeased when I offered that if he had apprehensions about hiring a babysitter, he was welcome to take time off work to do the legwork required to find the perfect one.

I arranged for Danielle's babysitter, Tanya, to come over and hang out with Violet for two hours while Elliot was at school. It would be a trial. Tanya had specifically mentioned in her return texts that she would bring a princess sticker book for she and Violet to do together. This was going to work out just fine. And suddenly the $10-per-hour cost sounded affordable. Cheaper than a divorce, or a burial.

Tanya knocked on the door. Violet ran toward it wearing her purple Rapunzel dress and shouting, "Stickers!" She had taken the bribe.

Tanya, with straight blonde hair, stood in the doorway wearing a Princess Jasmine t-shirt and Vans sneakers covered in tiny Genies, holding the promised sticker book. She was really blurring the line between knowing her audience and red-flag territory.

Tanya crouched down to Violet's level. "You must be Princess Violet."

Violet nodded, but found my leg and clung to it.

"Danielle raves about you," I said.

"I just love Owen. He's such a sweetheart."

Red flag number two.

Violet was eyeing the sticker book in Tanya's hands, but stayed glued to me, her little fingers gripping hard. "Violet, this is Tanya. She's the fun person that's going to play with you." I was doing the fake excited-mom voice to pressure your kid into feeling okay about something they don't. "And there's the super fun sticker book we talked about." *Had I mentioned this was going to be fun?* A slight grin eked out of Violet, but this was new territory for her. She hadn't had to separate from me and into the arms of a true stranger, ever. I tried to ease myself away from her.

"Mama, I needs you!" She was holding her arms out, her face worried. I willed myself to be strong and to lug my own childhood baggage out of the way. "Hold you, hold you," she said, pushing herself into my arms.

I bent down and she hugged me tight. Tanya looked on with a warm but clueless smile. This right here was the moment that I had spent the past two years—well, eight—running away from. The moment where my mother heartstrings got yanked from my ribcage and twanged by teensy fingers. *You can do this, April. Normal people do this. Like every day.* I knew that I could stay here until the end of time, hugging and reassuring Violet, and my four-year-old self standing on the dock of Little People's Landing. It was a total mindfuck that, in order to restore sanity and become a better mother, I had to separate from my child, which actually made me feel like a worse mother.

But then I did it. I pulled out of the hug, overriding my primal instincts and Violet's death grip. I looked into her eyes, past her just-forming tears, and saw the strong foundation I'd laid since the beginning. "I love you and you're going to have so much fun with Tanya." *FUN.*

Tanya picked up on the cue and took Violet's hand, leading her to Stickertown. "Let's see which princess we can find first." But Violet wasn't interested. And then came all the tears. And wails.

"Ma-ma. I needs you," she cried, reaching out toward me as Tanya held her back, like a stage-four clinger.

I bit my lip as I ascended the stairs, waving to Violet and pretending to be confident. "I'm gonna be right up here, Baby Girl." *Jesus Violet, I'm just going upstairs.*

She sobbed and begged for me to come back. Upstairs was too far. I knew that working moms would've had a field day with this pathetic spectacle, but it was monumental for me and I gritted my teeth, hating every heartbreaking second of it. I wanted it to stop, but needed it to work. I put my hands over my ears to block out Violet's protesting cries, and sat on the edge of my bed. I could have chosen to get under the covers and contract into a tight ball for the next few hours, but there was no way I was going to spend good money to suffer. And I needed to finish CeCe's order. I pulled my hands away from my ears, cautiously. There were no screams, just the sound of Violet and Tanya eagerly searching for stickers downstairs.

Embarrassed, I sat down, flicked the sewing machine on, and carefully set an applique and shirt under the metal foot and needle. I began, again.

৵

Hiring a babysitter had gone smoothly, overall. Tanya and Violet played together like two peers, except that one of the peers changed the other one's diaper.

That week, I got a much-needed personal break from caretaking *and* I cranked out my boutique order without being rushed or having to multi-task. And some days, I even used Tanya-time to shower. The best of all worlds. What felt impossible without a babysitter was actually quite easy with one—a total game changer. Why hadn't anyone told me? *I hate myself.*

৵

Finally, I had a box of finished inventory, complete with ruby-red tissue paper and a branded sticker to seal it with. I knew CeCe would be pleased.

As Tanya and Violet laughed hysterically downstairs at Olaf sliding through a town on his belly, I slipped on my only pair of designer jeans, along with a black tank top, a teal cardigan, and trusty black ballet flats. I looked well-assembled, kind of like June. June lite.

I pulled out of the garage while blowing kisses to a happy, waving Violet in Tanya's arms. I was so proud of my sweet, resilient girl.

As I rolled up in front of the Costa Mesa boutique, I noticed it was next to a vegan cupcake shop and a bone broth bar. Yes, a bone broth bar. The boutique was called "CeCe's by the Sea" and it looked like a Red Lobster mated with a weed and crystal shop.

As I got out of the van, I glanced in the rearview mirror. Violet's car seat was empty. *Oh shit, where did I leave her? I did a double take, panicking. Did I leave her on top of the car? Why would I have put her on top of the car?* And then I remembered that I was on a rare solo excursion. My pulse returned to normal.

A tall, red-haired woman stood behind the glass sales counter. She wore all white and her wrists glimmered with clanging gold and silver bangles. Her hair was short, yet teased so aggressively that her face looked like the center of the sun, orange wiry hairs radiating around it. She was hard to look at directly, and when I finally did sear my eyeballs to get an up-close glimpse, she looked like some kind of a shaman, with giant fake lips. When her eyes met mine, she did not smile.

"Um, hi, I'm the friend of Martha's. With the shirts. Are you CeCe?"

"I've been expecting you. Let me see the shirts."

No time for niceties.

I opened the box and CeCe grabbed the shirts without regard for my tissue and stickers. "Love. Love. Love," she kept saying as she pulled out each shirt one by one, and then, "Loathe," when she got to the squirrel. My heart sank. I should've gone with the horse instead of the squirrel. *Damnit. Always go horse.* She held up the squirrel shirt to examine it closer. "But someone else may love it." She curled her top lip and worked her tongue extra hard as she spoke. The shirts sat in a heap on the counter. "Beautiful work. Let me write you a check for what we agreed on."

I wanted to tell her we hadn't agreed on anything yet, but I worried that she would try to lowball me if she knew I did the work without knowing a price. But before I could utter a word, she whipped out a checkbook, scribbled something, and firmly handed me a check for $300. The name section was blank. I was startled with how abrupt things felt, but $300 was more than I had made caretaking around the clock for nearly a decade, so I went with it.

"I hope your customers like them." I motioned to my shirts.

"Oh they will, Dear. They will eat them up like flies on a fresh turd."

I curbed my laugh. I couldn't tell if CeCe knew how cuckoo she was or if this was some sort of test. I felt like I was in a *Saturday Night Live* sketch—the last one of the night that goes off the rails.

"Let me know if you'd like more," I said.

"I already want more. Your shirts would be perfect for a pop-up shop I'm doing at an exquisite home in Newport Coast. Could you join us for a pop-up shop next week?" I could barely handle how her inflated lips contorted when she said "pop-up shop." If Aaron had been with me, it would've been over. Our hysterics would have gotten us kicked out immediately.

I looked away from her mouth and tried to focus on what she was asking. "When is it, and what is it?"

"They're a real hoot. I gather my favorite designers and the hostess invites everyone she knows to shop. There's champagne and ahi. The pop-up shop ladies would just die over your stuff." I didn't miss that I had been included in CeCe's favorite designers.

"Sounds, um, great. I have two kids, so I'd have to get childcare."

"Get childcare, Honey. Don't let those leeches suck your dreams." All I could do was blink silently as she continued. "It's next Thursday and I should tell you that you will make a lot of money there. For someone like you." I guess my Lauren Conrad ballet flats weren't fooling anyone. "These ladies have more money than Duggars have babies." Then she waved her hand at me like she was shoo-ing away a fly. I felt like I'd been tazed by all the things that had just been spoken aloud by her. I hurried out the door.

Safe in the car, I held the $300 check. I knew it wasn't a fortune, but I had earned it. CeCe left a bad taste in my mouth that no mint could ever cover, but she was currently my only ticket to freedom and sanity. I did the vague math on all the babysitting and take-out dinners "a lot of money" could buy. For that, I could put up with an unhinged, offensive shaman.

I couldn't stop thinking about the comment she'd made about leeches sucking my dreams. *I love those leeches, you bog woman.* It was strange to be on the other side of the comment—to be one of the "working" moms. Yet it still stung because I wasn't really a working mom either.

That night, after the kids had been fed, bathed, chased, sang to, rocked, kissed, and snuggled, Aaron sat on the couch watching *Stranger Things* while I messaged my village, asking who could pick Elliot up from school next Thursday so I could bask in ahi and champagne at the pop-up shop. Chloe came back with a quick yes. One down. Violet was covered after a quick text to Tanya who was even available to do two more days that week so I would have enough time to create sufficient stock. Aaron sat next to me, oblivious that having his childcare covered on the daily was an intrinsic right as a working father.

Next up: deciding on designs, sizes, and styles. No squirrels. I would have to put in a new rush order for blank t-shirts, something I hadn't done in years—calling in a business order. It felt good to be back. My sewing time would have to be used wisely in the next week if I wanted to make enough shirts to capitalize on all that money that supposedly flowed like Duggar babies. I was shooting for fifty shirts. Fifty shirts could buy a lot of sanity.

CHAPTER THIRTEEN

Human Time Bombs

*T*he week had flown by, like a Kindergarten half-day. I had hustled, knowing that more inventory meant more meals I didn't have to make, more showers, and next, maybe even a house cleaner. My fingers were sticky from spray adhesive, and my neck and back ached from slumping over the sewing machine for hours on end, a part of the process I had forgotten. A massage had recently edged its way onto my wish list.

I had been so immersed in getting everything done for the pop-up shop that the time spent with my kids was actually a welcome break. I felt more playful and present when I was with them. Candyland and finger painting could be fun when they weren't the only things you were doing. But something always had to give, and this time it was Aaron who wasn't getting a piece of—or any direct-deposit hand jobs from—this new working me. I knew my pop-up shop sewing overload was temporary, and that Aaron, and our skanky reality TV, would all still be there once I got through Thursday, so I kept my head down and worked into the nights.

Late Wednesday night, the warm glow from my sewing lamp illuminated the fruits of my labor. Fifty-five shirts sat there, all sewn, tagged and nicely folded. Goal exceeded.

I fell over onto the bed, my shoulders burning like when I nursed Elliot and Violet around the clock. I lay there, on top of my nest, looking like a frozen crime-scene victim. I stared up at the ceiling, concocting a plan in which I didn't have to brush my teeth or go pee or turn the lights out before closing my eyes and falling asleep. Catheters needed to be more accessible to the public.

Just then, my phone dinged. It was Tanya. A late-night text from the babysitter was never good news.

> I'm so sorry but I have a fever and a sore throat and I don't think I should watch Violet tomorrow.

I sat straight up. This couldn't be happening. And also, *of course* this was happening. "Not so fast with those plans, Ma'am," the Motherhood Police were reminding me. I wanted to text back *fuck fuck fuck fuck* but instead I replied to Tanya with forced sympathy.

After all of my hard work and money spent on babysitting, I couldn't fathom missing the pop-up and its monetary reward. But even more than that, I couldn't imagine taking Violet with me and trying to do anything productive while she went on one of her giggling and running rampages in someone else's lavish house, surely full of fragile, diamond-encrusted leopard figurines. I couldn't do it. And I couldn't ask Lucinda, who was out of town. I would have to ask for Aaron's help.

"Tanya just cancelled for tomorrow. She's sick," I said as I descended the stairs.

"That sucks. I'm so sorry." Aaron's voice had the slight disconnection one can only have when the bad news doesn't directly affect them.

"Can you work from home tomorrow with Violet? I really need your help."

"I wish I could, but we have a huge meeting tomorrow about the pickle-art mishap." He looked genuinely bummed that he couldn't help, and I understood. Kind of.

"Fuuuuuck," I said as I breathed out fire and walked into the kitchen. Here I was, once again, in the role of master juggler. *Why the hell did I do this to myself again? My head was right. My heart is an idiot.* It was late and I was weary. But I needed to make a plan. I knew what I had to do. And I hated it.

I shuffled to the snack cabinet and began preparing a diverse assortment of crunchy bribery that would hopefully keep Violet occupied tomorrow as the both of us did our best to make it through the pop-up—and her no-nap time—in one piece. I packed all the healthy stuff—freeze-dried green beans, protein bars, dehydrated bananas, an apple, two small tangerines, and beef jerky—into her favorite pink lunch bag. Then I moved onto the not-as-healthy, bottom-of-the-cabinet back-ups from parties and holidays, should she go berserk: Twizzlers, Cheetos, M&M's, and a lollipop. Those would go into Elliot's old Minions lunch bag, which would be used like a fire extinguisher behind glass.

☙

The next morning, I had set my alarm early enough to have kid-free time so I could shower and dress myself for the pop-up shop without a person attached to me. The house was dark and quiet, Aaron still snoring away. I needed to wear something stylish so CeCe's fabulous people believed I was one of them—or at least fit to be in the same house with them. I slipped into a black-patterned maxi skirt with a flowy tank top and a chambray shirt— also known as a "jean shirt" everywhere outside of California and New York. The outfit was just neutral enough to slide under the radar and not raise any waxed eyebrows. I pulled out my jar of jewelry from the halcyon days of blow drying and accessorizing and reached for my silver bracelet and teardrop earrings.

Downstairs, I had ten minutes before Elliot would need to be woken up. If I hurried, maybe I could eat breakfast alone and sitting down. But when I shut the fridge door, there he stood already, groggy, and in his too-small Mario Bros. jammies. "Whoa, it's morning and you took a shower, Mom?"

"I know, big change for me."

At 9:30 a.m., only Violet and I remained. She was wearing her special Ruby Riot "Oc-pus" shirt. If she had to come, she could at least help with marketing.

With Violet buckled in her car seat, snack and diaper bags packed, various princesses secured, and the box of inventory loaded, I began to pull out of the garage, but then stopped. I ran back inside to grab my Ergo baby carrier. I hadn't worn Violet in it for quite a while since she now preferred combat to snuggling, but I needed to have all the tools at my disposal today in case my only choice was to strap her to my body like the explosive she sometimes was.

We passed Elliot's school, waving at the playground and saying, "Hi Elliot!" The canyon behind his school looked greener than usual this foggy morning as we passed the gated subdivisions on our way to the freeway toward fancy Newport Coast. Violet made no peep from her seat in the back. I was so used to constant kid engagement, that sometimes I forgot to just let quiet children be.

"Do you want to listen to 'It's a Small World' song?"

"Yes," Violet answered, very ladylike. I hit play and we both started singing along with oomph, right until the jolly, prepubescent voices warned about the world of fears.

"I needs Small World ride!"

Many Southern California kids had an early and intimate relationship with all things Disney, something that only Orlando kids could understand.

"Not today, Sweetie. We have to show off Mama's shirts instead." *Those things are equally fun, right?*

Violet wailed. As I pulled up to the lush, gated entrance into the Newport Coast neighborhood, I cracked my window as little as possible to give my name to the gateman, worried that people with howling toddlers weren't allowed. But the gates slowly opened and before us, the Pacific Ocean revealed itself. We were high up on the apex of a hill, no fog.

"Look, there's the ocean, where mermaids live." Violet stopped crying and craned her neck to see Ariels.

I followed my GPS to a stunning mansion that looked like a bloated version of a quaint French cottage. I wanted to hate it. I wanted to think it was too big and too obnoxious and the people in it were too rich, but it was truly breathtaking and I wished it were mine, with the distant ocean dancing in the background, the blooming roses next to the shorn landscaping, and the giant wooden door that looked like something from a fairytale, vines swooping around it. Suddenly, the feeling that I stood out overtook me. Would people take me and my designs seriously or would they pity me and my TJ Maxxi skirt? Had I remembered to brush Violet's hair?

I gathered the arsenal of bags and slung them on my shoulder.

"We going to a party, Mama?"

"Sort of."

"I eat cake!"

"No, not that kind of party." I took Violet's hand and we walked toward the massive, enchanted door. I knocked.

"Come in," a voice called, much like Ursula in her underwater cave. *Come in, child.* CeCe walked toward us, wearing a gold pantsuit with a sheer but sparkly floor-length robe and holding a full glass of champagne. "Wonderful to have you here." She did the double air kiss thing as if she hadn't previously shooed me out of her shop. Crostini crumbs rested in the corners of her cartoonish mouth. I tried not to look. She peered down at Violet. "And what is this? I didn't realize you'd have a business partner."

"I didn't either, but our babysitter cancelled at the last minute," I said, realizing that CeCe probably had no idea the catastrophe that was. "This is my daughter, Violet."

"I much prefer roses to violets," she said from up high, taking a sip from her champagne. One of the dangling mouth crumbs fell into her glass, making its way to the bottom in a bubble trail. My politeness withered as I tightened my grip on Violet's hand.

"Let me show you to where your shop will be set up," she said, walking away. I re-slung all the bags over my shoulder, picked up an unsure Violet, and balanced the shirt box on my hip while following CeCe past my dream kitchen, where a woman was setting up a handmade soap display, and then into my dream sunroom.

"Here it is," CeCe announced, holding her hand out like a game-show hostess. The sleeve of her wizard's robe billowed like a flag.

The sunroom was a gorgeous alcove with an oversized white couch and glass tables with fat crystal bowls sitting on them like hens. The window looked out over the shimmering ocean. I should've felt tranquil, but I was too tensed up just thinking about how much wrangling it would take to make sure Violet didn't break anything or get the pristine white couch dirty. I cursed myself for not making a specific snack bag of all white foods.

"Ladies will be popping in your shop throughout the day. A little wombat told me that one of the women will be stopping by later with Jessica Biel," CeCe explained before vanishing. *Excuse me, what? A little wombat? This lady's smoking goddamn goofballs all day long.* But wait, had she also mentioned that Mrs. Justin Timberlake might show up and give her husband over to me today? I set Violet down and grabbed my phone to message Aaron.

> I know you have meetings
> all day, but FYI, I may be
> making sweet sweet love
> to Justin Timberlake later.

I methodically laid my shirts out on the couch so that each design could be seen. I organized them in rows, by color and size. Violet was helping by climbing up on the white couch, with her shoes on.

"Oh no, Honey. We can't get up there. We'll get it dirty." I struggled to unbuckle her little sandals while she pulled away from me, eyeing my immaculate display job. I would have to pull out the big guns sooner than I wanted to. "Do you want a snack?"

She aborted her tyranny and came skipping over to see what was in the pink bag, stopping at the freeze-dried green beans. She crunched away, buzz saw mouth in full effect. My stomach turned. There was no getting out of here without her making a huge mess. Thankfully CeCe hadn't made me put down a cleaning deposit.

Two maturely-dressed middle-aged women (read: more iridescent pantsuits) walked by and peeked their heads into the sunroom. "CeCe's brought a babysitter. She thinks of every last detail," one said to the other.

"Oh, um. I'm not a babysitter," I kindly explained. "I make children's shirts and this is my own daughter." Both ladies went silent for a moment with wide eyes and zero wrinkles. I couldn't tell if they thought I was crazy or incredible, or if they were both having simultaneous strokes. I began my saleswoman pitch to hopefully make things less weird. "I make these one-of-a-kind shirts for kids. No two are alike, as you can see. Kids can wear their favorite animal or something they love, like this guitar. And I sew them myself."

As if rehearsed, Violet paused her crunching, looked down at her own shirt and said, "I love oc-pus." The ladies' heads swung down toward an angelic Violet. Their faces finally slackened.

"Isn't she darling?" one said to me.

"Didn't Candace's friend's sister's daughter have a baby in the last year?" one said to the other.

"Yes. Did you know they already have a pony waiting for her?"

The other one gasped in pleasure. Then they turned to me. "Do you happen to have any shirts with horses?" I had their motherfucking number. I made a point to include a shit ton of horses in my stock, at the expense of squirrels, the poor man's horse.

While the ladies debated the merits of pink versus coral, my phone dinged. Aaron had messaged back.

> You have every right to bring sexy back with Justin Timberlake because I've basically been having an affair with Sheriff Hopper from Stranger Things every night this week.

At least Justin and I had Aaron's blessing.

"Miss, I'm going to take these two here because I don't know which size she is." I was in awe of rich people's love of buying gifts for people they barely knew—and in multiple sizes. But I found rich people much more tolerable when I was personally profiting off of them. I wrapped the shirts in red tissue paper and put them into a small brown paper bag with handles. I tied a strip of leftover fabric around the handles into a soft bow. It was a little polishing touch that I had come up with years ago.

"Just adorable," one of the women said on their way out.

So far, so good. I had already made enough money to hire a cleaning lady, one time.

☙

People trickled in and out, everyone oohing and ahhing over the uniqueness of my shirts and some monetizing their delight. It felt damn good to be seen. And paid. I was already out of horses.

As I covertly counted my money, I looked over to see Violet straining to pick up one of the glass bowls. "Those belong on the tables," I said, rushing over to help her set it down gently. There was far too much glass on glass in this room. She changed her target, laughing and running over to the shirts. She swiped them off the couch as if her hand was a rake, and cackled. "Violet, please," I begged, reorganizing. She went back to the bowls, put her hands on one and looked right at me, testing. "Stop," I said sternly. I was getting impatient. So was Violet, who flopped on the floor, amid snack wrappers, and rubbed her eyes. In addition to closing in on nap time, the newness of the experience was wearing off for her. Red tissue paper had been danced with and thrown and now it was just plain annoying to be confined to a room in which she couldn't touch anything. I was wearing down with constantly keeping one eye on her, one on glass bowls, and one on shirts, wrapping them up, and taking payments. Three eyes. I needed three goddamn eyes.

Violet lay on the floor, spinning in circles, when two chatty women who looked to be in their late thirties—and who weren't Jessica Biel—came through the doorway. I greeted them with a little less enthusiasm than I started with two hours earlier. Both women smiled aloofly. One, a muscular blonde, was wearing ripped black skinny jeans, high-heeled booties, and an off-the-shoulder t-shirt with the words "Spiritual Gangster" across her rack. Her eye makeup was so thick that it was hard to tell what she really looked like underneath it all. She motioned to her friend. "Jen, look at these . . . Jagger would love this robot one."

Jen was the toned-down version of her friend. She had almost the exact same blonde hair and chiseled arms, but she wore very little makeup and had on Nikes. She wasn't responding to her Spiritual Gangster friend because she was so focused on Violet, who—for the moment—looked serene on the floor.

"She's such a doll," Jen said to me.

"Sometimes," I replied, with a slight motherly chuckle. Jen's head tilted and she looked at me as if I had said I hated my child. She clearly wasn't a mom.

"These are just so freaking cute, I can't even," the Spiritual Gangster said, handling every single shirt with her bright red talons. "I'm gonna get these as favors for Atticus's birthday party."

Jen turned her focus away from Violet and her ungrateful mother and picked up a mermaid shirt. She rubbed the applique with her thumb. I thought I caught a wistfulness in the way she patted the shirt after putting it back with the others.

Her friend was going to town. "I should get one of these for Mari too. She's obsessed with horses. Do you have any with horses?"

"Fresh out. But the cat is cute. I've found that nine times out of ten, horse lovers are also cat lovers." I had no real facts to back this claim up.

"The cat *is* really cute. I love this red-striped pattern on the light blue."

I felt a tug on my leg. It was Violet and she was rubbing her eyes again. "Mama, I wanna go home." I picked her up, but she resisted, kicking my knees furiously. I tried to lower her safely, but she wouldn't straighten her legs to stand. She neither wanted to be held nor put down, a mythical middle ground that made my muscles shake as I tried to force her into picking one.

"Aww, she looks tired," Jen said. There was something in the way she looked at Violet, as if the entire world should revolve around this little dumpling and what kind of mother was I not to dote on her every need? I'd seen grandmothers act in a similar way to Jen—namely one at PetSmart a few weeks back. Maybe she and Lucile were on different sides of the same coin. This thought made me pull back and empathize, until Violet started swinging her arm of destruction at the shirts.

The Spiritual Gangster was holding at least five nights' worth of pizza delivery in her hands—and still shopping. Rewarding a screaming child with junk food would make me a trash parent, but it was time. I dug deep in my purse for the Minions bag and handed it to Violet, whose eyes lit up. She snatched the bag from me and sat down quietly by herself, unzipping it.

"I'll take these," Jen's friend said, patting a stack of shirts. I tallied up her total, took her money, and scrambled to get her bags thoughtfully tissued before Violet smashed M&Ms into the floor. My stomach growled. She wasn't the only one who needed a snack bag.

Before I could hand over the paid-for shirts, Violet interrupted. "Wook Mama!" She had torn into the Cheetos bag and was gnawing through them at a fantastic rate. She clapped her hands, misting a light fog of Cheetos dust toward the couch. I ransacked my purse for a wipe while one of my three eyes stayed locked on her. But she was knowingly headed for the white couch with her orange-powdered fingertips leading the way. Before I could act, she thrust herself onto the spotless couch cushion.

"No!" I yelped.

Jen and her friend stood there, unable to look away. I rushed over to the couch and gently (okay, forcibly) cinched Violet's wrists like a nabbed criminal's. She wriggled and giggled as I managed to lift her up, thinking it was a game. A silly hogtying game. You know, totally normal.

There, on the couch, was a large streak of orange soot. I buckled, letting her run free, and scrubbed the couch furiously with the wipe intended for her hands. I looked up at the two women, who turned around immediately, pretending they'd seen nothing. The Spiritual Gangster leaned into Jen and not-so-quietly said, "That poor little girl. Dragged around while her mom works. Just like that gypsy couple in front of Home Depot with the accordion." Jen looked back at us with concern, but it was unclear if it was more for me or for Violet. I was putting money on Violet. "Who lets their toddler eat Cheetos, anyway?" the friend added as they walked out.

The two were gone. But their words were not.

I stayed with the stain and rage-scrubbed it until my phone lit up, interrupting me. It was an actual call from Chloe, who was supposed to be picking Elliot up from school in thirty minutes. "Everyone okay?" I asked worriedly, hoping it wasn't a broken bone or active shooter.

"Savannah threw up at school. I just picked her up and won't be able to come back to grab Elliot for you. So sorry."

Everything was falling apart around me. There would

be no romp with JT. Nor selling out of inventory. I abandoned the orange skid mark and picked up Violet's dolls, spilled M&Ms, and the larger Cheetos crumbs like I was on fast forward.

Suddenly, a gaggle of women entered my shop. They held champagne glasses and tiny toasts with something white and creamy on top, and moved as a herd. They didn't even look in my direction. I dashed to quickly throw a shirt over the orange shame.

"Get out!" one said to the group, pointing.

"Oh my God, look at the guitars," another added, rushing over. "Bowie would love this." They swarmed the couch like a flock of tipsy seagulls and began grabbing the shirts. *Mine mine mine.*

The chaos scared Violet and she dropped *le résistance* and came running over to me. I needed to speak up and tell everyone that I must grab my shirts and leave, but this could be one last huge sale—the difference between a year's worth of organic strawberries versus conventional. I dug through one of my bags and excavated the Ergo carrier. I plopped Violet in the front, our united hearts beating fast for different reasons. Her face was right in front of mine.

"Mama, I wanna go home," she begged, rubbing her eyes hard.

"I know, Baby, we will soon," I reassured her. I instinctively bounced as I tried not to think about Elliot standing at the pick-up line all alone, lost. I had never been a no-show at pick-up. It was one thing to let your kid down because of some unforeseen event. A flat tire? Fine. One could even argue it's good for them. Life happens. But peddling t-shirts to pay for sanity because being a mother was more taxing than I thought it would be? Harder to justify.

The feeding frenzy finally subsided and all of the women stood in front of me with shirts in hand. They were so caught up in their chatter that they didn't notice how hard I was working to quickly bag their items while wearing another human being, or that Violet was now trying to claw her way out of the carrier as I frantically folded red tissue. There was so much to handle that I wanted to scream. The overwhelm flashed me back to being in labor with Elliot, trying to push him out and Martha locking onto my eyes and saying, "Just keep going. That's it. The only way out is through." All I had to do was get through this moment, make my money to pay for my freedom, and then race to get to Elliot.

I stuck my hands out to give the women their perfect little bags of shirts, but Violet's paws batted them away in protest. The escalation of her physical commotion finally pulled the women out of their fizzy champagne cocoon, and they were forced to pay attention to what was happening right in front of them—a mom trying to be something more.

They looked mortified that an upset toddler should be a part of their pop-up shopping experience, and I didn't blame them. I hadn't wanted it to be a part of my selling experience either. I dropped the bags on one of the glass tables and walked away. Too much was going on around me. I breathed out hard. *Fuck this shit.* I was near eruption and needed to get Violet off of my body, like when they tell you to put the crying baby down before you lose it. I pulled my arm back like a contortionist and attempted to undo the carrier clip on my upper back, but Violet bucked, making the tension in the strap so tight that I couldn't unlatch it.

"Violet. Stop. It."

She reached her orange Cheetos hand back and then bitch-slapped me square in the face. SMACK!

The flock of women looked up from the table of bags, aghast. They didn't know that this wasn't my first time being slapped in the face, in public, by a toddler. I had been initiated into this part of motherhood by Elliot and his slap heard 'round the world in Toys R Us, years earlier. But the rage that came from being open-handed slapped in the face this time felt just as visceral as the first.

My cheek stung hot and I couldn't see for a brief moment. It was either because my eye was hit, I had blacked out, or both. My hands quivered, like they were contemplating rising up to give a slap back. My adrenaline told me to fight and hit back the thing that had just hit me, but my mothering sense was telling me to protect my offspring. There was an all-out war inside my body. I had to pause and deliberately force my hands to slow down, my right one coming up and grasping Violet's hand tightly and then quickly letting go.

When my brain came back online, my mouth was agape and I looked down square at Violet, who was well aware that something colossal had just occurred and it might not be good news for her. I wanted to give her a tongue-lashing and possibly a caning to discipline her in some way that would matter, but I also knew that she had been pushed by this day just as I had. This was all her fault and yet all my fault too. It also felt like Tanya's fault.

I tuned into the loud whispering coming from the women exiting the room with their bags, remembering that there had been an audience. And a merciless one at that. "I would never let my kid get away with that," one woman muttered, throwing a condemning look directly at me. "Some people just shouldn't be parents. That's why this generation is so entitled," said another. I shook and felt tears well up and blur my vision, so I bit my lip to squash it, just shy of making it bleed. I wanted to upstage Violet's bitch slap and punch these women in the fucking whitened teeth. How could they eat up my shirts and then spit out my heart?

Violet, who was still in the carrier on me, had been silent since the slap, but the soft sound of her now-calm voice peeped up. "I sowy Ma-ma." I looked down into her tired eyes, our bodies pressed into each other. She laid her head down on my small breast that made a perfect little pillow. I couldn't bring myself to be verbal quite yet, so I kissed her hot, weary head and quickly threw everything into my box and bags.

I ghosted from the house of horrors, weighed down not by clanking chains, but by Violet and overflowing bags that nearly fell off each of my shoulders as I sprinted out to my minivan, hoping to avoid CeCe and an explanation. As I exited the grand gates, I saw a black limo entering on the opposite side. It had to be JT—and what's her name—because nothing would complete this day quite like missing out on my celebrity crush by sheer minutes. I pressed my hand up to my window as our vehicles passed like ships in the night.

As I sped onto the freeway towards Elliot's school, I was ravenous. Even though Violet had snacked the day away and fresh ahi was on the breath of every person who came in my room, I had eaten nothing. I plunged my hand into the center console, looking for a stowed-away snack—

anything would do. Even an old bank receipt or a squirt of sunscreen sounded delicious at this point. Lucky for me, there was a granola bar from the Mesozoic Era. But at least it was still in a wrapper.

I screeched into the nearly empty parking lot of Elliot's school. The pick-up line and all its drama had driven off twenty minutes ago. I got out and peeked through Violet's window to find her sleeping. She was the only child on Earth who refused to fall asleep in the car, but today she was zonked out. I cracked the window just a smidge, shut my door, and ran into the school's front office which was just steps from where I parked. I ran through the front doors, hoping Elliot would be there waiting for me instead of in a stranger's car on the way to the state line.

There he was. He looked so small, sitting in an oversized waiting room chair. My shoulders dropped. "El, I'm so sorry," I said as I moved in and gave him a hug. I pulled back and looked at him, holding his shoulders. His eyes were wet.

"Where were you, Mom?"

The office lady not-so-stealthily side-eyed our exchange.

"I was at a work thing, and then Savannah got sick and they couldn't get you. I rushed straight here," I explained, realizing that none of the logical details would change his emotional state. I remembered what it felt like to be a kid and to think that your parents had forgotten you somewhere. It felt like you were in a nightmare.

"I thought you were at the end of the line of cars and I kept waiting and waiting and then when I didn't see you . . ." The reliving of it made him crack. ". . . I got scared." I wiped the warm teardrops off of his cheeks and hugged him tightly, while looking over his shoulder to make sure Violet and the minivan were still there. I felt seasick. Being home with my kids meant that I hadn't experienced many moments like this. It felt awful.

"Let's go, Honey."

He stood up and grabbed his backpack. "Where's Violet?" he asked. I waited until we were outside, away from the nosy office lady, to answer him. I'd been judged enough that day and leaving children in cars—even for two minutes in the shade within your eye line—was a touchy topic.

As we pulled out, Elliot said, "I was wondering if maybe we could go get that Pokémon pack that I've been wanting. You know, since it's been a rough day and all."

And there it was. That edge. That spot where an already gut-wrenching parenting moment is splintered into something even more complicated and seemingly manipulative, and there's no way out that doesn't feel like total shit. After leaving Elliot for dead after school, all I wanted to do was comfort him. The last thing I wanted to do was to say "no" or negotiate about Pikachus. And yet.

"Not today. I think we could all use some down time." In the rear-view mirror, I saw his head drop. My nausea returned. Maybe it was the archaic granola bar I'd mainlined minutes before, but it was most likely the familiar parental guilt.

We pulled into the garage. Four more hours to go before Aaron would hopefully be home. I felt grateful to be walking into a house with no glass tables. I had $1,200 of blood money in my pocket, but I was pretty sure it hadn't been worth bringing myself and both of my kids to our collective knees. Everyone had been traumatized today.

All of my rules had been slapped out of me. When Aaron walked in the door, the only light in the room was the glow from the TV that shone off of our three faces watching back-to-back *Cupcake Wars*. A bowl of spent edamame shells sat on the coffee table. Dinner.

"Why's it so dark in here?" Aaron asked, turning on the kitchen light. I recoiled like a vampire. I might've even hissed. Violet went running toward him with sudden, full energy.

"Dah-dee, dah-dee!" He picked her up and they melted into a big hug. I opened my mouth to speak, but couldn't think of how to sum up all the violations of the day, so I shut it. Aaron walked over to me on the couch and kissed me on the head.

"JT must've worn you out," he whispered into my ear.

"I wish," I groaned. Aaron moved over to Elliot and gave him a kiss on the head too.

"Mom forgot me at school," he chimed. *Great. Thanks, Elliot, for always keeping everyone up to date with the latest.* Aaron's eyebrows raised. To hear that I wasn't completely on top of managing the kids was new to him too.

"It turns out I can't be a stay-at-home mom and a working mom at the same time," I said throwing my hands to my sides, just like the emoji. "And I've scheduled an emergency session with June tomorrow, so I don't have to download my whole day to you. Instead we can watch rich people go on exotic trips with people they hate." I was referring to *Real Housewives*. "On second thought, let's skip that one tonight. I've had my fill of rich people."

"Man, it must've been really bad then," he joked as he headed to the fridge. Even though I didn't want to recall my painful day entirely, it was unusual that he completely took the out and didn't inquire further at all. Just like forgetting to pick up children from school was a new occurrence in my life, so was Aaron and I not engaging about our days.

⚘

After the kids were asleep and we pillaged the snack cabinet in tandem, Aaron and I sunk into the couch.

"This day," I said, exhaling.

"Yeah, no kidding." He must've been referring to his own tough day dealing with whatever the cute little pickle incident was. He picked up his phone. I'd shown too much restraint all day. I couldn't help myself.

"So do you want to know *anything* about my day?"

"Sure," he forced, eyes still affixed to his phone. I said nothing. He finally looked up. "Are you going to tell me or not?"

In the history of marriage, those words never ever led to anything good.

"Never mind," I said.

He ran his hands through his dark hair and pressed his palms on the sides of his face. "Look, I care, April, but I had a rough day too. I just want to chill out. You told me that's what we were gonna do since you see June tomorrow. Am I wrong, did you not say that?"

"You had a rough day too? Did you have to wear another human being on you during your meeting? Did someone slap you in the face in front of fancy people drinking champagne who said you shouldn't be allowed to have children? Did your son cry in your arms because you left him somewhere?" I unloaded on him like a baby with reflux. I didn't want it to be a competition for whose day was harder, but, well, it was, and mine was. There was nothing at Aaron's work that could've trumped my day unless there was a gunman and a white couch.

He threw his arms up. "I know, I know. Your day is always harder than mine. Your life is always harder than mine."

"It actually is, Aaron, because I'm multitasking every single fucking moment of my life while people accost my face."

"I know being with the kids all day is hard, and God, I wish I could make it easier for you, but I can't. It's not easy to sit here and see everything be so hard for you. When do we get to the part where something gives you some relief? Wasn't a babysitter supposed to help? Wasn't getting back into sewing supposed to help you? I haven't seen you in a week for *this*?"

I felt like I'd had the wind knocked out of me by a four-square ball, like in fourth grade.

"I'm allowed to have a hard day too," he said, looking away and shaking his head. I was silent on the outside, while a storm surged inside, his shaking of the head noted in the internal scorebook of marital misdemeanors. He was right about asking when the fuck would anything give me real, tangible relief from the shackles of motherhood. I was as frustrated about that as much as he was. I had been making progress, until today, when it all shit the bed. This day had almost broken me and here I was six hours later, facing the final blow. It was too much, again, so I saved myself, again. I stood up and walked to the stairs.

"You're just going to walk away? Is this a new thing you do?"

I stopped before the first step and turned around. "This day needs to end. I can't possibly handle one more thing. Even if you think I should be able to."

I turned back around and went upstairs. He let me go.

CHAPTER FOURTEEN

Asking for a Unicorn

I didn't move a muscle during my eleven hours of sleep, and I had a crick in my neck to prove it. It was astounding how much more rested one could feel when they went to bed at 9 p.m. instead of midnight. When I awoke to Violet's yells, I actually felt human, for a moment.

Despite the marital tension that awaited me, which had become annoyingly common as of late, I felt relief that at least I wouldn't have to be both a working and a stay-at-home mom today—and that Lucinda was coming to the rescue while June would surely help me make sense of yesterday's collapse and what it meant for the future of my mental health.

On my way to Violet's room, I heard Aaron and Elliot laying in his bed, talking intensely about a topic near and dear to their hearts: why Ariel from *The Little Mermaid* didn't write a message to Eric, describing the whole voice debacle and urgent need for a kiss. Elliot was passionately arguing that if Ariel could sign her name on the contract with Ursula, that meant she must know how to write the English language and therefore could've easily sidestepped the entire ordeal by reaching out to Eric via pen and ink.

I stood in Elliot's doorway as Aaron passionately nod-ded in agreement. I hated that Aaron and I had unfinished business from last night and the day already felt shaky because of it. I didn't want to contemplate what to say or not say, or if I should even look in his direction, and who owed who an apology. I wanted one damn day without heaviness and for everything to just go back to functional, even if it meant sweeping this corpse under the rug. We were both doing the best we could, for fuck's sake.

And then it happened. Somewhere between the internal evaluating and accidental meeting of eyes with him, I just let go. There was no pat on the back nor applause when it happened. I simply smiled at him, surprising even myself. The amount of energy it would've taken to teeter in relationship purgatory was far more than it took to just move forward, and my subconscious knew that before I did.

Elliot threw the covers off both of them and came at me. "Mom, today is desk sale day at school. I'm gonna go find stuff to bring."

Desk sale day was when all the third graders brought their personal junk to school and sold it to each other. Pretty much Marie Kondo's worst nightmare. They used "scholar dollars" (AKA the hush money they'd earned for following the prison rules in class) and Elliot could make it rain scholar dollars with all the rule-following he did, which meant that he would come home with more junk than he left with. The Bin of Pointless Crap wins again.

"Hi," Aaron said to me, putting his arm around my waist and leaning his chin on my head. I couldn't tell if this was denial, acceptance, or the gateway drug to divorce. But life went at warp speed with kids, and sometimes there just wasn't enough time to handle every little marriage dispute with the utmost care. Sometimes letting things go was an act of grace, not disconnection, Right?.

I plopped myself comfortably on June's couch, like a teenager at a friend's house, then noticed she had what looked like a fresh manicure—nine hot pink fingernails and one black pinky nail.

"What a pleasant surprise to see you so soon," she said, taking a seat. It pained me not to be telling her a success story.

"Everything started out so promising. But then my career ended in a great glass room with a toddler and a bag of Cheetos." June's eyes dilated incrementally as I kept listing off the atrocities of the previous day. "I was naïve to think I could be a mom and do anything else outside of that. My heart is an idiot."

There was a long uncomfortable silence. June sat with her chin resting on her hand and her foot bouncing. She looked like she was trying to figure out where to go next with me and was without something immediately helpful to say. I waited, staring at the carpet so intently that I could see the microscopic loop of each fiber brushing up next to my Toms.

"Let's go back to the part that sounded do-able. How do we get you back to that place?"

"I guess I could just keep it simple with the shirt orders and only take a few," and never do a pop-up again, I said, completely deflated, nearly mumbling.

"Hmm. Sounds like you don't want to do it on a smaller scale, like when things seemed to be working. Is that right?" I felt a splash of embarrassment, as if I was asking for a unicorn. But I was only asking for equal opportunity. Aaron had that unicorn.

"I want to say yes to things, like Aaron does. He gets asked to do art shows and doesn't hesitate one bit. He doesn't ever have to get a babysitter because I am his built-in babysitter. I didn't sign up for this. Who wrote these rules?" I breathed out in frustration.

"I hear you, April. Motherhood invites us to reassess the things we gave up to become mothers—and even wives. Some pieces you can take back and some you can't, as is part of any life transition." Her words touched me in a low, painful place.

"When Aaron and I met, we were both following our dreams. He loved my independence and I loved his creativity. We were equals. And then we weren't." My throat burned its familiar burn as I worked through the tightness of my anger. "I cannot make peace with this. I want to, but I can't." I imagined a giant curtain, faking all us women out. The second we have a baby, the curtain drops and we see that equality was a total fucking lie. This gig is biologically unequal out the gate.

"It doesn't matter how woke my husband is, June, I'm the one whose breasts leaked when my babies cried. I can't regain my sanity as a mother because in my quest to get it back, I push it further away. Trying to make money to buy the help I need just makes me need more help." *It was a masochistic riddle. That's how I would describe motherhood from this day forward.* "And it all hinges on my babysitter's ability to show up. Everything I worked for."

My voice became deep and urgent. "Can you be real with me?"

June nodded.

"Is any of this shit you're offering me going to work?" I

had been searching for some elusive, microscopic place of balance and now I wasn't even sure it existed.

She took a deep breath and closed her eyes for a moment. "There's a lot to unpack here, but in ten years of doing this work, you are the first person to ask me that question directly. And it's a valid one."

We sat staring at each other, in the stillness of not knowing what to say or how to fix anything. I wondered if June was going to answer the "valid" question or just hand me a prescription for whatever people take to make motherhood feel less unjust, which at this point sounded amazing. I broke gaze from her and nervously brushed my hand back and forth against the grain of the couch's fabric until she spoke.

"No two moms are the same. We all come to motherhood differently. Things like hiring a babysitter, wearing eye shadow, or getting a manicure actually help some of us to feel like our old selves again." She wiggled her manicured fingers. "Some respond to these quick fixes and others need more."

I now understood how the search for one's old identity could sometimes be misinterpreted as vanity, but I didn't feel any better.

"April, you have a unique self-awareness that borders on anxiety. You aren't afraid of deep emotions and you ask hard questions. That's why quick fixes don't work easily for you. They don't address the root of the issue and so it keeps coming up. I can see that clearly now."

It made a fucking lot of sense, and I knew it meant there was probably no way out for someone like me. Martha was right. The only way out was through.

"There's no magic pill," June continued, "to erase the

dark while leaving the brilliance. Time, maybe. Your kids will grow."

Great, I'll just wait this out for sixteen years. No big deal.

"There are pharmaceutical options, and I can refer you to someone, but those come with trade-offs as well."

"Do you think I'm depressed?" I almost welcomed a diagnosis so we could just wrap this whole thing up and put it to bed with a little Prozac.

"You're more an intensely thinking and feeling mother of young children than clinically depressed. You're doing your best with who you are, like all of us."

Her words stung for some reason, perhaps because they were so true. I suddenly understood that if I were to give myself some compassion and truly believe that I was doing my best as a mother—flaws and all—I would have to retroactively extend that same grace to Marnie. She was also a mother doing her best with who she was, even though it didn't feel good enough to me. But what was I supposed to do with those conflicting feelings?

"It's okay to feel more than one way about motherhood," June said. "You can love parts of it, and love your children fully, but also find yourself in a blinding rage from the amount of sacrifice."

She must've known "blinding rage" would make me laugh, because it did. June never joked, and this was perfectly timed. Then she sat up tall in her seat, like someone pricked her with a pin. "I have a poem I think you might love. Let me find it." She slid a few books out of her bookshelf, opening and shaking them. A folded piece of paper fell out of the fourth one. "It's called *The Shoelace*, by Charles Bukowski. Take it with you to read." She handed me the tattered paper. The poem was handwritten. I wondered if the handwriting was hers, or if it had been passed down to her.

She checked the time.

"I didn't mean to downplay the legit support you've given me here, June."

She smiled in her humble, June way. "You've worked hard here. I commend you for that."

I wished I could be more like her: calm, yet in charge. She could sort things out with care, just like I wished I had done last night with Aaron.

"Your family is fortunate to have you," she said, standing up.

"Let me call my husband real quick and have you say that to him," I joked.

"Husbands are a different thing entirely."

"Well, your husband is lucky to be married to someone like you, who can untangle the knots we humans tie."

She tried to repress her guffaw. "Thank you, but we don't agree on much," she said, smiling painfully. *Come again?* I didn't know how much I could ask, but she offered an opening. I took a leap.

"So he doesn't think he's lucky to have scored you?" I instantly regretted it when I saw her look away and smooth her hair behind her ear. Her scar.

"I'm sorry, April. I shouldn't have said that." Her voice became strained. "Our time together is about you and I want to honor that."

"No, I'm sorry. I didn't mean to pry."

She smiled warmly, but with a lilt of what looked like regret. I hated myself for having prodded her too far. Me and my senseless questions and love of honest human connection. No wonder Marnie didn't have the patience for me.

"You didn't pry. I know it's hard for clients to have a one-sided dialogue in here. There's more I'd like to say that I can't, but I can tell you that it's far easier to make sense of someone else's life from the outside than my own from the inside. We are all human." *If you were really human, June, you would just spill it instead of leaving me dangling on a goddamn cliff, but whatever.* "What are you thinking about a next session?"

I felt lost at the thought of not having June to help me, like a baby without its lovey. But I needed a break from the straw grasping, even just temporarily. "I'm going to just be for a bit. And spend the money I made from the pop-up shop. It wasn't a total failure," I said with a grin and dollar-sign eyeballs.

"Good for you. Really good."

Not knowing when I might see her next, I unabashedly went in for a hug that was maybe also an apology for digging at her personal life. She accepted and hugged me back.

"I really hope our paths will cross again," she said, her hot pink- and black-tipped fingers squeezing my forearm.

CHAPTER FIFTEEN

Superheroes

*A*fter leaving Mother Roots, I was sick of soul searching and wanted to have some fucking fun for a change. I texted Danielle to see if she and Owen could meet up at Costco for some cheap-ass hot dogs, bulk buying, and another playdate in a place of business. Shopping with your own children was risky enough, but including other people's children was next-level. Especially with Owen. But the payoff of getting to do a normal mom activity with Danielle was worth the gamble of a possible disaster.

They were totally down.

In front of Costco, I was about to click the button to open the van door when Elliot stopped me. "Mom, wait. Let's do it on the count of three. One, two, three!" He loved pressing the buttons for the automatic van doors at the same exact time, to create a spaceship experience. Or something. The doors opened in unison.

The three of us walked up to the Costco "dining" area, which resembled a roller-skating rink snack bar meets an airport concourse, and ordered our dogs. We saw Danielle sitting with Owen, who was deep-throating a whole dog while holding a second one in his other hand. She waved us over.

"I'm sorry I've been so MIA," I said, hugging her. "These shirts have been kicking my butt." All three of the kids laughed at the word "butt."

"Tanya told me she was spending lots of time at your house and I could hardly believe it. But good on you."

"Well, I was just at my therapist's office today for an emergency visit, if that gives you any indication of how things are going."

"Oh right. I forgot about that whole OC housewife mix-up." Danielle sipped her Coke.

"It's funny, I really like her. I judged the shit out of her —oops, sorry kids—but I was wrong." My filter had fallen off. "But today she dropped some hints about being in a bad marriage, which just boggles my mind since she's basically perfect."

"Aren't therapists not supposed to talk about themselves?"

"She didn't come out and say it, but she for sure implied it."

"How can she counsel you when she's dumb enough to be in a busted marriage?"

There was Danielle's bluntness. I felt a jolt of protectiveness over June and regretted having told Danielle anything. She didn't have the context in which to place June and all of her loveliness.

"Well," I said, stalling. "I don't know that it's so black and white." I sounded like the person I was defending. "Just because she's human doesn't mean she can't be a good therapist." I was careful not to sound too defensive. It was delicate territory discussing new friends with old friends.

Before Danielle could respond, Owen suddenly stood up. "MORE!" He sounded like a tiny king.

"No, dude, we are all done with hot dogs," she said, wiping grease off his mouth and hands. His face squeezed up like he was about to burst into tears so she put her Coke straw into his mouth like a pacifier. He instinctually sucked into submission.

One of the perks of Costco was that the carts had two kid seats up front. Its girth made it a bitch to drive, although it was slightly more manageable than the dreaded twenty-foot-long car cart at the grocery store I mowed down every end-cap display with.

"Okay, what's on your list?" I asked Danielle.

"Dino chicken nuggets, those small bags of chips, Fruit by the Foot." Her list was my junk food list.

"Are you kidding me with Fruit by the Foot? They still make that?"

"I know, right? Owen loves those things."

"Can we get some Fruit by the Foot too?" Elliot asked, jumping up and down eagerly. If I allowed Cavities by the Centimeter into my home, I would have to micromanage it and the subsequent teeth brushing for as many days as fifty rolls lasted. I wanted nothing to do with any of it.

"Not this time, El." Or any time. I knew the low-hanging head was imminent. As Danielle walked over and reached for a gigantic box of Fruit by the Foot, I whispered in his ear. "That stuff's not good for you."

"But Mom, Danielle is buying it," he said loudly, holding his hands out in total kid despair, not picking up on my discretion. I winced, preparing for damage control, but Danielle seemed not to mind, nor even to question the 150 feet of yellow #5, red #40, and blue #1 she was humping into the cart. She was like a mom in the 80s, giving zero fucks.

"MOUF," Owen demanded, looking at the box and pointing to his pie hole. She ripped it open, pulled out a package, and handed it to him. He took one look at the little bundle of spiraled paper and red stickiness and shoved the entire thing in his mouth.

"Owen, you have to pull the paper off." She fished it out of his mouth. "He does this every damn time," she said to me, shaking her head.

"It's probably a lot to figure out with the paper and all," I reasoned, trying to make her feel like Owen's primal ways were normal. A little bit like June did for me.

"Would you like one, Elliot?" Danielle asked him, which felt like possible retribution to me. His eyes blinked widely and looked at me for the green light, his hands in praying position. I wasn't really sure why the toxic hot dog from ten minutes earlier was more acceptable than this junk, so I said yes.

"Wha 'bout me?" Violet said, like a damsel in distress.

"Of course you can have one too, Sweetie," Danielle said, handing an open package to her. Violet had never had Fruit by the Foot before, but somehow she instinctively knew how to carefully peel the red part off of the paper. Danielle noticed. "She's a genius."

Danielle and I did our best to chat between constant interruptions. For thirty seconds, we talked about her and Daveed's upcoming adult getaway to Napa, and the spa day she had planned for them, which had me drooling. Then there was screaming over a too-tight seatbelt which caused us to completely forget what we were saying, which rolled right into someone asking if they could get a life-sized Storm Trooper. The five of us looked like some kind of group neurosis, with two feet of sweet-smelling paper trails hanging from every child's hand, like Dead Sea scrolls.

Suddenly Owen let out a piercing yelp that was out of the normal vocal range for him. Danielle dropped the fat sack of round, red cheeses that resembled an overstuffed fisherman's net. I looked at Violet for a trace of foul play or guilt, but she looked as startled as we were.

"Shit," Danielle said, bummed but unfazed, as Owen doubled over, moaning. "Time's up on Owen." I looked at her, concerned. "It's this new thing he does when he has to poop. He screams bloody murder, clenches and resists and then when he finally does go, it's like a crime scene. I gotta get him outta here."

"Do you want me to get all this stuff for you and drop it off at your house?" I yelled as they fled. She waved a firm no.

The three of us remained.

"Mom, what does she mean that it looks like a crime scene? Does Owen have to go to jail?" Elliot asked.

"No, it was a joke." I hoped that would suffice. And it did, only because he noticed that Danielle had left their opened and partially-eaten box of Fruit by the Foot.

"What about that?" he asked, pointing to the ripped box, looking uncomfortable. If I had been alone, I would've dumped it off somewhere in the tire aisle, but I knew impressionable eyes were watching and any slight violation of the law would lead to hard-hitting questions. Danielle had gotten the last laugh, intentionally or not. "We're gonna buy it since we opened it, right?" he asked eagerly, hands in praying position again.

"We sort of have to, I guess."

He mouthed a "yessssssss." I could just picture his and

Violet's back teeth covered in sugary red blankets for the next three months, like tiny cakes covered in red fondant.

Our playdate had quickly turned into me finding the fastest way out, after snagging lunch-box usuals and splurging on some new towels that didn't stink. The outlying Costco gatekeeper—an insanely good-looking young man all us local moms referred to as "Costco Ryan"—snatched my receipt, put the highly official highlighter dash on it and released us into the outside world. It was piercingly bright outside compared to the fluorescence of Costco's innards.

I slid my sunglasses on, stopping in my tracks. There was June, walking in my direction. She noticed me too. Her smile was just as warm outside of the office as it was inside. Two curly-haired boys who looked to be somewhere around six and ten stood on each side of her. The older boy was wearing a boxy surfer hat with the California flag on it. The younger one was wearing an Iron Man muscle costume.

"Look at your adorable boys," I said, taking my sunglasses off. I relished in getting to see her children, a peek into her life. *So these are the work of perfect mothering.*

"This is Chase," she said, pointing to the older boy who waved shyly, "and this is Charlie—I mean Iron Man." He pretended to punch in the air. "And who are these two cuties?" she asked, gesturing toward my kids, pretending not to know. I wished Violet was representing herself more accurately, but instead, she was making a liar out of me by just sitting there quietly.

"This is Elliot, and this is Violet." I patted them each on the head. "And this is June, you guys. She's a friend of Mama's." *A friend Mama pays to cry in front of.*

"Mom." Chase said, pointing at Elliot's Minecraft shirt.

"I see you play Minecraft, Elliot," June said.

"Yeah. My favorite part is blowing up pigs with TNT," Elliot said, and Chase laughed.

"Well, isn't that lovely to know about a person?" I said, slightly mortified that my son outwardly spoke of getting pleasure from killing things, but then I realized that the more bananas my kids were, the more my tales of woe made sense. *Bring it, kids.*

Suddenly, there was a commotion just a few feet away. An older woman had lost control of her cart with an obscene amount of toilet paper and vitamins in it. It was gaining speed and about to careen into a parked car. She was yelling for help. Before any of us knew what was happening, Charlie went barreling toward the cart.

"I got it," he announced, in superhero mode.

"Charlie, no!" June yelled, turning to run after him. But it was too late. Tires screeched and a silver Range Rover slammed hard into the runaway cart and into Charlie, both bouncing to the ground hard, in different directions. Everyone gasped in unison, like a canned sound effect from a movie. The Range Rover revved hard and peeled out of the parking lot, leaving its mess behind. June raced over to Charlie, who laid on the ground.

Oh fuck. Oh fuck. Please make him be alive. No blood. No blood, please. My body felt like bricks. I wanted to do something. To comfort June. To rewind time. To turn into the Bionic Woman and go pull that Range Rover driver out by their hair, wherever they were, but all I could do was stand there, heavy. I fumbled my phone in my shaking hands, dialed 911, and breathlessly rambled about what had happened and where we were. My heart pounded inside my mouth. Onlookers were gathering and employees were scurrying over with hand radios. I ran over to June who was stroking the curly hair of a motionless Charlie. "Baby, baby, baby, baby . . ." she was repeating, breaking into tears.

"I need everyone to back up!" an employee yelled, crouching down next to June. She patted around Charlie's body, feeling for blood or a heartbeat or whatever a mother feels for when her baby is unresponsive. There was nothing anyone could do yet. I saw Chase standing there, frozen, his eyes transfixed on his mom, and on his brother's ripped costume.

"Do you want to come stand by us?" I asked, not sure if taking him further away was even a good idea. But he nodded and walked back with me and stood by Elliot. Violet, who was still sitting in the cart, reached for me. I scooped her up immediately, hugging her tight and then grabbed Elliot's hand, squeezing it hard. He squeezed back.

In what seemed like seconds and also hours, an ambulance arrived, sirens full blast. Violet covered her ears. There was movement and quickness and suddenly up from the chaos came Charlie on a gurney with his eyes open. Seeing June rejoice at seeing her baby's eyes open made me feel like I might collapse. She was holding onto the gurney, but looking for Chase in the crowd.

"He's over by us," I said, waving.

"They won't let him in the ambulance," she said desperately.

"He can come home with us. Just call me later. Do what you have to do. We'll be fine. We've got Minecraft." *What ridiculousness was I even saying? I blame the adrenaline.*

"Thank you." She climbed into the ambulance, ghost white, and blew Chase a kiss as the doors shut and the sirens re-blasted.

The four of us stood there, underneath the tall metal Costco canopy, watching the ambulance lumber out of the packed parking lot, dickhead cars refusing to move and give up their place in line for the up-front spots.

I looked at Chase, not knowing how to handle any of this. Elliot tapped my shoulder from behind. He was pointing at the box of Fruit by the Foot in our cart and then pointing at an unsuspecting Chase. I nodded yes to Elliot. "Do you want one of these?" he asked Chase.

"Sure."

"My mom never buys this stuff, but our friend had to poop so bad that they were going to take him to jail." Elliot made zero sense, which made Chase laugh. We all laughed. *Thank God.*

"Wait, do you have any allergies?" I asked Chase, remembering that these days, he could likely be allergic to anything and everything, could need an Epi-Pen on his person at all times, a special kind of cream for debilitating eczema, or a tranquilizer for when he ate anything with red dye.

"No."

How utterly refreshing.

"Mama, I have more Fruit Foot?" Violet asked, adorably. Elliot's hands were already in the praying position, his eyes wide open, hoping for another yard of sugar for both himself and his sister. Such a chiseler. But I took a lesson from Danielle's playbook and realized there were worse things in life, such as your kids not opening their eyes.

When we arrived at home, Elliot grabbed his iPad and took Chase upstairs to his room. Seconds later I heard the two boys laughing hysterically at the sound of oinks and TNT exploding. Violet corralled her mermaids in the family room and had them all gather around one that was laying on the floor, like Charlie had been.

I sat down on the couch, noticing that I was still shaking. Upon seeing me sit, Violet came over, climbed up into my lap, and curled into a tiny ball. I kissed her on the crown of her head and put my arms around her. Safe. The intense events played in my head, stopping only when I realized that it was almost dinnertime and Aaron would be home soon, or not. Despite just spending an hour at a grocery store, I had nothing to feed my family except for lunchbox-sized servings of beef jerky, hummus, carrots, and the motherfucking unending nightmare that was Fruit by the Foot. I would be calling out for pizza.

When I took my phone from my back pocket, I nearly jumped and dropped Violet. There was a missed call from an unknown number. It must've been from June. My phone's ringer and I were constantly at odds. I called the number back. June answered.

"Charlie's fine, thankfully. He's got a broken arm, some scratches and bruises, but nothing too serious, we think. But he will have to stay here overnight so they can monitor him."

"Gah. I'm so sorry." I didn't know what else to say.

"I have never been so scared in my life," she said, breaking. I sat there listening to her cry, trying to be strong for her instead of the tenderized slab of meat I really was.

"I bet." It didn't feel like enough.

"Thank you for taking Chase. I will probably send my sister, Cammy, over later to grab him. April, thank you. I don't know what I would've done without a friend there today."

CHAPTER SIXTEEN

The Revolving Door

*T*he next morning spit Violet and I out at Target, bright and early, because somehow there were no diapers left in the house, despite me swearing I had a whole box left. I threw on some jeans and put on a bra under the shirt I slept in.

I looked around Target's not-yet-packed parking lot at the handful of other moms in their minivans who also swore they had diapers that morning. It was like a cult—a cult where your days are spent driving from big-box store to the next, acquiring items you never bought for the first twenty- or thirty-something years of your life. Early-morning Target possessed a spa-like tranquility mixed with the heavy smell of plastic packaging.

"I needs fishy crackers!" Violet chirped as I lifted her into the bright red cart.

Pavlov's findings were in full effect. Every time Violet entered Target, the red bell in her head went off that told her a carton of Goldfish crackers would be hers. And she was right. It was a small atonement that would give me at least three minutes of peace and a way to distract her from the "Dollar Spot" section that worked as a lobbyist for the Bin of Pointless Crap. I was also not immune to Pavlov's poop theory, as usually right about the time I found myself in the furthest corner of the store, I would have to shit.

And I recently found out it wasn't just me. Danielle said this also happened to her. We Googled it and apparently it's a *thing*.

Hoping to get out in under ten minutes, I tried to stay the course, dodging the whimsical snares of the brightly colored seasonal tableware. I almost got snagged by the witty kids' plates with smiling vegetables and a cartoon bubble that read, "Lettuce be friends," but I kept steering the red chariot straight to the diaper section, which smelled like clean baby butts. I hoisted a box of disposables into the back of the cart, pausing as a flashback overtook me. Elliot was a newborn and I was cloth-diapering him, like all the "conscious" moms did. Nothing would touch his precious skin except pure, organic cotton woven by bunnies. But then there was endless laundry. And the inability to leave my home without hauling a bag of piss-filled cloths with me.

I lovingly looked at the disposable diaper box with deep gratitude. My phone dinged with an email telegram from CeCe with no subject, as usual. Had she found the orange couch stain?

CeCe D'Ambrosia
To: April Stewart
No Subject

The pop-up shop was a hit. Half of the people raved about you and your shirts. I have another one in two weeks. On a Friday. Can you come? No children. Love and light, CeCe.

How could such a short email conjure up five different feelings? I looked for the answer in the women's clothing section. My ego felt stroked and then slapped and stroked again and then kicked, and finally, outraged at her hypocrisy. She should more accurately sign her emails with "Curtness and judgment, CeCe."

"I needs get down," Violet barked. She strained to unbuckle herself so she could stand up in the cart's seat and send herself to the ER. It was the Mommy version of "last call." I needed to get to the checkout immediately. I found my way back to the white linoleum road and picked up serious speed. An elderly man with a basket full of enough cat food cans to last his lifetime snailed toward the one open cashier. I whizzed past him, doing a favor for everyone who didn't want to hear a toddler melt down. The cashier had Target-red lipstick, wrinkles, and a fanny pack. She scanned the diaper box without taking her eyes off a struggling Violet.

"I never liked that age," she said, matter-of-factly, handing me my receipt. *Well I never liked fanny packs, Karen.* Why the fuck did cashiers think they could comment on the one minute of life unfolding in front of them? They were only seeing a snapshot.

In the parking lot, Violet finally wriggled her way out from under the buckle and sprang up to standing in the cart seat as I lurched to stop it. "I out!" she celebrated. I lifted her down.

"You have to hold my hand, though," I explained. She put her starfish hand in mine, jumping and smiling the whole way to the car as if her feet had never touched land before. She looked up at me and grinned, showing her Chiclet teeth, happy-ass eyes, and pure toddler glee. I playfully lifted her up high on the next jump.

I opened the back of my van and set the diaper box

inside the trunk on a messy pile of blankets, two strollers, sandy beach toys, and the current pile of "things to donate." I tried to close it, but something was in the way and the hatchback wouldn't shut. I pushed a caught piece of blanket out of the way, which revealed another box of diapers—the ones I swore I had. *Of fucking course.*

In the driver's seat, I cranked the *Moana* soundtrack to quell Violet so I could sit there and reread CeCe's email, which felt like a temptation and an ultimatum—the universe cleverly asking, "So just how much do you like money and freedom?" I wondered what June would make of it.

Ohmygod June! The events of yesterday had slipped my mind in the urgency of diaper acquisition. I turned down the blasting, "SHINNNNNNNNNYYYY . . ." and called her.

"How are you guys doing today?" I asked when she picked up.

"Better. We just got home from the hospital."

"Wow, that's great. And how are *you*?"

"Tired. I stayed up making sure Charlie was breathing, replaying the scene in my mind."

"Yeah, that was really scary. Can you sleep today—do you have help?"

"Don't know yet. Before I forget, Chase told me that he thinks he left his hat in your car."

I cranked my head and looked around the van, past a singing Violet. There was Chase's hat sitting on the back seat next to a wad of wax paper.

"Yep, I see it right now. Want me to drop it off later and give you a break so you can nap, or just to say hi?" After I said it, I felt my stomach drop, thinking maybe I'd been too pushy, essentially inviting myself over to her house, even if in the name of Mom Code—the law of helpfulness that moms follow when one of our sisters is in distress.

June paused. It was a big jump and I understood. She sputtered and then, "You know what? I would love that. Chase said he and Elliot had tons of fun together, so he'll be excited too."

Relief.

As I hung up and waited for June to text her address, I realized that I had no idea where in Orange County she lived. It was a big place. I pegged her for Newport Beach.

&

When Violet and I arrived home, we opened the door to see an unusually tidy post-breakfast kitchen, complete with an empty sink and humming load of dishes mid-wash. We had left for Target while Aaron was still home and this must've been his doing. The hand-job equivalent for moms.

His good deed made me miss him. Us. I walked over to our dry-erase wall calendar and looked for a weekend day that was free. I texted Tanya, asking if she could babysit next Sunday so Aaron and I could go on a much-needed date.

The response dots appeared.

> I'm busy Sunday. But I could do
> Saturday.

I looked at the calendar and shrank. That day read, "Chalk-paint furniture class." It was a class at a hip little craft store that I'd been wanting to take since Elliot was small, and I'd finally scheduled it after my pop-up shop payout. Here I was again, having to choose between time with my husband and time with myself. The dishwasher changed cycles with a powerful whir and with that reminder, I chose my husband. I erased my craft class and wrote "Date," with a big heart around it.

I felt giddy. I had tonight with June to look forward to —with Lucinda coming last minute to watch Violet—and now a date with Aaron this Saturday. I messaged him with the good news.

> Hot date this Saturday. You. Me.

Holy shit. Where are we going?

> Anywhere without children.

Dear God, yes.

CHAPTER SEVENTEEN

Mr. Calvin

*M*om guilt was a cloud that sporadically hung over my relationship with Elliot. With his full-day schooling, and the addition of Violet, there was very little time just for him and me, like we had in our beginning. He remembered what it felt like to be an only child and spoke about it like a dead best friend. I treasured our fragments of alone time and found myself enjoying the peaceful, non-Disney-dominated car ride with him to June's house, where he divulged which of his classmates had said the f-word on the playground that day.

She lived only fifteen minutes away—inland, which was completely unexpected since June exuded a beachy vibe rather than a barren desert vibe.

We pulled up to a huge but plain-looking house that stood behind a gate. It was like an R. Kelly sex-cult compound. June seemed too down-to-earth for a monstrosity like this. I scrolled through our texts to make sure I hadn't mistyped the address, but sure enough, her voice greeted us over the intercom and the gate buzzed open.

I shriveled at the thought of June being so privileged, and worried that our developing relationship might suffer if she was living an entirely different life than me. My house could fit into her garage. Maybe we didn't have that much in common, after all.

"They must be rich. Way richer than us," Elliot said.

I parked the van next to a black Mercedes SUV. June was waiting at the front door for us with her usual bright smile. She was wearing one of those cold-shoulder tops that looked like your kids had taken scissors to one of your nice blouses.

"How are you holding up?" I asked. In light of last night's events, a hug felt appropriate. It was the first non-awkward one we'd had.

"Good, thanks to Cammy's cooking."

As she walked us into the foyer, Chase rambled down the massive, marble staircase. To the side of it was a twenty-foot golden obelisk that spanned two levels. Across from that was an oil-painting of a smug-looking man. We were in the lobby of a Trump hotel. *Kill me.*

As the boys raced up the palatial stairs together, June hurriedly walked me to a giant, open family room with natural light streaming in as the afternoon sun began to set.

"It's not what I would've done with the entryway," she mentioned, tucking her hair behind her ears. I now knew this was her tell for "embarrassed."

A warm, savory smell pulled my nose toward the kitchen, zeroing in on the Crock-Pot on the counter, which seemed strangely out of place in a rich person's house.

"That was Cammy's doing this morning," June said, noticing.

The cheerful, clean family room popped with tropical pinks, greens, blues, yellows, and tangerines against soft white walls and a tan couch. Cozy and unpretentious, just like June's office. The oversized dining table between the family room and the kitchen looked like a refinished barn door, and the chairs were a matte lemon yellow.

"Ooh, is this chalk paint?" I asked, taking a closer look at the finish.

"Good eye."

I looked around the room. "Where's Charlie?"

"Right over here," she said, quickly walking me past what appeared to be an office with the door cracked open. Next to the door, a sign on the wall—more like a plaque—read "The Boss." I stopped and squinted to see that below it, in smaller writing, it read "No whiners allowed." I peeked inside the open door to see a wall covered in awards and shadow boxes with medals. Above an ornate desk the size of my bed hung a large framed picture of a man running through the finish-line tape of some kind of race. Underneath it were the words "I run the day. It doesn't run me." I shuddered. *That's some serious control shit.* June doubled back.

"My husband is obsessed with running," she said with a smile that visibly hurt her face. We closed the office door and kept walking to a nook on the other side of the family room, where Charlie sat in a fancy beanbag, his legs covered with a patchwork blanket. His bright red Iron Man–inspired cast was perched on a stack of pillows, just like a nursing mom's elbow. There were random tapes still stuck to his body and a bruise on his left cheek. I wondered how many others he had.

"Hi Charlie," I said, remembering that I was essentially a stranger to him. He momentarily looked up from the *Avengers* show on his tablet.

He shyly said "hi", the opposite of his superhero swagger the day of the accident.

June led us back into the kitchen and pulled out a stool

for me to sit on at the center island. "Coffee? Tea?" she asked.

"Tea. Erry day."

I fixated on a long black panel of switches on the wall. Each switch was labeled with some kind of technical code that someone must've understood. Below was a small mahogany table with a bank of screens that looked like surveillance. I could feel the push/pull of energy in June's home. Feminine rustic was at war with the boardroom.

June dug through the cupboard, setting three black mugs on the counter so she could grab whatever it was she wanted from the back. The three mugs were tall, with "Chet's Coffee" written in gold lettering. She was sighing and struggling to find what she wanted through a bevy of black mugs. "Drives me nuts," she said half to herself as she finally reached what she was looking for—two light blue teacups with wide rims and small bases, like from the Mad Hatter's tea party. She put all the other mugs back, shaking her head.

"You must really like this Chet's Coffee place," I said.

"They're my husband's. His name is Chet and he likes to put it on everything." She went over to the wine rack and pointed to custom corks with the letter "C" on it. Then she walked over to a drawer and pulled out a barbeque tool for branding a steak, which I thought nobody actually bought. The iron had "CHET" emblazoned on it in all caps.

"Whoa," I said. *With a name like Chet, this guy was destined for douchery.*

June slid a bowl of various tea bags over to me. I chose peppermint.

"How is Chet doing with what happened to Charlie?" I asked, now that Chet had been brought up.

"He was most worried about me not getting identifying information about the driver that hit him."

I felt a prick of guilt. "Shit. I should've thought of that."

"I'm glad we didn't get it, April, although I'd like to give that driver a piece of my mind. Chet lives for litigation and would've made this person's life miserable, and dragged all of us into it. He gets back from a trip tonight and I wouldn't be surprised if he first goes down to Costco and demands to see video footage."

I grasped the mug and lifted it up to my lips. Too hot. June lowered her voice. "I would never have married him had I known better."

"What didn't you know?" I forced myself to take a tiny sip of the piping hot tea, to busy my mouth, so she would continue.

"At nineteen, it was fine that he was a bit of a bully because he was also charming and a really good dancer. I had different criteria for marriage back then. At least I have my precious boys, but I'm also stuck in a nightmare." She bobbed her tea bag up and down.

"What do you mean by stuck, like you can't divorce him?" I hoped the use of the D-word was not premature, although referring to your marriage as a nightmare probably meant it was warranted.

"Stuck, as in I've never felt like I could be a single mom. It's been my anchor throughout my kids' lives. When I want to run away from Chet, I tell myself, 'I cannot be a single mom, I cannot be a single mom,' and that keeps me going for a bit longer."

I suddenly felt like I'd been a huge whiner. I would most definitely not be allowed in that office over there. While I sat on June's couch at Mother Roots, complaining about my life with a well-intended, kind husband who didn't need to bitch-stamp his name on our possessions, here she was trying to keep herself afloat in an awful marriage that I clearly didn't even know the half of yet. I felt like a selfish jackass. But I would deal with my own feelings later.

"So you would leave him if you could?" I clarified.

"Yes. In a heartbeat if I had the money. And if he wasn't so vengeful."

My eyes momentarily darted to all the wealth surrounding them. She must've noticed. "He'd fight me tooth and nail for all of this. Even the kids—especially the kids. And he'd probably win, with his will to take people down." She looked over in Charlie's direction. "Which is why I knew I could never leave him." Her voice cracked.

My tears teetered. I was in awe of June and her ability to keep showing up to such a mangled relationship.

"I wanted to be strong for my kids. I'd rather have a loveless marriage and get to see them than break free and lose them." She turned around and hid her emotion by wiping her hands on a dishcloth for too long. I looked down at the chaotic grey and white marbled countertop wishing Harold and his purple crayon were here to draw her out of this.

"How long do you plan to stick it out?"

"I don't know. I just pretend that this ordeal isn't happening and try to distract myself." She flashed a self-deprecating smile and looked over at the chalk-painted chairs. "But yesterday, something shifted."

My eyes got big and I sipped my tea hard.

"When Chet was unfazed by what happened to Charlie and refused to come home early from his trip, I suddenly knew. I've stayed all these years out of my fear of his boys' club lawyer friends punishing me in court—and the aftermath. But for the first time, I'm more scared of us staying than I am of leaving."

"Oh June, that's horrible. Surely you'd have some rights."

"Normally, yes. But Chet had an agreement drawn up when we got married and I was dumb enough to sign it. He said it was something his dad told him we should have. It felt like a very adult thing at nineteen, so I signed it. And I'm embarrassed to admit that I have no idea what it said. I trusted Chet. I loved him. And I thought he loved me. Maybe he did. I don't know. It doesn't matter."

"There has to be a way to fight that, saying that you were young and didn't know what you were signing."

"There is really only one hope."

Whatever it was, I would do anything and everything in my power to make this thing happen. Mom Code to the infinity power.

"If I can get footage of him cheating on me, it gives me leverage and might be able to nullify some things. But it would have to be actual video footage—real evidence—not just receipts or texts."

"Whoa. You think he's cheating on you?"

She scoffed. "I *know* he is."

My jaw dislodged like a boa constrictor's. But then I picked it up off the counter in excited realization. "That means there's hope for you. I mean—I'm so sorry. I don't mean to gloss over how hurtful all that is."

"No, I understand. I actually feel the same way. His cheating isn't anything new and I buried that grief years ago."

I felt ill thinking about living and parenting with someone I knew was cheating on me, for years. That kind of betrayal was incomprehensible. I wanted to know all the details about it: when, how often, was it with one person or many, did he know she knew? And more importantly, I wanted to know how I could help her. I was trying to figure out how to ask all of this in a gentle way when Chase and Elliot barged into the kitchen, "starving."

June dished out a juicy pot roast, potatoes, and carrots into bright white bowls for all five of us, one on a special tray for Charlie. I hoped Elliot would not refuse to eat it. I crossed my fingers. Meals at friends' houses were one of the few times peer pressure could work in a parent's favor.

June left her bowl untouched and walked over to Charlie, who had fallen asleep in the beanbag. She sat down next to him on an ottoman and stroked his hair until his eyes opened. I jettisoned back to the images of the previous day. I wondered if she would ever look at her sons waking up the same way again. Chase and Elliot sat at the table, gobbling up their dinner out of genuine hunger and not just haste to get back to the iPad. Elliot even asked for seconds. Once both of their bowls were empty, the boys were gone in a flash.

As June fed Charlie his dinner, I sat in my own personal bubble of peace, the tender meat and flavorful veggies melting in my mouth. No one was almost spilling something on me, and my usual dinnertime "is-someone-falling-out-of-a-chair" reflexes were on pause as I absorbed not only my dinner, but all that had just been said.

A wind chime tinkled, like it was being stroked over and over. It was June's ringing phone, which lay on the counter next to me. I lifted it up toward her direction, my mouth too full to speak.

"Will you look and see who it is? I'm waiting for a call from Cammy about a prescription for Charlie."

I looked down and saw a picture of Snoop Dogg. Not like a super dope album cover graphic of him, but a real-life picture of him in the world with someone. He was hugging the person in the picture. My brain did not know how to make sense of this.

"Um, it's a picture of Snoop Dogg and someone," I said to her, laughing.

The wind chime kept on and on.

"Just let voicemail get it. I'll call him back later," she said flippantly.

I looked at the Snoop Dogg picture once more. It finally fucking registered. The person hugging him in the picture was *June*.

"Juuuuuune! This is *you* with Snoop Dogg! What?" I was standing up. "Wait, was that *him* calling you? You know Snoop Dogg, like personally?"

She giggled at me, amused. I was baffled. *Say words, June. What does all this mean?*

"He's been a neighbor for a long time. Sweetest guy, and his kids and their cousins play with the boys. He's probably calling to check on Charlie," she explained as if this wasn't the biggest news of *my* life. My eyes must've been popping out of my head, a la Large Marge from *Pee Wee's Big Adventure*. I couldn't wait to tell Aaron that we were within two degrees of Snoop Dogg—the actual fucking Snoop Dogg. I was beyond starstruck. Yes, his atrocious (and catchy as hell) lyrics went against every pro-female belief I had. But I also never claimed to be perfect.

"I take it you're a fan?" she asked.

"Yeahhhh. Just a little bit. I may or may not have sung

'Lodi Dodi' to my kids to calm them down as infants." I peered out the window like a stalker. "So, does he live right next to you or a few houses down?" I was looking for a house with a bumpin' party, fly hunnies playing volleyball, and maybe a dog statue out front with the words "Don Corleone" on its collar.

"Yes, he's on our street." She was withholding just enough specific information so I couldn't get myself into trouble.

"Mom, who was that on the phone? Someone was calling about me?" Charlie asked.

"Yes honey, that was Mr. Calvin."

"*Mister Calvin*? You get to call him that?" I nearly lost my gore. I walked in circles in her kitchen.

Then a door opened loudly somewhere in the back of the house. In walked a man whom I assumed was Chet. His most immediate feature was a Bluetooth wireless headpiece stuck to his ear and an oversized smartphone he wore in a holster on his belt—that, and his neon-orange running shoes that held up his chiseled, diamond-shaped calves. He was mid-conversation and his volume level was at about a three hundred. He was wearing shiny running shorts and had spiky gelled hair. "They're wrong. The average income in America is 150K. Look it up, morons," he said as he popped in the office.

"The Boss" was home.

"I'll call you back," he said, abruptly, tapping his earpiece and looking at me. I felt like an intruder and tried to make myself disappear into the stool.

"Chet, this is my friend April. She was the one there when Charlie got hurt," June said while moving closer to me, protectively. Chet didn't even look in her direction, his eyes fixated on me like the Terminator's. I felt like I might melt from his intensity when suddenly his seriousness morphed into a huge grin as he stuck out his hand for a hearty shake.

"Pleased to meet you. I can't thank you enough for all you did for us yesterday."

I shook his hand. The firmness of his grip was equal to the amount of overcompensating he was doing.

"I didn't really do anything. June was the one in there." Mom Code represent.

"So from the periphery, you probably saw the make, model, and year of the car that hit Charlie then, right? You probably also saw a distinguishable profile too?" he queried.

"No, no," I said, feeling cornered. "I was with my two kids, trying to keep them calm. And Chase too."

From the other side of the room came a soft voice that rescued everyone. "Daddy, do you want to see my red cast? I have superpowers in my arm."

"Hey, Chief!" Chet said, turning toward Charlie and walking over to his son with a wide and deliberate gait. His severity oozed with every move. I looked at June with sympathy, wonder, and deep concern. Our eyes met. Hers were apologetic. So were mine.

"We need to go home, it's getting late," I said. "I'll go grab Elliot." I began walking to the marble staircase. Soft music suddenly piped in, as if I was in a waiting room. It sounded familiar. I was ashamed to admit it, but I recognized it as a Muzak version of Jimmy Buffet's awful song "Cheeseburger in Paradise." I looked back to see Chet in front of the panel of switches. He must've turned it on—another power play for Team Boardroom.

I found the boys in the first room at the top of the stairs, having a Lego battle.

"How dare you destroy my battle station, infidel!" Elliot said in a character voice as Chase crashed a ship into his building. There were mouth sound effects of explosions and long, slow deaths. I knocked on the open door.

"I'm sorry to break up your fun guys, but Elliot, we have to head home." Right on cue, he gave the sound of eight-year-old resistance.

"Awwwww, Mommmmmm." And then came the bargaining. "Can we just have ten more minutes?"

"No." The immediate harshness in my voice was in direct relation to how badly I wanted to avoid any more interaction with Chet, and Elliot must've picked up on it because he started cleaning up immediately. "I'm impressed that you guys played with Legos instead of iPads," I said, trying to change my tone to a lighter one.

"The iPad died," Chase said. *Ah yes. Of course. Stupid me.*

As we reached the bottom step of the staircase, I could hear Chet in the middle of a conversation with June through the instrumental condiment-listing part of "Cheeseburger in Paradise."

"What I don't understand is, how were you so distracted that you didn't stop him from running off into a parking lot like that?" He was blaming her for Charlie's accident.

"Chet, kids run off. And they do it quickly. He was standing right there next to me and then he wasn't. It happened in seconds. It's not like I wasn't paying attention." She wasn't backing down. *You fucking tell him, June.*

I made my footsteps loud on purpose. Chet's demeanor

did a one-eighty as the boys and I walked into the kitchen. Chet's penetrating, shit-eating grin was back.

"Dad!" Chase yelled, running toward Chet. They hugged. The boys' affinity for their father certainly had to make June's decision to leave or stay that much harder.

June walked Elliot and I outside. "Well, now you have met Chet."

I didn't know what to say back, but what came out was, "I guess so." I wanted to tell her that I couldn't imagine living with him, much less being married to him, but none of that was helpful to say to someone who was stuck. You don't tell someone stuck in an elevator how you couldn't imagine being stuck in an elevator. You try to slip them a tortilla through the doors so they don't starve to death.

I gave her a long hug. "Thank you for having us over tonight. The dinner was unbelievable. And so was the fact that you know Snoop Dogg."

She smiled and folded her arms to keep herself warm in the night air as Elliot and I got into the van. Those damn cold-shoulder shirts were too drafty. I wished they would die.

"I haven't really shared my story with anyone other than Cammy. Real friends are non-existent. Most good people don't stick around because of Chet." The sadness on her face broke my heart in two. I couldn't imagine how she had stayed so quiet for so long. How she'd survived without friends. I would've been telling my story to anyone who would listen.

"I wish I could do something to help you."

She gave me puppy-dog eyes, but no specific instructions on how to help.

As I pulled through their fancy drive-thru driveway, I considered canvassing up and down the street, searching for Snoop Dogg's house. It had to be obvious which one was his, right? Hoopties in the driveway, a yard full of Dobermans.

When Elliot and I arrived home, Aaron was sitting on the couch chatting with Lucinda, both indulging in a glass of wine. They were all smiles, naturally. Violet came running over and hugged my legs. Lucinda stood up.

"I should probably get going. The toga party starts in two hours and I gotta get the rest of the gold leaves glued onto my costume." I never imagined I would be jealous of a senior citizen's social life.

"I got to have dinner sitting down because of you," I said to her as I gave her a big hug. "I hope this one behaved for you." I pointed at Violet.

"She's easy-peasy."

No she's not. Say she's a wretch and you don't know how I do it every day. Lucinda's words felt like more of Marnie's gas-lighting—a grandma tag-team—even though I knew that wasn't her motive. I was looking forward to someday being a grandma. It sounded like the ideal way to have children in one's life—all the fun without the monotonous caretaking and crushing responsibility aspects. As a grandparent, you got to let shit slide and the consequences of doing so didn't directly affect you—you'd even be dead before these kids grew up to be adults that had to hold jobs and not die of diabetes.

I sat in the big comfy glider, on the downhill side of bedtime, cradling Violet and singing one of our favorites from *Beauty and the Beast,* about the Beast's metamorphosis from total dicknut to being dear, and so unsure. The second I fled her room, I ran downstairs, side-stepping all the toys and books on the floor to text Aaron, who was detained in Elliot's room.

Big news.

I attached a .gif of Snoop Dogg morphing into an actual dog. Minutes later, Aaron walked downstairs briskly.

"So what is this about Snoop Dogg?"

I paused for a moment, relishing the delicious news that was mine to divulge.

"He's June's neighbor," I said, straight-faced.

"Holy shit. So she lives Snoop Dogg–adjacent?"

"Yep. And not only that, but they are frieeeeends." His knees buckled. "And he called her while I was there. And I was holding her phone, so I was basically touching him."

"What does this mean for us? When can we go visit him?" He was only half-joking. I broke a smile as our familiar banter returned. "I feel like everything I knew before this moment means nothing. We know Snoop Dogg," he said on his way to the cabinet for a celebratory snack.

"How can you eat at a time like this?" I asked.

"Snoop would want me to eat."

"I also met June's husband who was a total fucking piece of work."

"I don't want to hear any words come out of your mouth that aren't 'Snoop' or 'Dogg' right now."

"Good point. Back to Snoop Dogg."

Aaron rummaged through the pantry, finally settling on a small bowl of Market Street's more cardboard version of Triscuits, aptly named "Straw."

"Okay but really, what was her husband like?"

"There was so much to take in, but first and foremost, his name was Chet."

"Say no more."

"I'm dumbfounded. If June can be married to a guy like this, then nothing makes sense anymore. She wants a divorce, though."

"Did she tell you that?"

"Yep. He's a bully. I saw it. And he's cheating on her and she knows it." I slapped the coffee table with that news. It was like a reality show come to life.

Aaron's jaw dropped just like mine had about two hours earlier, except his was full of Straw.

"If she can catch him in the act and on video, it could be her escape plan."

"This is your therapist, right?"

Why can't anyone give this poor woman a break? I felt protective over her again.

Our night together happened like it used to, with our new favorite housewife reality show spin-off, *Vanderpump Rules*, lots of pausing and chit-chatting, and zero tension. When we found ourselves yawning for the tenth time, we looked at each other and simultaneously said, "Bed."

Something about the playful and strain-free night we'd had, plus feeling grateful that Aaron wasn't Chet, made me feel like I could possibly entertain the idea of putting a small deposit in Aaron's account. I wouldn't go so far as to peel off my warm clothes and engage in actual sex, but I was willing to give and knew that I had to strike soon before he reached for his phone and killed my generous state of mind. "If you were looking for a hand job, I might be offering one." I smiled cheekily. His eyes lit up like a torch. "I'm *always* looking for a hand job. Amazing." He spared no time and took his tight boxer briefs down. He was already hard, as most desperate-for-sex husbands are at the sound of their wives' voices saying the word "hand job."

I grabbed the lube out of his bedside drawer, making a mental note to put it up higher, somewhere where children couldn't find it. I squeezed it on my hand and it made the usual, unfortunate fart sound as it splattered. I began. Aaron laid back in ecstasy as my forearm went to work.

We're almost out of fish food again. I should get some tomorrow while I'm out. I need to return that too-small swimsuit I got for Violet. Maybe tomorrow night I'll find a good recipe for cheese enchiladas and make those for dinner. I wonder if there is a brand of enchilada sauce that is less spicy for the kids. I should ask about that on the Facebook mom's group when I'm done.

My forearm slowly began to burn.

I should really strengthen my forearms so this doesn't hurt in the future. But wouldn't that be kind of weird to just focus on the forearm muscles? Everyone at the gym would know it's for giving hand jobs. They would call me the "hand jobber" behind my back. I would be a legend there.

The burning intensified. I switched hands, which in hindsight was always a bad idea and elongated the entire process. I took an intermission to quickly lube up my other hand, and then went back to work. *Oh shit, this arm is even weaker than the other one.* But I kept on, using my pain-coping strategies from birth class to help with the searing forearm pain. I wanted to tell Aaron to focus and to hurry up, but I knew that the quickest way to finalize this was to cup his balls with my free hand.

When all was said and done, I washed my hands thoroughly and hopped into bed next to a tranquilized Aaron who hadn't moved a muscle since the event. He smiled at me lovingly. His demeanor had completely softened, much like the Beast's after being in Belle's care. Maybe the easiest way for Belle to have gotten her father back was to have given the Beast a hand job. It wasn't right, but it was just a thought.

Knowing that Aaron had been sexually pleasured by me meant that I could actually lay down and fall asleep without the normal nightly guilt. Some nights I felt more guilt than others—and some nights I was asleep before I even remembered to feel guilty—but tonight I got to be free, and feel like I had been enough for everyone that day, namely the person lying next to me.

He got under the covers, limply rolled over my way and kissed me. "Thank you for that."

"You're welcome," I replied, trying not to sound like Maui from *Moana*, but damn it if every utterance of those two words didn't sound just like him.

I laid there, feeling grateful for Aaron. It didn't mean our marriage was ideal, nor that either of our needs were always being met, but he didn't wear his phone in a holster and that felt like a really important detail.

I floated toward sleep. Before it overtook me in the dark room, I turned to Aaron. "Goodnight, I love you."

"Love you too, A.B." And then he whispered, "We know Snoop Dogg."

CHAPTER EIGHTEEN

Choose Your Own Adventure

*T*he week had been a blur with more bodily fluids than usual. Violet caught the stomach flu and I waited in fear for the next victim to fall, while nearly turning to voodoo to get the vomit smell out of her car seat. I found myself texting regularly with June as our friendship continued to level up. I asked for Snoop Dogg's address in at least half of those texts, as it had become a joke between us—but she still wasn't giving up the goods. Each time I worried about the ethical nag June might be feeling about our relationship outside of Mother Roots, I remembered the loneliness in her voice that night on her driveway, and the thought vanished. She deserved friends.

I hadn't forgotten about CeCe's email, still dangling in my inbox. With all the laundry, homemade chicken soup, and extra snuggles, there had been no time to email her back a "suck it." Or probably a suck it. The traumatic memories of the pop-up shop were fading, yet the cash remained—cash to pay for a real adult date at a real adult restaurant with Aaron, where I would wear eyeliner. I'd been dreaming about it all week, especially when elbow-deep in puke.

Since it was Saturday, the kids woke up before the sun. I believed it to be part of some pact all babies made on the "other side," before they came down the ol' birth chute. "Resist everything when you get down there, especially on weekends!" their leader must've ingrained in them. I'm pretty sure #resist was invented by kids.

I parked Elliot and Violet in front of the TV downstairs, granola bars in hand, and returned to my bed for as long as they would allow. I looked over at Aaron, who was sleeping like a husband. On our lunch agenda today was telling him that sleeping in was my sex.

His body began to outstretch on the bed like a spring flower blossoming, one of his arm stems instinctively unplugging his phone from the charger on his nightstand. He scrolled. We hadn't even made eye contact yet. I touched his arm to bring him back to me.

"Aw shit. I have to go into work today."

"But you can't."

"CEO's in town last minute and is stopping by the office. Everyone has to be there so he feels like we're all committed or whatever." He got out of bed, walked over to the closet and began rummaging. "Shit. I don't even have any clean work clothes."

"Wait, what about our date?" I shot upright in bed.

"What date?" he said, picking up wrinkled pants off the closet floor.

"Are you serious? The date I had planned for us today. I have Tanya coming and everything."

"I didn't know we had a date today." He sniffed the pits of shirts from the floor.

"Yes, yes you did. I messaged you about it. You responded. It's on the calendar downstairs." It was unfortunate he was getting hammered from work and from me, but there were facts here.

"Well then I'm sorry, but I have to go," he said, almost falling over while attempting pants.

I felt like I was in a *Choose Your Own Adventure* book and there were a variety of paths I could take here. One choice would've been for me to say: "Bummer, but we'll have our date again sometime soon. I'm really sorry that you have to go into work today, but don't stress, I've got the kids and dinner covered. See you whenever you get home." But that was a choice I was incapable of making. Instead, I went the other direction and ran toward the burning building.

"Does the CEO really expect you to be in the office on a Saturday, last minute? None of you have lives, or families?" I was standing next to him in the bathroom while he trimmed his beard hairs that fell to the wet sink, sticking.

"Apparently, or I wouldn't have gotten the email."

I clenched my jaw and hands, knowing that there was no way around it. The fear of being fired motivated his every move, even though he was too valuable, productive, and likable to ever be let go. Even though I had no fear of being fired from my job as "mom," I tried to be sympathetic since he was the breadwinner. It had to be unsettling that his employer held the power to pull the rug out from under him—and us—at a moment's notice. I understood that his fatherly duty to provide for us fueled his primal need to stay in his boss's good graces, but surely there were ways to avoid being a perpetual doormat.

I swallowed my anger and imitated June, choosing my words carefully. "What would you do if I wasn't here today, and you couldn't find someone to watch the kids?"

"I'd have to stay home, obviously."

"Right. You would have to choose your family."

"Oh come on, April, I'm not *not* choosing you today. This is for my work, our family, this house." He motioned toward our newly remodeled, outhouse-sized bathroom that cost as much as a year of private school.

"You are for fucking sure not choosing me today," I said, adamantly. "Spending time with your wife is less important than going above and beyond for your job, yet again. What if you simply said no to them?"

It was like he had blacked out. Full go-mode.

"I have to go," was all he said as he rushed by.

I heard him hit the last step, onto the hardwood floor downstairs.

"You going somewhere, Dad?" Elliot asked him, confused. I could hear their conversation as I stood in our bedroom doorway.

"I have to go into work, El. Huge bummer."

"On a Saturday?" Elliot asked with the appropriate amount of bewilderment. *Yes, my son, ask the hard-hitting questions.*

"Yeah, I know. But I'll be back later, and tomorrow we can do something together."

"But what if you have to go into work tomorrow too?"

"I won't. It's just for today."

I could hear Aaron gathering his things in his work bag.

"But Dad, how do you know that? What if your work tells you that you have to come in again?" Elliot's chiseling was finally benefiting me. Aaron was getting annoyed, his voice impatient.

"Elliot, it's just for today. I'm sure you, Mom, and Violet have something fun planned."

With the sound of the garage door closing, I slid to the floor of my closet, amongst the dirty clothes, and kicked the empty laundry bin. This felt like the last straw in a rapid succession of short straws. Maybe something vital *was* broken in our marriage, something that I hadn't seen before today, something that small deposits couldn't fix. It was impossible for us to get on track for more than a few days. Hours? It was never like this before kids.

Crushed and feeling sorry for myself, I tried to muster up the energy to go downstairs and change Violet's ten-pound morning diaper. Maybe I could salvage something from this wreck since Tanya was already coming. I clicked on the chalk-painting class's webpage from my phone. "SOLD OUT," it read. I groaned and sorted the clothes into the appropriate hampers while I was down on the floor. When I stood up, I was startled to see a concerned Elliot standing in the doorway.

"What are you doing, Mom?"

Contemplating divorce on the floor, and you?

He shuffled over in his giant shark slippers and hugged me. I put my arms around him and rested my chin on his scruffy head. "Are you sad?" he asked, which broke me. I wiped my eyes with my wrists.

"Yeah. I'm sad that Dad had to go to work today. We were planning a special lunch date together."

"But we can still have lots of fun that is funny," he said, quoting *The Cat in the Hat*. "Dad said you had something *fun* planned for Violet and me. What is it?" He was jumping up and down. "Is it the toy store?"

Not only had Aaron flaked on me, but he'd gotten the kids' hopes up, telling them that I had something of substance planned. I sent Elliot downstairs, assuring him that I would figure it out, while I canceled with Tanya.

I stood in front of the mirror looking at my disappointed

face. A couple of gray hairs poked out at my hairline, front and center. Short ones, like antennas. I plucked them with tweezers, but as I tilted my head into the light, I saw about ten more. I set the tweezers down and wondered how little I could do with my hair today to be presentable. It was somewhere between straight and wavy, right around scarecrow. Something serious needed to be done and it needed to include water.

I disrobed, catching a glance of my small pancake breasts in the mirror. It stopped me. I nostalgically cupped the empty ghosts of my beautiful, full nursing rack.

The steamy warmth of the shower beckoned me and I complied, cracking the door in case of a kid emergency. The hot water hit my forehead and then trickled down the back of my body, causing pleasurable goosebumps all over until I sensed a child in the vicinity. "Which one of you is here, and what do you need?" I said, turning around to see Elliot standing behind the clear curtain like an axe murderer.

"Violet is trying to eat my granola bar."

"Do we have any more?"

"Yeah."

"Then can you just give her one?"

"Yeah." He ran back downstairs.

I shook my head.

By getting my hair wet, I had committed to a full blow-dry and flat-ironing—an ancient ritual only done on the solstices. It was the least I could do to tend to myself on this already craptastic day, even if I had to start and stop the blow dryer one thousand times to referee fighting.

Underneath the whir of the dryer, I mentally went through the short list of fun, cheap things I could do with the kids. Most "fun" child-based events were, in fact, not fun for anyone but the child, and even their happiness wasn't a given. Pumpkin patches, fairs, carnivals, bounce houses, and theme parks were all hellmouths for parents. No sleep-deprived mom or dad actually wanted to stand around and pay for overpriced things their kids are whining for, while listening to other kids do the same. It didn't take me long as a mother to figure out that the only reason parents went to shit like that was to pass the time—to get to the promised land of bedtime faster, while taking pictures they could post on social media to show how fun parenting was, while secretly wanting to gouge their eyeballs out with a corn-dog stick.

There was always the beach, but it had too much sand. And sunscreen. And sunscreen mixed with sand. There was really only one option left. Go to the dreaded park.

When Elliot was a toddler, I walked to the neighborhood park every single day. It was my lifeblood. I would eyeball the other moms and wonder *which one of you bitches is about to be my new BFF?* I was desperate for adult contact, even in the form of listing our baby's sleep (lack of sleep) schedules back and forth in mind-numbing detail. But by the time Violet arrived and my mommy friends were set, going to the park had lost its charm.

"Do you guys want to go to that new castle park today?" I asked.

Elliot was measured. He looked at Violet to see what her reaction was and if he should agree or disagree. Sadly, she didn't really know what a park was because of the curse of the second child, but she had heard the word "castle" and was in.

"I wanna see pin-cess!"

The only thing left to do before leaving was to get

both kids dressed and their teeth brushed, have Elliot use the bathroom, pack snacks and waters, find the sunscreen, gather the playground toys, argue over appropriate socks and shoes, and oh yeah, I still needed to eat breakfast.

By the time we actually made it out the door, it was lunchtime and both kids were hungry again. I may have screamed.

The newly redesigned park sat on a fat sunny hill, the industrial-grade plastic castle glimmering next to two massive wooden play structures. For the first five minutes, I wondered why I hadn't given the park a fair shake, as I soaked in the sunshine, fresh air, and colorful spongy turf beneath my feet. But at that six-minute mark, I remembered why I had avoided it like the plague as I ran around the sides of an elaborate jungle gym, trying to keep an eye on Violet, making sure she didn't stage-dive off the tall open landings that seemed to be every three feet. Violet was squealing like a kid who had grown up inside a basement for two years and today had finally broken free. But I couldn't relax for a second, with all the big kids careening past her as she toddled along the wobbly bridge. Meanwhile, I hoped Elliot wasn't lying dead in the castle since I couldn't look away.

Elliot was alive, and suddenly right next to me. "There's a kid that won't let me go into the dungeon. He's blocking it and says I can't go in." *Ah yes, the requisite shit bag kid blocking something at the park.*

"Tell him it's public property and you can go in if you want."

"I said he wasn't the boss of me. He said that he was."

I non-consensually scooped up Violet from the bottom of the slide and walked with Elliot over to the castle.

"There he is," Elliot pointed.

"Try to go in and see what happens."

Elliot walked toward the castle entryway and there was the kid, standing in the doorway, holding a large stick, like motherfucking Lord of the Flies. The kid shook his head "no." And of course he had a faux hawk.

I walked over, saying nothing, but moving closer to him, a cold dead look in my eyes and a thrashing toddler in my arms, like a deranged human chainsaw. I squinted, but the kid didn't crack. I would have to utilize more intense, yet legal, tactics if I was going to regulate. While constraining Violet, I leaned into Faux Hawk and put on my best breathy ghoul voice. I got right in front of his face. "Hey, friend. How about you let the other kids in the castle or I will unleash this wild animal on you."

Violet was a weapon, vigorously flapping her arms and legs, screaming to get down. I moved in closer to the kid who was flinching at the flailing toddler body parts coming for him. He immediately dropped his stick and ran.

"You are awesome, Mom," Elliot said running through the castle door, flashing a thumbs up my way. An escaped Violet galloped behind him. But seconds later, the fun came to an abrupt stop. "I have to poop," Elliot panic-whispered. I glanced around for a bathroom, but didn't see any. Surely they wouldn't rebuild a park without bathrooms. But they did. And so, the three of us cut and run.

We screeched up to the closest frozen yogurt shop and busted out of the van like a bunch of terrorists. After Elliot got colonic relief and Violet got sprinkles, all was well.

When we returned home, Elliot reunited with his iPad while I sorted out the events of my frustrating morning with Aaron, all in my head, as I scrubbed the sink spotless.

Now that I wasn't micromanaging Violet on a deathtrap play structure, my mind was free to go through the entire thing with a fine-toothed comb, but I needed June, the ultimate detangler.

The marriage excavation accompanied Violet and I outside as I monotonously pushed her in a chunky, pink, plastic car, up and down our cul-de-sac. *I'm the only one who even plans special dates. His work always wins out over everything. How much more of this can I take?*

And then the self-judgment came in. *But this is part of the deal with being a mother. Why can't you just accept it, April? Accept it and all your problems go away.*

And back and forth and back and forth, until the day rolled into the evening and it was finally time for a napless Violet to submit to slumber. Elliot sat on the couch, reading a comic book. I had no idea when Aaron would get home, so I assumed I would be on full bedtime duty. I couldn't bring myself to check in with him. I was still too mad.

While the kids resisted brushing their teeth, my phone dinged with two texts from Aaron.

> I'm almost home. I can put Elliot to bed if he's still up.

> BTW, total waste. CEO never even showed. So pissed. At least me and the crew got to drink some beers while we waited, but what a joke.

I felt heat surge from my chest to my eyes and then spread throughout my entire body. Numb. *Of course the*

CEO didn't show up. *Fuck all you dipshits, but mostly you, Aaron.*

When the garage door opened below, it was fortunate that Violet and I were sitting in the glider reading *Yummy Yucky* behind her closed door because I was seething. Aaron and I were going to hash this shit out tonight after the kids were asleep. This motherfucker wasn't going to stand me up ever again.

After I heard Elliot's door shut, I strategically emerged, finding three missed calls from June, and a text asking that I call her as soon as I could. *Shit.* Was it Charlie? Or worse, Chet? I stole away to the garage, sat on the concrete step and called her. She picked up immediately.

"I'm sure you're in the middle of bedtimes and all that," she said.

"No, it's fine."

"Remember when you said you'd be willing to help me? Can I take you up on that—tonight?"

"Oh my God, what's going on?"

"I'm nearly 100% sure Chet's spending the weekend with someone in Las Vegas, and I'm finally ready to get my evidence."

"Wow, okay. Wow." I paced between our cars.

"But I can't do it alone. I can't confront him all by myself. I'm really scared, April. Will you go with me?"

I felt Mom Code zap me at my core, like a baby kicking inside the womb. "Of course I will go with you."

June audibly exhaled.

I had said yes before doing the math, but I had to go. I was so livid that my gut was calling the shots. It was not like me, leaving my kids on a whim (or at all). But goddammit, I was going to do the thing that Aaron had the luxury of doing every single day—driving away. The kids would be fine. Aaron wasn't a shitty dad, just a shitty husband. Sometimes. Today.

"Thank you. I can do this. We can do this. I owe you," June said.

"I know one way you can pay me back."

"Anything."

"You can tell me where Snoop Dogg lives." I tried to lighten the mood, yet crossed my fingers that I might also finally learn where Snoop Dogg called hizome.

June laughed. "Well, I do have something he gave me that you could have. Good enough?"

"Fuck yes. Is it weed?"

"You'll see. And don't worry, everything's on me. I'll fill you in when I pick you up after I drop the boys at Cammy's. Text me your address. How long do you need to get ready?"

I wanted to leave before I changed my mind, or saw Aaron. "Like twenty minutes."

"I'll be there."

We hung up and I screamed out loud and then slapped my hands on my mouth, both thrilled and petrified. I zipped upstairs on my tiptoes, like a cat burglar, and threw a random assortment of clothes and toiletries into a bag—a few of my nicer date-night outfits, sexy heels, a bikini, and eyeliner—it was Vegas, after all. I rejoiced at having showered and blow-dried my hair earlier that day. "Live every day like you might go to Vegas after bedtime" was my new motto. I waited on the porch, hiding from my neighbors and Aaron, behind a pillar.

I felt alive.

June pulled up in her black SUV. I gingerly closed the passenger door behind me, wanting to draw zero attention.

In hindsight, sliding in through the window may have been more fitting for the moment.

"Hi," she said, a palpable thrill in the air.

"Thank you for rescuing me," I said.

"Me rescue you?" she asked, backing out. "Aaron's with the kids, right?"

I shook my head yes, then stared at my phone. I knew I needed to tell him I'd left.

> I'm on my way to Las Vegas with June. She needs my help to catch Chet cheating.

I hesitated before hitting the send button. There would be no going back. But if Martha was right and I was going to fuck my kids up no matter what, I might as well enjoy myself a little. *I might as well spark some motherfucking joy, isn't that right, Marie Kondo?*

Send.

The response bubbles immediately lit up.

> What??

> I'm confident you can figure things out without me.

> When are you coming back?

> I don't know.

> Seriously?? You're going to
> Vegas and don't know when
> you'll be back?

> Affirmative.

I didn't know why I was using soldier lingo, but it felt right.

> You gotta come back A.B. Tom
> and I have plans to go surfing
> tomorrow morning for his 40th
> birthday.

> Well your babysitter just
> canceled.

My phone rang and it was, of course, Aaron. I sent it straight to voicemail, which made me feel queasy, with a wave of whathavelfuckingdone? This trip wasn't intended to be a punishment for him, but it was unexpectedly playing out that way. A split second later, the queasiness turned into a rush of freedom and power, like I was wearing a pair of brass TruckNutz. There was no looking back. And I would find out if our marriage could withstand an unexpected trip to Vegas.

CHAPTER NINETEEN

Junebug

*D*o we have to dress up as maids or some shit? What is our actual plan?" I asked.

"There's no elaborate plan. All I know is that Charlie asked me if I was going to a place called Las Vegas this weekend. I told him no and he said, 'I thought Dad told you on the phone that he couldn't wait to see you at Mamelle, the best topless pool in Las Vegas.'" Her eyes widened as she flipped her blinker and we hopped on the 5 freeway.

"Did Charlie ask what a topless pool was?"

"Yes. And when I told him it was a pool where you didn't have to wear a top, he said, 'Mom, I never wear a top at any of the pools I go to,' so I think I dodged that bullet, but our family calendar showed Chet away on business this weekend, and now I know where, specifically. That's a first."

Wait just a minute.

"Are *we* going to have to be topless at a pool with twenty-year-olds who've never nursed babies?"

"Not sure." She looked like the yikes emoji with the teeth showing. "I got us a room at the Paris hotel, where Mamelle is. My only plan is for us to be detectives and see what we can get on video, if anything. I know it's risky." A silence hung between us as the heaviness of the situation sunk in. "But I can't have Chet see me or else he will pre-emptively come after me legally. That's where I need your help most."

"But he's met me. He fully scanned my soul with his eyeballs."

"I doubt he could pick you out of a crowd, or if he did, he might think you're just coincidentally there."

"True," I said, wondering if staying home for a knock-down, drag-out fight with Aaron would've been the safer bet. "So, um, with Chet, are you at all worried that he might be mad if he finds out? Like maybe try to hurt you? Or me?" I wasn't sure exactly where Chet sat on the psychopath spectrum, but I knew he was for sure on it.

"I've got it covered."

"Did you hire a bodyguard, or do we have pepper spray, or did you bring a handgun?"

"Bingo."

"Wait, Chet is enough of a threat that you actually brought a gun?"

Her head locked forward to watch the road. "When you marry a sociopath, you spend a lot of time at gun ranges."

I sighed loudly, with a little moan of horror at the end, realizing that sometimes Mom Code can kill you. I put my head in my hands. A thrilling girls' trip to Vegas in the name of justice for women everywhere was now a possible double homicide. I thought of Violet and Elliot's faces when Aaron would break the news to them that I'd left. Or worse.

"I know it's a lot," June said. "Maybe this is the perfect time for Calvin's gift."

"Yes, please, for the love of guns that we hopefully don't get shot by, what is it?"

"Open up the glove box."

I clicked the button in front of me on the dash and the glove box slowly dropped open. Inside was a small package wrapped in Iron Man wrapping paper. "I even wrapped it for you."

"Mr. Calvin would've wanted it that way," I joked. I took out the red-wrapped packet and began to open it. I carefully tore the sides of the paper and unfurled it in my lap, like Charlie Bucket in *Willy Wonka and the Chocolate Factory* opening his winning ticket. There laid three thick joints. "There has honestly never been a better time for this than right now," I said, dead serious.

"There should be a lighter in the glove box," she motioned.

I held up one of the joints, inspecting it like I remembered doing the few times I'd smoked weed in college. As I flipped the chubby white paper tube over, I noticed there was handwriting on it. It said "For Junebug."

"He calls you Junebug?" My head tilted in such awe that my skull almost rolled off my spine.

"It's what he used to call his uncle. I don't know," she said, brushing off the fact that Snoop Dogg had a pet name for her. "He gave me these a couple months ago and said they were something called 'Girl Scout Cookie OG.' I don't know what any of it means. Maybe it's his favorite kind of marijuana." She shrugged.

There were many things to consider here. First and foremost was that the fingers of *The* Snoop Dogg had touched these joints, as had his pen, which weirdly seemed as exciting as his hands. It would be sacrilegious to say no.

But didn't I need to also keep myself together to help June? In the first hour of newfound freedom from my family, was I really going to smoke weed in a car on the way to Vegas?

Yes. Yes I was.

I held the joint up to my mouth. Night had settled into the sky, helping hide the questionable decision-making going on in the car. "Are you sure you're okay with me doing this?" I asked.

"I just dropped a lot on you. Go for it."

I flicked the lighter and held the flame to the end of the crinkled paper. The white wrapper lit up orange as the green leaves crackled inside. I sucked deeply, as long as I could and then exhaled the smoke, hoping for a graceful blow-out without coughing. Just like riding a bike, I didn't forget how. *Still got it.* A large, stanky waft of smoke clouded up the entire front seat.

June cracked her window. And then it came. The coughing until I nearly vomited.

"You all right?"

I held my hand up, working my way through it, shaking my head and stifling the coughs with my fist. The all-over body tingle came immediately after the coughing ceased. I smiled in slow motion. All my worries drained out of me and were replaced with an inner bubble bath. I took enough hits to feel beautifully limp.

Cradled in the soft front seat, looking out the windshield at the red tail lights all moving toward Vegas, nothing else mattered. Until I felt a sudden need for music. It took all of my strength to turn my one-ton head, but after what was surely twenty minutes of trying, I looked at June out of my half-mast eyes. "Can I put some music on?"

"Sure," she said, laughing at me.

I scrolled through the music on my phone, for how long, I'll never know. Ninety-nine percent of it was terrible kid music. I saw seven albums entitled "Music Together," and started giggling. "You have to hear this shit, June."

I pressed play. It was the folky "Hello" song that we were forced to sing at the beginning of every Music Together class, which was led by a woman wearing bellbottoms and with hairy pits and white woman dreads, banging on a huge drum at the local community center. When the flutes came in, I lost it. I laughed so hard I couldn't breathe. My bladder control had to fight for its life. I tried to speak but couldn't, which made June laugh almost as hard as me. Saccharine kid music was funny enough sober, but it was hysterical when high. The two of us laughed for what felt like ten minutes straight. We listened to the entire song. On repeat. It got funnier every time. June was holding it together better than I was, but it was clear that she hadn't avoided a contact high.

We exited off the freeway in a town called Barstow that appeared to exist solely for high people with the munchies. She pulled up to the front of a gas station, which sat below a towering dirt hill. Being high in public as a mother was another new thing I was experiencing that night.

❦

As we continued to drive through the dark desert, my high began to wear off. "I can't believe I smoked Snoop Dogg's weed. It's like he and I are married now."

June's enthusiasm barely reached neutral, making me feel like a celebrity whore.

"Isn't there a famous person you're into, that you'd want to meet? Or bone?" I asked.

"I just don't get that starstruck."

"Like not even one person? What about a buff longhair like Jason Momoa?"

"Almost every important person I've met has been a huge letdown. Chet and his Hollywood friends have introduced me to so many famous people who are truly terrible human beings. I'm just jaded. Don't mind me. Go ahead with your Snoop love over there."

My high was now completely gone at the reminder of Chet's sour influence on her life and our reason for going to Vegas.

"And maybe to Jason Momoa," she said, with a wink.

The next three hours passed with the kind of organic sharing that only happens when sitting next to someone for an extended period of time in a moving vehicle. We talked about early sexual fiascos, including the frat guy with the stirrups hanging from his ceiling—and also things like hemorrhoids and cracked nipples.

As we passed the last of the stubble-covered mountains that led into Sin City, the brightly flickering city lights awoke in the distance, cheering us on. Once in the city, June deftly navigated her way through the jumble of nightly traffic on the Vegas Strip. The radiant flashing lights and gigantic signs pulsated with promises of fun and entertainment, but we were there on business.

It was nearing midnight as we pulled up to the Paris hotel parking lot, which was in the back, away from all the glitz and glamour. Stepping out of the car and into the hot night air felt like a baptism for me, since I reeked of pot smoke. I had forgotten that this time of year, outdoor Vegas felt like the inside of a fevery mouth. I was probably the only one who actually liked it. We got our belongings from the trunk and strolled toward the back glass doors. The ass end of the casino.

"Wait," June said, stopping and unzipping her bag. She pulled out a large hat and pair of sunglasses, and put them on. She looked like a movie star trying to fool the paparazzi. "In case we see Chet while checking in," she said, shoving me in front of her, like a human shield.

When we opened the gold-handled doors, Vegas overtook me. The cold, filtered air, the non-stop sound of dinging, the colorful carpet, the smoke, and the people. Oh the disgusting people. The sandals-and-socks wearers, the novelty-sized drink carriers, the ass-hanging-out-of-the-miniskirters.

June and I walked along the indoor French cobblestone street toward the check-in desk. The back-door seediness was replaced by the expansive casino area with high, open ceilings and attention to detail, right down to the ornate Parisian streetlights and metal Eiffel Tower leg jutting through the building like Godzilla. Vegas's flaws and its glory held a special place in my heart. Aaron and I had been regularly visiting Vegas since our college days of young love. We both equally liked the gambling, the people watching, and the amounts of sex we had there, before children. On the hardest days of parenting, he would look at me and say, "Vegas," and we would both close our eyes and pretend we were there, doubling down, and drinking lava flows by the pool. It felt wrong not only to be there without Aaron, but not even to be in contact with him. It was like I was living in some parallel universe where we never got married. But perhaps this is just what I needed—to be in the world as just myself, a woman attached to no one.

The best part of Vegas casinos was that children were basically illegal. There were always those few parents who thought it appropriate to bring kids to a playground filled with booze and tits, but aside from that, the ratio of adults to children was perfection.

We walked through a sloppy-drunk bachelorette party in front of the check-in desk and June lowered her sunglasses while nervously scanning the surroundings for any sign of Chet. She was keeping chitchat to a minimum.

"How many nights will you be with us?" the gentleman concierge asked with a smile. I wondered the same thing.

"Just one, for now," she said.

I felt the urge to text Aaron that I would probably be home tomorrow, but June was already walking to the elevators, and he didn't deserve it.

Once the elevator doors dinged us to the 22nd floor, I started to settle into what it felt like to be on a trip alone without a stroller, car seat, and a Pack 'n Play. I felt carefree as I pulled just my suitcase down the long hall to our room, noticing the hypnotic patterns on the carpet. My high from the pot had transitioned nicely into a natural high from autonomy.

When we walked into the gold-and-ivory-striped room that looked more circus-like than Paris-like, June quickly plugged her phone in a charger and asked me to do the same. "If we're gonna get video, we can't have a dead battery derail this whole thing," she said.

Next, we flopped on the king-sized bed. Bed bugs be damned, it felt good to mess up someone else's sheets. We laid there, in silence, soaking in the stillness and hopefully not too many stray pubes from strangers. It didn't matter how nice a Vegas hotel was, Vegas was Vegas. I could've easily fallen asleep right then and there.

"Ready to be a detective?" June asked.

"I guess. Does it mean I have to put on a swimsuit?"

"Well, only the bottoms," she said, smiling like Elliot when he's chiseling. I buried my face in a pillow.

"I'm going to change into one too," she said. "Best to be ready for whatever."

I hesitantly made my way to my bag. "I'm just going to warn you, I will be wearing the boy-shorts version of a bikini because it's been a while since I've done any landscaping down below," I said, sliding my stark white legs into black and white polka-dotted swim shorts.

"No judgment," she said, pulling out a strappy, crocheted purple and gold number. I was 100% sure that June's nether regions were perfectly coiffed all the time.

Standing in front of the wide bathroom mirror, amidst the marble everything, I made a sad attempt at applying eye shadow. "Why am I so terrible at this?"

"Here, can I try something on you?"

I turned to June like all Plain Janes turn to their hotter, more skilled friends with ten times the amount of eye shadows and lip glosses.

"Close your eyes," she said, bringing a thin brush up to my eyelid. I obeyed. She painted and brushed and lined. "Okay, open."

She had given me the most picture-perfect smoky eyes. I squealed like Violet. "I've always wanted smoky eyes!" Like most women when put in the hands of a talented make-up artist, I was pretty sure I was model beautiful. A quality eye job was so powerful that it could change the way a person walked.

We put on the finishing touches—a breath mint for my weed mouth and bronzer for June—and stopped for one last look in front of the funhouse-sized mirror by the door. We were both in tight pants, low-cut drapey tank tops with our bikini tops peeking out, and fuck-me heels.

"I'm just missing one thing," June said walking toward the bathroom. She carefully lifted something from a box that was tucked away in her bag. She bent over, gathered her hair in a tight band, shimmied something on her head and stood upright. She was wearing a wig. It looked just like her long, wavy hair, but now she was a redhead. Then she put on a pair of Warby Parker cat-eye glasses and turned to me. "Would you be able to recognize me in this?"

"Whoa," I said, stunned by her ability to be gorgeous no matter what she did. "No."

We walked back down the long hallway to the elevators, this time with a sway in our hips that hadn't been there before. Heels + Vegas = sexy swagger, no matter the reason for being there. A funeral in Vegas + heels? Swagger. A medical-supply expo in Vegas + heels? Swagger.

"Where are we headed first?" I asked as we cascaded downward in the '90s rock-blaring elevator alone, staring at an ad for $9.99 prime rib.

"I think we start at Mamelle. It's the only specific information I have, so it seems most promising."

The elevator doors telescoped open, welcoming us into the land of old dudes wearing Tommy Bahama shirts and young dudes wearing Hollister. I spotted a sign that pointed the way to Mamelle, next to a royal blue upholstered seat in the round that sprouted up into the ceiling and fanned out like a flower. We followed the arrow.

June's eyes constantly scanned right and left, and her

walk was focused. I was on the lookout for Chet too, but fell behind while getting drawn into the sensorial delights—the R&B group performing "Uptown Funk" and the cheers from the craps table, which was Aaron's and my favorite Vegas game.

We eventually reached the front entrance of Mamelle, which was a tall, black wall for privacy with a sheet of water pouring down it, spraying over the illuminated letters of "Mamelle." June turned to me. She was breathing deeply, fanning herself and walking in a circle.

"It's okay, I'm here. We can do this," I said.

She stopped circling, closed her eyes and opened them again, looking straight at me. "Will you go in there and try to find him?" I could tell she knew the weight of the favor she was asking. I rubbed my temples with my thumbs.

We had talked on the surface about going into Mamelle, but I had never formally said "yes." Mom Code rattled inside me like an earthquake, telling me that I must do this for my friend. But the most loathsome part of my body, that I was most insecure about, was my chest, or lack thereof. It was the part of me that I wanted to hide. The part that made me feel not good enough, not womanly enough, and unsexy. Going topless would mean no padded bra between me and the world. I imagined the stares, the laughs, and how I would become a part of someone's epic Vegas story: "Remember we went to the topless pool and there was that dude there, but it was a lady? That was hilarious!"

I put my hands on my head, covering my eyes with my palms.

"I know I'm asking a lot, April," June said in a respectfully desperate way. This day had already seen so many new sides of me—the me that leaves her husband and family on a whim, the me that smokes weed, the me that walks like a sex kitten in heels, with flawless smoky eyes—why stop there? What did it really matter if I became part of someone's funny Vegas story?

"Okay," I said, looking into her eyes, which were welling up with gratitude. "No crying right now," I reprimanded. "I don't want you to get me started. I'm about to look like an idiot and it's exponentially creepier if I'm crying while doing so." She obeyed. I had another question. "So, if I see Chet in there, do you want me to just video whatever I see?"

"Yes. But make sure you're close enough. A jury has to be able to tell it's him. That's the most important part. It has to be clear."

I nervously vanished behind the wall of water.

On the other side was a nearly topless D-cup desk attendant whose name tag read "Jessica."

"Hello, velcome to Mamelle. How can I help you?" she asked in a forced French accent dripping with lip gloss, like she was the duster in *Beauty and the Beast*.

"Um, I'd like to use the pool."

She glanced at my chest and back up to my face. I started to sweat.

"'Zis pool?"

"Yes, the pool I just said I wanted to use."

She looked at her computer screen and clicked feverishly on the mouse, which I assumed was some sort of alert that the scenery at the pool was about to degrade. Maybe she was preemptively doling out refunds.

"Follow me," she said, stepping out from behind her desk and showing a tiny Moulin Rouge–inspired costume that outlined her derriere like the peach emoji. She led me back into a fancy changing room and handed over a key to a locker. "Zis is where you may put your things. And I vill just need to take your phone."

"Wait, you have to take my phone?" I asked, trying not to sound like I was too eager to take naked photos of other people.

"Vee do not allow any picture taking at Mamelle and therefore vee require that vee hold your phone at zee front desk, and you vill receive it upon leaving." She held her hand out for my phone.

This could've been the perfect excuse for me to not have to bare it all, but I knew that even if I couldn't get video, it would be helpful to at least see if Chet was there. Then we could wait for him outside, all night if we had to.

I handed my phone over. She pulled a cloth case out of her overflowing bra, lowered my phone into it and gave me a numbered tag. "Zee entrance to zee pool is over there." She pointed to a door made of hanging ribbon. "And ven you are finished, you come out zee way you came in. Any questions?"

I had about thirty, but instead tried to play it cool.

She walked out and I was left alone. There was no one else in the locker room. Slow night. Or maybe everyone else was smart enough not to go to a topless pool.

I took off my pants and tank top. The heels would be staying on. Maybe my long legs could make up for my lack of sexiness on top. I paced in my bikini and heels. It was the moment of truth. But first, sunglasses. Totally normal at night. I swallowed hard and untied my black bikini top from the back of my neck, and undid the clasp. It fell forward into my hands. I was officially topless. The draft of air on my nipples, coupled with being half-nude in public, sent me into a panic. I bolted through the ribbon door, not knowing what stood on the other side of it.

As I birthed myself into the pool area, strobe lights hit my barely A cups from all angles. Through the colored, pulsing lights, I saw a smattering of people lounging on chairs—about a dozen men and two women—both wearing their motherfucking bikini tops!

WHAT THE ACTUAL FUCK?

I turned right around, soaked in embarrassment. I flew back into the locker room and bungled my bikini top back on with haste. *Oh fuck this. Fuck this a million ways.*

Like a complete bozo, I didn't realize that this was a top-optional pool, and now I had to go back out there and look for Chet. How much had anyone seen? I wanted to put this whole charade behind me, so I discreetly eked my way through the hanging ribbons, making zero eye contact, and heading straight for the bar in the back. There hadn't been an uproar of laughter, so maybe no one had noticed. I kept my head down while ordering a smokescreen mojito and began to scan the premises for Chet with my sunglass-covered shifty eyes. All I wanted was tea. And more weed. Pounds of weed.

Young guy. Tool. Tool. Young guy. Tool. Although there were tools there, my completed scan showed none of them were Chet. Great, I could be done with this godforsaken place. As I turned to leave, the bartender set down my drink.

"Don't forget your drink, ma'am." At least he got my gender right.

I grasped the cold, wet glass, and in an attempt to just GTFO, I sucked down the entire mojito in ten seconds and scrammed. It had mint in it, after all. It was basically peppermint tea. I hoped my bowels would show mercy on me. I stopped at the desk on the way out to retrieve my phone.

"Leaving zo zoon?" Jessica asked as she slid me the bill and my phone. I said nothing, grabbed my phone, threw cash down, and escaped.

As I rounded the tall wall, I saw red-headed June sitting on a slot machine chair in the near distance. The booze I had pounded was starting to hit me.

"June!" I yell-whispered. She looked up, eager for the word. I rushed over. "You are never going to believe this."

"What? Was Chet there?" she asked, and then paused. "Are you laughing? You smell like rum." I was trying to hold it together, but the events of the last fifteen minutes were piling up. She eyeballed me, impatient.

"First, Chet was not there. Second, I went topless at a pool where everyone else was wearing a fucking top."

"Wait, you *didn't* have to be topless?"

"No." I snapped. "I walked out with my nipples on parade, like a freak, and everyone else was wearing tops."

June unsuccessfully tried to hold back her laughter. "I'm so sorry." She was doubled over. "Did anyone see you?" she asked, grabbing my arm.

"Just everyone. Strobe lights were hitting me. I think I blacked out for a second," I said through laughter that made me fall all over the slot machine chairs, drunk. I stood up and waved my hands in my face to get air. "It was horrifying, but now that I'm not there anymore, it was hilarious!" We could barely breathe through our cackles. People were starting to look at us.

We regained our composure and wiped our eyes. I couldn't remember the last time I laughed that hard. I instinctually clicked on my phone to message Aaron all about it. Then I remembered. I scrolled through my messages, wondering if he had sent a text. He hadn't.

"I really had no idea that topless pools were actually top-optional," June said. "I assumed they were strictly topless."

"You and me both, friend," I said, raising my hand for a high five from her. She raised her hand to consummate the fiver but never followed through. Her face fell.

CHAPTER TWENTY

Dorothy and the Scarecrow

*J*une silently pointed behind me, mouthing a single word. "Chet."

I froze. My neck wanted to turn right around and see for myself, but I kept still as she slid over, directly in front of me so that she would be blocked from Chet's view. I studied her eyes, trying to see the reflection off of them. They were alert at first, and then they began to fill with tears. I felt the overwhelming need to comfort her or to take action, but I had no idea what was specifically happening behind me. I tried to be her rock, even though the mojito and my empathy were making it a challenge.

Finally, she softly spoke into my ear. "He's sitting at a table in the café and he's with a woman. He keeps kissing her." June's voice tightened at the end.

"Let's get you to a chair and out of sight. Then I will make my move," I suggested, calmly, like a stewardess during an impending plane crash. June nodded blankly, and we both shuffled to a chair like we were in the three-legged race, keeping our alignment. She sat down and swiveled away from the scene. "Are you okay?" I asked. She didn't respond. Of course she wasn't okay. "Wait here." I squeezed her shoulder and dashed off toward the café.

Chet and a young woman, who was in the same type category as June—stunning and blonde—sat at a wrought-iron café table, overlooking the casino walkway, like they were on the Champs-Élysées. Romantic French music spilled into my ears as I casually got closer, using the nearby foliage for cover. I lifted my phone up, moving my thumbs to pretend to be casually texting, but tilted the screen just so, capturing Chet and his faux-June in the frame perfectly. His face was in clear view and as intense as I remembered. He was still wearing those goddamn neon orange sneakers.

I steadied my shaking hands as I pressed the red record button. Chet and his lady were sitting so close that his legs were like outside barriers to hers under the table, blocking her in. He leaned over and kissed her with his entire Terminator face and tongue. She appeared to enjoy it. I gagged. What was this woman's story? Was she paid for?

I glanced over at June, who had turned herself so that she could peek at the action from behind a slot machine. After five long minutes of watching Chet and his orange sneakers prey on this woman, I hit the red button again and stopped recording. I pivoted around and walked back to June. She stood up, silent, and we both walked away from the scene of the crime.

"Will that work, was it enough?" I asked her with sadness.

She nodded yes.

I put my arm around her and swept us away to a dark bar I'd been to before with Aaron, finding the most tucked-away spot in the back. She plopped herself down on the plush chair, much like I remembered doing on the couch in her office.

"How dare he." June slammed her fist on the table. Hatred dripped from her voice. It was jolting to see June in this state. She was the stable one. "What a piece of shit. How could he lie to me and our boys? Is she his mistress back home or just some floozy he paid for? I don't understand." It was the first time I'd ever heard June swear. I liked it.

Suddenly, a cocktail waitress who couldn't read a room walked up with her chirpy, eager spiel. "Hi ladies, how's it going? Can I get you one of our delicious drinks tonight?"

Still numb from the mixture of pot, rum, and adrenaline, I shook my head no.

"I'd like six shots of tequila, please. Limes and salt," June said like a boss. My eyebrows lifted. The night was taking yet another unforeseen turn. "I did this to myself. I stayed with a man who I knew had the capability to disrespect me and our boys. I deserve this."

"June, no. This isn't your fault. You stayed to protect everyone from Chet's wrath."

"Did I? Or did I stay because I couldn't face it?" She was angry and grasping.

"Chet would've made your life miserable if you left, right? Give yourself some slack, you have a mercenary husband."

"I let this happen," she bellowed from a low place. "I didn't stick up for myself or my boys. I tried to hack off the pain and the disappointment every day and now look where I am."

The jolly waitress appeared with the bounty of tequila shots. "Enjoy, ladies!"

Fucking Vegas.

June took off her glasses, wiped her eyes, and surveyed

the row of shots before us. "I didn't expect this to hurt so much. Chet repulses me, but seeing him with that other woman reminded me that he didn't cut off that part of himself, like I did. He just looked elsewhere. Why didn't I?"

I spoke softly, knowing I was treading on fragile ground. "Because you were busy being Chase and Charlie's mom."

"But why didn't I go looking for that different kind of in-love love—that need to be desired? And why didn't Chet tell me to go? He kept me as much as I kept him. I stayed out of fear, but why did he stay?"

I recognized what was happening. Despite her training, degrees, and office bookshelf, she couldn't see the big picture of her own life, just like she had told me.

"Chet is a power-hungry, egocentric control freak. He didn't let you go because he wouldn't be able to control you." I was not choosing my words carefully anymore. June didn't make a peep. "The guy has his name on everything in your house. He might as well have wallpaper with dick pics."

"This is such a fucking wreck." She put her hand to her head.

I noticed the "fuck" upgrade.

"You are smart, strong, and will do anything for your boys. You will all come out of this." *Or would they? How the hell did I know?*

June suddenly pulled her head away from her hands to examine them. She turned her left hand over, fixating on her sizable, sparkling wedding ring. She quickly slid the ring off, put it in her change pocket in her purse, and zipped it closed. A flurry of unexpected emotions stirred up inside me.

"Please have one or three of these shots with me," June

said. I momentarily ignored her to tug off my wedding and engagement rings. "What? You have a respectable husband."

"This isn't about him. It's about freedom. I want one night where I don't belong to anyone."

June didn't ask any questions. We were both speaking deep truths and trying on new identities. I put my rings inside an empty mint tin in my purse.

"Now that that's settled," she said, pointing down at the table. My mouth gushed saliva just thinking about the awful taste of tequila. But I couldn't let her take shots alone, in Vegas, while feeling utterly unloved. She licked and salted her hand, passing the shaker to me. Once ready and salted, I held my glass up.

"This is for you, June. A therapist I deeply fucking respect, and a friend that I am quickly growing to love." I touched my glass to hers, our misty eyes met, and we both tilted back the repulsive Mexican honey, scrunching our faces up and nearly gagging while sucking on limes.

She picked up another shot. "Too soon?"

"Nope," I said, matching her.

"This is for you, April. My only client-turned-friend and one of the few people I've let in. You were worth going against protocol." Clink, tears, down the hatch, and gag.

Thankfully there was only one set of shots left. My insides were revolting and I felt like I might throw everything up, but there was a rhythm I didn't want to disrupt, so I grabbed my last shot. June followed. I held my glass up, again. "This last one is for my new BFF, Snoop Dogg."

"To Mr. Calvin," she said.

The third shot burned my soul.

"What do we do now?" I asked.

"I don't know about you, but I'm getting laid tonight."

Come again? "It's been too long." She looked around the bar. She had my support, but as her friend, I did have to ask some protective questions before we stood up and the tequila went straight to our brains.

"Two things. First: will this hurt your case?"

"No one will know a thing," she said, tugging on her red hair.

"Second: how do you know who will and will not take you back to their room and cut your organs out?"

"Not sure. But I have a decent radar."

I looked at her like *yeah, but your husband is pretty much the serial killer type, soooo.* "Trust me, the radar has been updated."

"Well then, how can I help you get laid?" I said, smiling big. Almost too big. I felt a twinge of jealousy that June had free reign to go hand-pick a random man and be pleasured by him, if all went well and she didn't end up dead. I hadn't been in this position since I was eighteen years old. I rubbed my hand against the slick emptiness of my ring finger.

"Where do nice but attractive guys hang out here?" June asked.

"Gay bars?" But then I remembered an article about the guys from *Chippendales* and *Thunder From Down Under*–type shows actually being great lovers since they make women feel special for a living, or some shit like that. I told June.

"Are you suggesting we go to a strip show?"

"Maybe?" I questioned too, shrugging my shoulders. She looked skeptical. "Okay then, how about we try the next hotel over and see what we see?"

June laid cash down on the wet table and we both stood up. The warmth of the tequila raced upwards to my brain. "Aw shit," I said, feeling wobbly on my heels, like a freshly born baby deer.

"I got you," she said, steadying me. We linked arms and walked out of the bar together, like Dorothy and the Scarecrow. I was definitely the Scarecrow.

As we walked back through the cobblestone streets of the Paris hotel, June stayed subdued, watching her back. But once we walked out into the street and then through the filigreed doors of the Bellagio, she loosened up and forgot about hiding. Her alcohol smiled at every passing man. All of them grinned back, and some even turned around to watch her pass. I yanked on her arm. "Be careful. Making eye contact makes them think you've signed a contract to blow them. Eyes down until you find one you really like." But she couldn't help herself. Something had opened up in her and she was reveling in being seen in an entirely new way.

Off in the distance, the sound of thumping hip-hop music lured me like the Pied Piper.

"Oooh, let's see what's over there!" I pulled June in the direction of Jay-Z's "Izzo." The booze in my body demanded my muscles move to the beat and find my way to the dance floor. The physiological urge couldn't be fought. *I needs Izzo!* She pointed to the bar and headed off to grab a drink.

Not two seconds after stepping into the small sea of other people obeying their alcohol-induced physiological urges, a dude wearing a long drink around his neck that looked like a dong—a terrible phenomenon only found in Vegas—grinded me hard from behind. The me of twenty years ago might have let the ass humping go on for a bit before politely dancing her way to the other side of the floor, but the me of tonight turned around with gusto. "No way. Get the fuck off me."

The guy made a sad face and danced his way to some other shaking ass nearby. I got back into my groove when 70s-era Michael Jackson came on, until I remembered *all the details* from the *Leaving Neverland* documentary. *Jesus, April, let yourself enjoy something. Sometimes bad people make good art. Also, 70s-era Michael is surely the safest Michael.* I closed my eyes and sang all the words. I was free. This was heaven on Earth.

When I opened my eyes, I saw June chatting with a clean-cut guy with an old-timey haircut. His jawline was manly and defined, like Gaston's. I stretched my neck to get a glimpse of what he was wearing, when suddenly a man in a number 18 Denver Broncos jersey came into my line of vision and moved toward me, gyrating.

"I noticed you were staring at me," he said, grinning.

"Nope. Just looking for my friend," I said flatly. I turned around to get back into my MJ zone, alone. But there he was again, in front of me.

"That sounds cool, I have a friend too."

I was done. Trying to dance in Vegas was not worth it. I shook my head and turned to go find June, until the guy shouted at my back.

"No wonder you're single. Learn how to relax and have some fun, bitch."

I stopped dead in my tracks. I felt like Anger, Elliot's favorite character from *Inside Out*, bright red with smoke fuming out of my ears. Lots of things had changed since I last found myself drunk, dancing at a club without a chaperone, but apparently guys on dance floors still had the lock on deciding if a woman was fun or not based on their willingness to be dry-humped.

I walked like an Army general toward this bag of shit. He smirked until I got right in his face. I wished I'd had Violet as a weapon again.

"Let me tell you something, Peyton Manning. You know nothing about me. I am a fucking. Fun. Ass. Woman," I said as I poked his chest hard with each word. "I smoke Snoop Dogg's weed, I go to topless pools, and I help my girl over there get laid in Vegas. So why don't you go reread the manual on what to wear when trying to pick up a female and then jack off into a John Elway poster." I whisked around and walked off before he could respond. *"Female?" "Jack off into a John Elway poster?"* Really, April?

I spotted June cozied up to the good-looking fellow at their own tall bar table in the back. Visually, the two were a perfect match—their beauty equal. The guy looked trans-fixed on June, who glowed as a drunken red head. I approached the table, hoping he had promise and was not a total douche.

"April," June said when she saw me. "This is Dylan." She tucked her fake hair behind her ear.

Dylan wore a Mister Rogers cardigan, his buff arms nearly tearing out of it. He reached his hand out to shake mine. "Nice 'ta meet ya," he said with an intoxicating Aus-tralian accent.

I wasn't sure what to say. *My friend wants to get laid, but I need for you to treat her really well* didn't seem appro-priate. Instead, I asked, "What brings you to Vegas?"

"My work is 'ere, and grad school. I was just telling your friend Alyssa 'ere about it."

I looked at June who was apparently now going by "Alyssa." She winked. *Smart, June, smart.*

"He helps people die." June was grinning and drunk.

"Excuse me?" I said.

"No—well, yes. But let's be clear 'ere. I work in palliative care," he explained, blushing.

"I know you don't kill people." June patted his arm like she'd known him longer than three minutes. "But you do help dying people feel more at peace as they make the transition into death," she said beaming, as if directly at me to say, "LOOK AT THIS TREASURE I FOUND!"

"Next you're gonna to tell me you spend your free time holding babies in the NICU," I joked.

"That *has* actually been part of my rotation for school. Death and birth: same deal, different ends."

This guy was a fucking diamond in the rough. Trying not to jump the gun and show my full approval, I had a few more questions. "So you work, too?"

"Yeah, nights. At the Excalibur."

"Oooh, blackjack dealer? Pit boss? Magician?" I wanted to know the behind-the-scenes secrets of whatever he did.

"Not quite."

"*Thunder From Down Under* dancer?" I asked. June and I cackled, but then realized he *did* have an Australian accent. And he wasn't saying no. There was a pause and then Dylan shyly nodded a small yes. June and I looked at each other, eyes wide, trying to seem chill.

"Now that ya know that about me, would you like to go, or keep talking?" he asked June, as if there was a code of conduct for admitting you're a male stripper. I found his respect for informed consent sexy.

"I'll stay," she said, with zero hesitation, hanging on

him. He smiled at her and snuggled in closer. Dylan was everything she needed right now. He could help her transition from this life to the new one as a single mother that awaited her in Orange County, with lawyers, video evidence, and custody battles, while also turning her out in the bedroom.

Before I walked away, I gave a final smile to the two, like a blessing. Sure, there was a slight chance this death doula was a wanted criminal, but I agreed with June that he was worth the risk.

CHAPTER TWENTY-ONE

The Blue-Eyed Man

I walked under the Bellagio's glass-flower sky, alone, and suddenly felt painfully aware of it. The glow from the colorful, luminous ceiling highlighted the couples underneath. I'd been completely alone for less than five minutes and here I was, weirdly pining for my husband who I was mad at and had intentionally left behind. I felt like slapping myself. *Wake up, April, this is what you wanted. Enjoy it.*

I abandoned the garden of lovebirds and spied a bank of felt-covered craps tables. I might as well. It was Saturday night, which meant the tables were full and the bet minimums were at their highest. I remembered how savvy I felt when playing table games in Las Vegas, especially craps. There were lots of confusing ins and outs with various ways to bet, and what each dice roll meant, and I could hold my own among the men wearing diamond-encrusted watches. I refused to be the woman who stood behind her gambling man because she couldn't possibly understand the game like he could. Back in the day, when it was my turn to roll the dice, Aaron would do his best craps dealer voice—similar to a hot dog vendor—and say, "We've got a hot lady shooter here! Lady shoooota!"

I watched the tables carefully, trying to get a feel for which one had the most winning energy. A packed one on the end erupted in shouts and high fives. I turned in their direction, watching from a few feet away, seeing if the table's good luck was beginning or ending, and contemplating spending money on gambling. I could probably justify it as "self-care."

In all the hopeful faces cheering around the sacred, green felt, one caught my eye. He had dark hair and a baby face like my kindergarten crush, Drew Beaverson. He must've noticed my intrigue because he scooted over to make room for me, motioning that there was a space if I wanted it. I stepped forward and wiggled my way between the shoulders of the lively players, who had just hit their winning number. I smiled at the man with just enough reserve to avoid entering into a blow job contract. His eyes were a brilliant blue.

"I hope you're more good luck for us. This table's fire," the blue-eyed man said.

"Don't go jinxing it," I replied with a flirty smile.

I reached into my wallet, past the pictures of Elliot and Violet, and pulled out three fifty-dollar bills from my pop-up shop earnings. I set the money on the soft green. The table's stick man pulled the cash toward him with his wooden rod, looked at the bills for a second like they might be counterfeit, and then finally changed them out for rubbery chips. He slid the chip stack over to me, along with six dice.

"Good luck, lady shooter," the stick man said. I liked the power that came with being the shooter, but not seconds after joining the table. These people had worked hard together and formed unbreakable bonds. I couldn't just walk up and insert myself into the profitable world of their creation. I hesitated.

"It's not as scary as you think. Pick two and give it your best shot," the blue-eyed man guided me, as if I were a craps virgin. I slid my bet out on the come line. *Oh honey, I've been doing this shit for years.*

I picked through the dice, grabbed two, tapped them on the spongy felt wall two times, and lifted them up and forward just enough so they kissed the table's opposite wall. They fell down with a seven showing. The table cheered.

"Okay, okay, I see. You're not new at this," the blue-eyed man said, laughing and sipping his cocktail with an embarrassed, cute smile.

The stick man slid everyone their payouts and then glided the dice back to me. I rolled again. It was a six, which was a good solid number in craps. We all put our bets out across the board. A black-haired woman wearing a shiny pink jacket, and with a terminal case of resting bitch face, threw her chip out, knowingly. I rolled the dice again, the eager faces at the other end of the table fixated on the red cubes as they landed. The table roared in drunken hysteria. I had hit the six again—a payday for everyone. The blue-eyed man put his hand up for a high five. I gave it to him, gladly. The other players looked at me, tipping their non-existent hats in my direction. Confident, and with total support from my loyal tablemates, I picked the dice up once again and rolled. An eight. The table buzzed with payouts and new bets. They had faith in me. Look at how much happier I was in my new life.

The blue-eyed man threw out a chip to the stickman, and smiled at me. "Hard eight for the lady shooter." He

had put a bet on the table for me, as a reward for my performance. I felt a slight obligation along with it, as if the
harmless flirting had advanced into something else, but
everyone was waiting for me, so tap tap. I rolled the dice.
Everyone's necks craned to make the call.

It was a seven. I had crapped out.

In unison, the entire table made an "aghhhhhhh"
sound, like fifteen Elliots being told their screen time was
up. Some people even walked away from the table in disgust, shaking their heads. Those that remained looked like
the deflated balloon from the Bin of Pointless Crap. I felt
ashamed. I had let everyone down, including the blue-eyed
man who had put his money on me. Maybe my luck had
turned *because* he had attached strings.

"Sorry everyone," I mumbled in the table's direction. I
looked down at the few chips left in my hand instead of
the disapproving faces. The craps table had treated me just
like motherhood had—one minute I'm up, the next, I'm
down. The sweet spot had been so fleeting.

"It happens," the blue-eyed man spoke up. "I crap out
so much that I won't even roll."

I laughed out loud. Only in Vegas could a stranger say
they "crap out so much" and have it not refer to their shit-
ting habits.

"New shooter!" the stickman announced. At the end of
the table, sorting through dice and preparing to roll was
another woman. She looked to be in her mid-sixties, with a
kind smile, porcelain skin, and her brown hair in a small
bun. She was petite, wearing a striped sweater with a collar sticking out, and standing next to a tall, good-looking
man with grey hair, who was quickly setting his bet out
before she rolled. I was captivated by something about her.

Instead of putting my own bet out on the table, I watched them intently.

She rolled the dice with a similar lift and drop style to mine, except she added a playful blow right before she let them fly. The dice revealed an eight. The fair-weather table clapped at the solid number and spread their bets out. Aaron and I always bet on an eight, but I was too engrossed to ante up. The tall man with grey hair bent down and gave his lady shooter a kiss on the cheek. My eyes zoomed to the woman's left hand, which displayed a shining gold wedding ring with a row of four large diamonds. I checked out the tall man's left hand too. He had a matching four-diamond ring, but with a chunky gold band instead of her thin one.

I felt weak. I looked around at the faces surrounding the table, desperately searching for someone. A young-looking man with freckles placed his chip down, unsure, asking the dealer what the "come" line meant. A girl leaned on him, carrying a purse that was screen-printed to look like a ghetto blaster. They looked about fifteen. After listening to the dealer's instructions, she laid down her bet after his and they looked at each other and shrugged their shoulders, innocence pouring out of their eyeballs. The blue-eyed man asked for another drink as the scantily-clad cocktail waitress barely stopped to take his order.

Drums beat in my head. "Circle of Life" was playing in my bones.

Goddamn Disney. My brain could only think in Disney metaphor, but it was fucking onto something. I scanned the craps table Circle of Life, stunned at what I saw before me. I recognized my past and future selves standing there, betting with their partners, while my present self stood there, betting with the blue-eyed man. Amidst all the temptations that could be brushed under the dirty Vegas rug—sex with a good-looking stranger (or at least more flirting), gambling all my money away, doing more drugs, and drinking until I couldn't see straight—all I wanted was Aaron. The old Aaron. Before kids.

The inner drums dwindled as dice thumped on the table, and then a quick second of silence until the table let out its unified "aghhhhhhh." The lovely lady shooter had rolled a seven, just like I had. I looked in the woman's direction, to give a sympathetic salute from across the table, but the tall man with grey hair was already softening the blow of crapping out with his arm around his wife, kissing the top of her head.

"Damn. Looks like the table's gone cold," the blue-eyed man said, shaking his head. "You still in?" he asked me with a not-so-innocent smile this time, his hypnotic baby blues shimmering like the ocean outside the window of the glass pop-up shop room.

I felt a knee-jerk repulsion that quickly turned into alarm, so strong that I felt like I couldn't breathe. I bolted from the craps table without explanation, speed-walking in heels toward a cluster of Britney Spears–themed slot machines blaring "Hit Me Baby One More Time." I found an empty row and sat down on a sticky vinyl chair, my breath shallow and shaky. What the fuck was I doing in Vegas, alone, and with my wedding rings off? I didn't recognize myself. Nothing made sense, including the spread-eagled, schoolgirl Britney Spears on the slot machine in front of me, staring at my ridiculousness. I needed someone familiar. I was utterly lost.

I dialed my mom. In hindsight, a senseless choice. She

answered, groggy. It was the middle of the night for her, and me. I didn't know what I even wanted to tell her.

"Mom, I just needed to hear—"

She interrupted, her voice hazy. "Marnie, Sweetie, it's Marnie."

I screamed decades of anger into the phone at her. I hoped it melted her ear off. Extending that whole "doing our best as mothers" compassion to my mom was as hard as I imagined it would be. *Shocker.* An illuminated Britney Spears looked on, ogling my gaping mother wound. Martha. Maybe Martha could talk some sense into me. But it was all misplaced. I was the only one who could talk myself off this ledge. And I knew what to do to get myself down.

I fumbled my purse open, on a hunt for the mint tin that safeguarded my rings. I slid them back on, where they belonged, as fast as I could. I had wanted to let loose and experience some independence, not explode my life. Thank god Simba had brought me back.

Just then, my phone dinged. My heart jumped, in hopes that Aaron had cosmically felt me put my rings back on and was messaging me apologies and peach emojis. But it was a buttload of missed texts from Danielle.

> OMG Owen won't stop crying.
> I've never seen him like this
> before.

> He won't let me put him down
> and we leave for Napa
> tomorrow. I'm dying. Why didn't
> you tell me two-year molars
> were such misery?

He's sticking everything in the
back of his mouth. I just had to
fish a Jenga piece out of there.
What do I do? I'm at a total loss
here, April.

And why won't you text me
back??

I just cancelled our trip. I can't
leave him like this. Shit.

I couldn't get into teething and Danielle's trip being
swallowed up whole. Mom Code had already whipped my
ass and the events of the last eight hours were finally
catching up with me. I was so tired I felt faint. The stamina
of my mother self in Vegas was quite different than that of
my maiden self, and all I wanted was bed. And food. In
bed.

I speed-walked my way from the Bellagio back to the
Paris hotel, alone. I couldn't remember the last time I'd
walked this far in heels, and my feet ached. I missed
Aaron's arm to steady me as I weaved through the crowds.

On my way to the elevators, I stopped at the casino
mini-mart and picked up some snacks to hold me over until
breakfast: Pringles, an energy bar, a one-hitter of Advil,
and the world's tallest water. On an end-cap sat a mini slot
machine that Elliot would've begged for had he been there.
I stood in front of it, barely awake, but judiciously weigh-
ing the pros and cons of bringing a slot machine into our
lives, for my sweet El. I picked it up and set it on the
counter along with my snacks.

"I'll be right back," I said to the cashier. I walked past rows of chocolate dice, shot glasses, snow globes, and a mug with protruding jugs that read "Mamelle," searching for a Violet-worthy item. In the back corner was a rack of stuffed monkeys with Velcro hands wearing Las Vegas t-shirts. I scoffed. It was the kind of toy junk that I found hardest to reckon with. "Who buys this garbage?" I grumbled out loud as I picked a pink one out, answering my own question.

I made the ascent to the twenty-second floor carrying my black plastic bag of nourishment and child atonement. The doors opened and I walked down the long hallway alone. This time, the fun and excitement did not walk alongside me. The Ghost of Vegas Future had visited me, and now I ached to be kissed and hugged by the people I had earlier been so happy to run away from. But being alone in a hotel bed was a decent consolation prize.

I lay there solo, crunching loudly and thoughtlessly in bed, crumbs falling on the sheets. All I wanted was my lifeline to Aaron and for everything to go back to normal with us. Well, not everything. I texted him.

I miss you.

The response dots lit up. I sat up in anticipation, brushing crumbs off of my chest and sheets. He was awake, even though it was way past our bedtime. The dots kept bouncing and bouncing, as if he were writing a novel on the other end. Then his lengthy message came through.

He was there.

Are you okay A.B.?

>Yes. Too much to type.

When are you coming home?

>Tomorrow. I mean today. Ugh, it's late.

I'm sorry I was so thoughtless about everything. I saw the heart around our date on the kitchen calendar. I'M THE WORST.

>Yes, you are.

>And I love you.

I slipped under the hopefully-not-semen-stained covers, finally able to truly bask in the alone time, knowing that Aaron and I had at least made contact.

CHAPTER TWENTY-TWO

The Green-Eyed Man

*S*orry," June whispered, shutting the heavy door.

A stripe of light streamed in through the gap between the bulky, velvety drapes and the large window. It felt like it must be late morning. I gradually opened my eyes. There were no breakfasts to immediately make. Heaven. But my mouth felt like a sand dune and my head pounded. I took a five-minute drink from a water bottle I'd apparently spooned with all night.

"How'd it go?" I asked, returning to the fetal position in bed, like I longed to do every morning of my life.

June opened the drapes up a touch more, letting in the daylight and a view of the Vegas-sized Eiffel Tower. Her wig was off and her purple and gold bikini straps were missing out from under her tank top. She sat on the edge of the bed. "It was amazing. He was amazing. That was long overdue." She was radiating in an entirely new way, which I didn't think possible.

"So I was right about these dancer guys being good in bed?"

"You have no idea. Good in bed, good out of bed, good back in bed, good on the floor, good in the shower, and then, good at making me breakfast."

"He totally rocked you like a little NICU baby." We laughed with a racy cackle.

"He did," she said fanning herself, "I'm getting all worked up again." She hopped off the bed and started gathering her things.

"Did you get his number?"

"No, no. He was unreal, but it stays here. I have to focus on what I need to do next, and how." *Then he must not have been that good, June.* "How was the rest of *your* night?" she yelled from the bathroom, packing up all her pots of eye shadow.

"Crappy."

She peeked her head out of the bathroom doorway, concerned. "Let me see your left hand."

I pulled it out from under the covers. "I thought I wanted a break from everything in my life, which I did, but not like this."

"And what did it cost you to figure that out?" She had stopped packing and looked at me with a seriousness, like she hoped I hadn't done irreversible damage to my marriage.

"Only about sixty dollars at a craps table."

She clutched her chest. "You had me scared for a second." She picked up a too-long decorative bed pillow and hit me with it.

Oh my god, men are right. All girl's trips do end with a pillow fight.

We threw ourselves together—hair up and hoodies— grabbed our things from the barely-used room, and jetted. June didn't have any of her concealment items on.

"Do you think you should wear something in case we see Chet?" I wasn't sure how high the terror alert was now that the footage had been successfully captured.

"Right," she said, sliding on sunglasses and pulling up her hood. She looked like all the other hungover people riding an elaborate escalator maze through advertisements for magicians and one of the nine-hundred Gordon Ramsay restaurants in Vegas.

When we emerged from the casino into the hot underbelly of the parking garage, June stopped. "Oh shoot, I meant to get a water. I'll go back. Do you want one too?" she asked.

"Sure. Give me your suitcase and I'll get us loaded in the car."

She handed her bags to me and clicked the car unlocked. I popped open the back passenger door and slid our suitcases on the back seat, when something pink caught my eye. It was a zippered bag with handles, like the kind you get at Victoria's Secret, free with purchase, and it was crammed halfway underneath the front passenger seat. I pulled the bag out to find that it was heavy and also unzipped.

The gun.

I suddenly remembered June had brought a gun with us. Its brushed-metal barrel revealed itself from inside the bag. Fully-armed camping trips with my dad as a kid where we shot targets and skeet had made me familiar with the anatomy of a gun. I didn't know the caliber, but I had shot one like this before. I double-checked that the safety was on, which it was, but the thing was loaded. I went to dump the bullets out of the cylinder when I heard a clattering in the near distance. I dropped the gun back into the bag and peeked my head around the car to see June, sunglasses off, face to face with Chet. I jumped back into the backseat in horror, and shut the door behind me. My heart was beating out of my fucking chest as I popped up and peered through the backseat window.

June was yelling at him. "You are a disgrace and a miserable excuse for a father. Our boys deserve better than you. And so do I." She briskly turned to walk away.

"Fuck yes, girlfriend!" I cheered out loud, alone in the car. Chet leapt after her like a python, grabbed her wrist, and flung her around with force. My stomach tumbled, and it all clicked. That monster had manhandled her this way for years. The reason for the loaded gun. And probably her scar.

My panic turned to lucidity as I snatched my phone, slid it to "video" and hit record. The courts might want to see this too.

Chet verbally laid into June, still holding onto her wrist tightly. "You know what, you just messed up." He began laughing manically. "As of now, your whole life is gone."

She pulled herself free and ran to the car. He ran after her with the bladed arms of an Olympic sprinter.

Oh shit oh shit oh shit.

June opened the driver's side door, sat down hard, and hit the lock button just in time.

Chet zoomed over to the passenger side, like a demon without legs, and clicked his door opener for her car. The doors unlocked. I crouched down low as the video kept rolling. Everything was moving slow. And fast. Chet slammed himself into the passenger seat in front of me.

"Get out of here!" June demanded, fumbling to put the keys in the ignition. He slapped her. She gasped. I tried not to.

"Let's just remember whose car this is, huh?" he said smiling through his teeth. "Everything you have is because of me."

"You are sick. And I am done. GET OUT!" She screamed from the darkest place inside of her.

In the blink of an eye, he lunged forward and gripped his hands around her neck. "You're done," he said as he tightened his grasp. "You were never good enough for me and no one else will ever want you."

I felt myself leave my body, and from where I floated above, as if time had stopped, I saw the entire picture of what was happening inside that car, including the pink bag sitting right in front of me. June gasped for air and flapped her hands against the leather seat as Chet overtook her. I slid the gun's safety off. I cocked it in an instant and steadied it up with Chet between the sight.

"Leave her alone," I roared from the backseat. He jumped, his startled hands freeing her neck. She coughed and coughed as she looked for the car key. I was incensed. "Get the fuck out of here!" I yelled, sitting up and securing my footing. The scared look on Chet's face filled me with confidence. He was bumbling for the door handle. "I said get the fuck out of here. You touch her again and I will blow your fucking brains out."

Maybe I'd watched a few too many *Die Hards* with Aaron.

Chet ejected himself from the car just as June got it started. With the gun still pointed at him, I climbed into the front passenger seat. He ran, looking back in disbelief and panic. I closed the passenger door and June slammed the car into drive. She was headed right past Chet, but at the last second, she swerved, perfectly clipping his legs, and bringing him to the ground in agony. I looked at her in total shock and adoration. She looked at me the same way. We were both juiced up. I fell back into my seat.

"What just happened?" I said, shaking.

June peeled out of the parking lot and onto Las Vegas Boulevard. I re-flipped the safety on the gun and stashed it back in the pink bag, wanting it out of my hands.

"I think you just somehow pulled a gun on Chet and saved my life."

"And I think you just ruined his running career."

"I know," she said with a slight smile hiding below her rattled demeanor. She breathlessly looked up toward the sky and said, "I'm sorry, Michelle Obama, but I couldn't go high. I've been going high for too long, and that man nearly took me from my boys." She broke down sobbing and fought hard to drive through the tears and wails, but they wouldn't stop. I steadied the wheel from the passenger seat. She rounded her back and dry-heaved, and we got the fuck out of Vegas.

✺

It took a good half-hour for both of us to calm down and speak again. Driving down the cloudless highway, my stomach demanded attention. How dare it want an actual meal.

"I know you had sexy breakfast, but can we stop somewhere?"

"Of course."

I felt around for my phone to check out what food was nearby. Dread set in that I'd left it back in the hotel room until I realized when I'd had it last. It was still on the back seat.

"June. I recorded it."

"I know. Remember, I was there in front of the café with you?"

"No, no, not that. Just now. Chet. Him yelling at you and then the other stuff in the car." I couldn't bring myself to say the word "strangle" out loud. "It's all on here," I said, scrubbing through the video, unwilling to watch the actual footage. She put her hand over her mouth for a short while.

"A Chick-fil-A!" I shouted. My favorite hangover food.

June pulled off the highway at the Nevada/California state line and parked underneath the abandoned roller coaster, next to a gas station and the Chick-fil-A. Its parking lot was empty.

"Fuuuuuuck, it's Sunday." Chick-fil-A: crushing dreams and LGBTQ people every Sunday since 1967.

Gas-station breakfast it was. A chew tin of shredded beef jerky, a bag of almonds, and a package of Haribos. When I returned to the car, June had news for me.

"I just called Cammy. She wants us to send her all the videos. She knows a lawyer who might be willing to help me immediately."

I sent the damning evidence into the ether.

"She's got the boys on lockdown at her house until I get there, and asked if I wanted her to call the cops. I said yes." She looked at me with both anguish and hope. The wheels were in motion and their lives would never be the same. Her eyes were red and bleary. She yawned.

"I'll drive. Hop out."

⁂

The drive home from Las Vegas felt a million times longer than the drive there, as was always the case. The reckless, excited energy of the Thelma and Louise–style trip had now been replaced with quietude, reflection, and residual shock. While June slept, I watched the lonely cacti and graffiti-tagged shacks, surely full of dead bodies, go by.

My mind floated in and out of all that had gone down, and what was yet to go down with Aaron, once I returned, which was tame compared to what awaited June. I still had some truth to hit Aaron with and I didn't know how he would react. Maybe June had been right that day when she said our husbands won't save us. But mine could sure as hell be an active participant in my salvation and he needed to hear that.

I wished I was coming back empowered and refreshed, having wrung out every last ounce of my short-lived freedom, but instead, I was returning absolutely spent—albeit with clarity—and needing to spend about four hours on the toilet. I was also coming home with the new knowing that it was, in fact, possible for me to yank off my own leash.

My phone dinged. It was a text from Marnie. *This is gonna be good.*

> I just had the most bizarre
> dream that you called last night
> and screamed into the phone.
> Can you imagine?! Give those
> angels hugs and kisses from
> their Marnie.

As we neared our familiar Orange County roads, canyons, and big box stores, I knew that the cycle of exhaustion and overwhelm would start all over again, likely the second I stepped in the door. June had slept so soundly that she only opened her eyes when I stopped at the traffic light nearest to my house. She sat up, wiped the drool from her mouth and stretched out of her passenger seat pod. She looked over at me.

"I didn't mean to sleep that whole time. Sorry."

"You deserved it."

I pulled up in front of my own house, where our journey had begun, grateful that the neighborhood kids weren't outside with water balloons and fart guns for my homecoming. We both got out of the car and hugged a long goodbye. I felt the power of what we had experienced together, which was much greater than anything that could've happened on the couch in her office, or even in a Costco parking lot. Our trip had been therapy in itself. Life was savage.

I grasped the shiny brass handle to my front door, not fooling myself, knowing exactly what I would return to. And I wasn't wrong. The house was a wreck, with the same messy laundry baskets full of indistinguishable clean or dirty clothes in the same spot as when I had left them, the usual smattering of snack bowls, miles of Fruit by the Foot wax paper, and the TV screen showing Netflix's judgmental question, "Still watching?" Re-entry was hard and fast, and kids weren't even in the picture yet, until the sound of giggles and splashes echoed from upstairs. I wanted to be back in Vegas and also right where I was at home, all at once. The eternal rub of motherhood: wanting to be present and also not.

"Ma-ma!" Violet squealed.

"Mom!" Elliot called.

Their sweet voices snapped me back into the moment.

I came upstairs to find Violet and Elliot in the bathtub, both standing up to hug me, their wet eyelashes glistening.

"Mom, where were you?" Elliot asked.

"Helping a friend."

"With what? Where'd you go? What were you doing? I smell gummy bears," he pressed.

"I brought you guys a surprise," I sang, as a distraction. He grabbed his towel and hurried out of the tub, kissing me as he flew past.

Violet reached out her wet arms. "Owl towel," she said, referencing her yellow hooded towel with owl eyes. I wrapped her up in it and held her close.

"There's something for you too, Violet!" Elliot yelled from downstairs, having gone through my bag like a TSA inspector, except a thousand times faster. Hopefully he hadn't found the rest of the Junebugs.

Violet wriggled away from me and ran downstairs with the hood still on her head—her owl towel floating behind her bare butt like a cape.

I turned to Aaron who was standing just outside the doorway. He looked spent—fractured, even. I was unsure if his shattering had come directly from my desertion, or from having to wake up early with kids, alone, entertaining and feeding them all damn day. He pulled me into his chest and hugged me tightly.

"I missed you so much," he said, kissing the top of my head like the grey-haired man had done to the lovely lady shooter, in what felt like another world.

I stood on my tiptoes and kissed him on the lips, tears falling down my cheeks.

"What happened to you?" he asked, wiping away the wetness with his fingers. I couldn't find words yet to capture all I'd witnessed, so I burrowed myself back into him, feeling loved.

I'd been loved by my children for close to a decade, and I'd been loved by Aaron for double that. Their love for me was the only thing that wasn't fleeting in my disorganized life as a wife, mother, and daughter. I had intimately walked with June through the wreckage of a broken, abusive marriage and there were no similarities between that and this. Also, Aaron had to do better. For me. For us. The frenzied framework of modern parenthood wasn't going to change, so we had to—*he* had to—if we wanted to survive it, together. Yes, he needed to more equally share in the labor of our little family—and I would be starting that conversation right after I ate a meal that didn't come in a chew tin—but there was something else.

I looked up at the green-eyed man. "I need your help. And I need you to notice when I need your help. Before it's too late."

"I get that now. But how will I know?" He was being sincere, not a dick.

"Remember A.B.?"

"Yeah, I think I married her."

"When you can no longer find her in me, go get her and bring her back. She gets lost in motherhood."

"I will. I promise."

I believed him. Enveloped in his arms, safe and understood, I wanted to take this feeling and bottle it. Free of resentment, tangled emotions, and flagrant dad privilege, it was just like the old days, before we'd had kids. But I felt the approaching demands and minutia of parenting waiting to wear me down again. The rollercoaster of cryptic fevers and spilled bubble solution would try to undo me. I could bet on it. And I would likely need another getaway by next weekend. Maybe even tomorrow.

"I need another escape to look forward to. And sleep. I need to sleep." I suddenly remembered. "Sleeping in is my sex."

"What does that—"

"Mom, you got me an ATM machine?!" Elliot yelled.

"I'll explain later," I said to Aaron, taking his hand in mine and walking downstairs. "It's called a slot machine, Elliot. It's a game."

Aaron fished coins out of a change bowl for Elliot, while Violet did reckless somersaults on the couch with her new monkey. Elliot put the coins in the slot machine and pulled the lever.

"Mom, look, I got three cherries!!" he said jumping up and down, the coins clanging in the metal tray.

Next up: craps.

⚮

Aaron and I lay in bed early that night, phones far away and legs intertwined under the covers. It all felt simple again. The morning would surely change that. But at least I was looking forward to sleeping in. It was small, but it was something.

THE END

ACKNOWLEDGMENTS

I imagined writing this meaningful section while sitting alone, with a full teacup nearby, somewhere with a breathtaking view so I could really reflect on the bounty of generosity I've received, as I breathed in the fresh jasmine, or whatever. But as fate would have it, I'm at home because kids and summer, and my entire family is within throwing distance of me—one on an Xbox, one asking how to spell "sprinkles," and the other one eating toast loudly. It's sort of poetic, isn't it?

Yeah, I didn't think so either.

Thank you to She Writes, a truly groundbreaking indie press who believed in me, my voice, and this project. Brooke Warner, you are an inspiration. To my She Writes support team, Samantha Strom and the rest, thank you for putting up with my detailed (*cough* neurotic *cough*) emails and revisions.

Thank you to my amazing publicists, Marissa DeCuir, Ellen Whitfield, and the entire JKS family. Marissa, thank you for crying at happy things as much as I do, and for referring to me as your Jenny Lawson, even though I don't come close. And Ellen, from day one, working with you felt like I was working with a dear friend. Thank you for that.

A very special thank you to Marnye Young and my stellar audiobook team at Audio Sorceress, whom I have so much respect for, especially after going on the self-loathing (and fun!) ride that was narrating my own audiobook. If you'd like to hear me attempt Australian and French accents, along with numerous other voices while reading every single word in this book—check out the audiobook.

Much appreciation to my friends who consensually, and non-consensually, listened to me talk for years about this formerly intangible child of mine. Eternal love and thanks to Mary Becker, Clare Burley, Jeanine Tiemeyer, Chloe Myers, Valerie Farino, Becky Leonard, Mari Rockwood, Amanda Cagle, Jaime McNitt, Danielle VanGundy, Edith Presler, Lauren Flanagan, Michael Blash, and everyone I left out, which will surely hit me after publication. Just write your name in here: Thanks to my best friend in the world, _____. Now we're good. Extra thanks to Jennifer Gagliardi who not only let me download the book's entire plot into her while we ate breakfast one morning, but also for showing up as my official photographer.

Thank you to Pam England, Virginia Bobro, Britta Bushnell, and the entire Birthing From Within family who have always been so supportive of me, even though I wasn't as into yurts, kale, and rituals as the rest of you. You completely changed my lens and taught me what sisterhood (barf, I know, sorry) really was, and you're one of the reasons I try so hard to create it for others.

Thank you to a badass group of writers whom I didn't know I needed in my life like one needs oxygen—both Pescadero crews. It wasn't until I met you all that I finally settled into my writer self. I came for the writing instruction, but I stayed for your vulnerability, humanity, topnotch humor, and Slayer weed. I don't fully get how knowing people for only a handful of days can bond you to them for life, but it fucking can. A special nod to Shaheera Huggins for her steadfast support and willingness to mail my edited manuscript back to me all the way from Australia. Am I the only one who feels paralyzed by the idea of international mailing?

Many thanks to the queen of this Pescadero crew, Janelle Hanchett. Thank you, Janelle, for answering eager messages from a blossoming writer who was desperate for guidance. Your no-bullshit attitude, mentorship, and editing of this book taught me more about the craft of writing than any college English class.

Thank you to the others whose expertise graces these pages: Stephanie Rayburn, for your laser-focused edits and spelling catches, and to Nicole Frail, for your feedback, edits, and validation, as well as introducing me to my agent extraordinaire, Joseph Perry. Joe, you made me believe in agents again. And men.

To my *Adult Conversation* readers and podcast listeners, thank you for laughing with (at) me. Thank you for showing up for and supporting my rants, videos, podcasts, and the detailed Korean spa recounting. An extra special thanks to the heroes who financially support me and my endeavors via Patreon. I would take a bullet for you (rubber riot bullet, but it's still a bullet). To every last one of you in my Adult Conversation world, you make me feel less alone in this thing, which I hope makes you feel less alone in this thing. Now let's all go to the mall and get BFF necklaces together.

To my mom and dad, who are surely questioning their parenting choices—namely not having me evaluated by the school counselor before it was too late—thank you for doing just the right amount of right that I find myself a moderately functional adult, and now look at me, authoring a book. Also, thank you for doing just the right amount of wrong to give me lots of material to pull from. Seriously, you guys gave me so much good that I can never repay you. Thank you for believing in me.

And to my mother-in-law who defies all villainous labels, thank you for always supporting my harebrained projects (including this one), and for so frequently stepping in so I could step out. I was the lucky one when I inherited you.

This book had two doulas. Jessica Chapman and Kathie Neff held the cold washcloth to my hot head from the beginning of an idea to the moment I screamed and finally birthed this thing into the world. Thank you, Jessica, for being the same person as me, for leaving me messages sobbing because parts of the book hit you so deeply, and for responding to every single anxious message I left you about the book's story, a character, or a line of dialogue. You are this book's co-parent. And to the other co-parent, Kathie, thank you for keeping me on track with your supportive words, nudges, and masterful edits, and for continually begging for the next chapter while I wrote the damn thing. I will never understand what I did to deserve your friendship and loyalty, but I'm eternally grateful for it. Most importantly, you owe the world a book of your own. I gave you a cash advance and I expect to see a return on that. Don't make me sue you.

Of course, a bear hug of a thank you to my kids, August and June, without whom this book would never exist. Thank you for being who you are, bullshit and all, and thank you for loving me, bullshit and all. We have a pretty amazing thing going and I wouldn't want to do it with anyone else but you two. Wub.

If you want to see how strong your marriage is, write a

book like this and then ask your writer husband to edit it. Lucky for us, Matt, ours passed the test (as of publication)! You have always been by my side, making me laugh, and making me feel supremely loved. In addition, you taught me how to write a book. Thank you for reading my pages on those late nights when the last thing you wanted to do was read one more word. Thank you for trying your best to be gentle with feedback. And thank you for talking me off the ledge when I nearly went into cardiac arrest after I read my shitty first draft. (Side note: thank you, Anne Lamott, for everything you've ever written.) My inner feminist is reluctant to admit it, Matt, but this book wouldn't have been possible without your support, cheer-leading, sacrifices, and stellar parenting. Thank you for everything, always.

Lastly, thank you to Naomi Stadlen and her book, *What Mothers Do: Especially When It Looks Like Nothing.* Back in 2007, while trapped in a parked car with a sleeping infant who would only nap after a long drive, I read Stadlen's words and, for the first time as a mother, I felt truly seen. Her book made me understand things I was too sleep-deprived to articulate myself, including that I wasn't crazy. Motherhood was. It's wild to think that here I am, thirteen years later, hoping to give the same to other moms.

Also, it appears I need a restraining order against "Circle of Life."

ABOUT THE AUTHOR

Credit: Jen Gagliardi

BRANDY FERNER is a mother, wife, and the creator of the *Adult Conversation* podcast, social media pages, and blog. Her writing has been featured in *Good Morning America*, and at *The New York Times*, *The Huffington Post*, Romper, CafeMom, and elsewhere. In addition to writing and fulfilling her kids' endless snack requests, she spent the past decade working as a doula, childbirth educator, and birth trauma mentor, ushering clients through the intense transition into motherhood. The insight gained from watching moms crack wide open—literally and figuratively—and her own experience as an independent woman who suddenly traded autonomy for snuggles, led her to say out loud the things that modern mothers are thinking. Sometimes it's serious, sometimes it's comedic, but it's always honest. She currently lives in Southern California, and her love language is sleep.

SELECTED TITLES FROM SHE WRITES PRESS

She Writes Press is an independent publishing company founded to serve women writers everywhere. Visit us at www.shewritespress.com.

Play for Me by Céline Keating. $16.95, 978-1-63152-972-6. Middle-aged Lily impulsively joins a touring folk-rock band, leaving her job and marriage behind in an attempt to find a second chance at life, passion, and art.

Wishful Thinking by Kamy Wicoff. $16.95, 978-1-63152-976-4. A divorced mother of two gets an app on her phone that lets her be in more than one place at the same time, and quickly goes from zero to hero in her personal and professional life—but at what cost?

American Family by Catherine Marshall-Smith. $16.95, 978-1631521638. Partners Richard and Michael, recovering alcoholics, struggle to gain custody of their Richard's biological daughter from her grandparents after her mother's death only to discover they—and she—are fundamentalist Christians.

In the Heart of Texas by Ginger McKnight-Chavers. $16.95, 978-1-63152-159-1. After spicy, forty-something soap star Jo Randolph manages in twenty-four hours to burn all her bridges in Hollywood, along with her director/boyfriend's beach house, she spends a crazy summer back in her West Texas hometown— and it makes her question whether her life in the limelight is worth reclaiming.

Warming Up by Mary Hutchings Reed. $16.95, 978-1-938314-05-6. Unemployed and depressed former musical actress Cecilia Morrison decides to start therapy, hoping it will get her out of her slump—but ultimately it's a teen who cons her out of sixty bucks, not her analyst, who changes her life.

A Tight Grip: A Novel about Golf, Love Affairs, and Women of a Certain Age by Kay Rae Chomic. $16.95, 978-1-938314-76-6. As forty-six-year-old golfer Jane "Par" Parker prepares for her next tournament, she experiences a chain of events that force her to reevaluate her life.